Praise for J. L. Langley's *With Caution*

"A J.L. Langley's book is a sure reading. You will find a good story, hot sex, a lot of humor and romance for your heart. Yesterday I bought three books, but when I had to choose from what book start my reading, I had no doubt: J.L. Langely will not deceive me."

~ *Elisa Rolle*

Rating: 5 Angels & A Recommended Read "Ms. Langley has continued her With or Without series with this incredible story. Remi and Jake are two very real to life characters that leap off of the page and draw the reader into the story from the very beginning."

~ *Teresa, Fallen Angel Reviews*

"With Caution is a must read novel. This is the kind of book that will have you up all night to finish and then leave you wanting more. I can not wait for more of J.L. Langley's books. I am especially looking forward to more stories in this wonderful world of werewolves and amazing men."

~ *Kimberley Spinney, Ecataromance*

Rating: 4.5 Nymphs "J. L. Langley pens a suspenseful werewolf tale of love, family and dark secrets. With Caution is an edge of your seat, romantic thriller."

~ *Water Nymph, Literary Nymphs*

Rating: 5 Blue Ribbons "WITH CAUTION is the third installment in J.L. Langley's With or Without series. This is without a doubt one of the best werewolf romance series out there. I am a big fan of J.L. Langley and I couldn't wait to read this book. WITH CAUTION definitely lived up to all my expectations and more. I absolutely loved this novel."

~ *Christina, Romance Junkies*

Rating: 5 Lips "With Caution is a hot and sexy tale that continues Ms. Langley's With or Without series with the story about Remi and Jake. ...As these two men come together, the emotions and the passion will burn you up at the same time that they touch your heart."

~ *Bella, TwoLips Reviews*

Look for these titles by
J. L. Langley

Now Available:

With or Without Series
Without Reservations
With Love
(Also in print anothology Hearts from the Ashes)
With Caution

Sci-Regency Series
My Fair Captain

Coming Soon:

Sci-Regency Series
The Englor Affair

With Caution

J. L. Langley

A SAMHAIN PUBLISHING, LTD. publication.

Samhain Publishing, Ltd.
577 Mulberry Street, Suite 1520
Macon, GA 31201
www.samhainpublishing.com

Editing by Sasha Knight
Cover by Anne Cain

12/08

First Samhain Publishing, Ltd. electronic publication: November 2007
First Samhain Publishing, Ltd. print publication: September 2008

Dedication

To Dick D and Kimberly Gardner. The two of you were lifesavers on this one. Both of your opinions and encouragement were invaluable to me. Here's to both of you, I'm looking forward to both of you being able to sign autographs for me.

Also, thanks to Andre and the rest of my family for putting up with my long hours, and as always thanks to my critique partners.

Chapter One

"I fucking love your mouth." Remi dropped his head back to the pillow, his eyes closed, taking in every little sensation.

The suction on his cock increased as the clever tongue danced along the shaft.

"Oh, fuck. Gonna come. Stop. Not yet..." Winding his fingers through his lover's hair, Remi fought the growing sensation. He tried to slow the inevitable by pulling those delectable lips off him.

A soft, seductive kiss tickled his stomach, making him loosen his grip. As soon as his hand fell to the mattress, his prick was once again engulfed.

Ass muscles clenching tight, he shivered. His balls drew closer to his body and his legs tensed. It was absolute torture. A tingle raced up his spine. *No, not yet.* "Oh God, oh—"

The wonderful warmth left his cock.

Remi half growled, half laughed. "You fucking tease."

A snort answered him, then his dick was gripped, held upright and laved from tip to balls.

Fisting his hand in the thick hair again, Remi pulled his lover's face closer to his groin. "*Yessss*, that feels good."

His legs were shoved higher, exposing him more, and that wicked tongue laved his crease, snaking down.

Riiiing.

The licking continued.

Remi tried concentrating on the slick caress over his perineum and the breath across his balls. It was so—

Riiiing.

Loud. It was loud, like it was right next to his ear. He looked around, his fingers letting go of the dark hair. He didn't remember there being a phone. It rang again and the moist warmth disappeared from his cock. *What the—?*

Blinking his eyes open, Remi squinted against the sunlight coming through the window. *Shit.* He'd forgotten to close the curtain, or rather the quilt he used as a curtain, again. What day was it? Oh yeah, Saturday. He'd just gotten off a twenty-four hour on, twenty-four hour off stretch.

His morning erection throbbed. The wet tip rested against his lower abdomen. Wrapping his hand around it, he squeezed it through the thin jock. "Fuck." *The dream.* He kept having the same damn dream over and over. Well, except for the ringing. The phone was diff—

Riiiing.

My cell phone. Reaching toward the phone on the nightstand, he glanced at the alarm clock. *7:02 a.m.* If that was Chay wanting him to go running, Remi was going to strangle him. He grabbed the cell and flipped it open before it rang a fourth time. "Yeah?"

"Remi." Sterling's voice cracked. "They're at it again. Please come get me, I can't stay here. You gotta come."

Remi bolted to a sitting position. His breath hitched and his hard-on dwindled, replaced by a knot in his chest. "Where are you?" Throwing back the covers, he jumped out of bed, looking around for his jeans. "Sterling, where are you? Are you in the house?"

"Hurry, Remi. They've been at it since six."

"What? Why didn't you call me sooner?" Remi snagged a pair of jeans from the floor at the foot of his bed. Loose change flew out of the pockets, falling onto the gray carpet.

"I thought you'd be running with Chay."

He froze, his stomach plummeted to his feet and a chill raced up his back. "Shh. Sterling, I told you not to mention him in the house. If Dirk hears—"

"I'm outside."

Making himself move again, Remi balanced his phone on his shoulder and shook the pants out. "Sterling, you can't let Dirk know I'm still friends with Chay. If he found out..." He shoved his foot into the jeans, not wanting to think about what would happen if the asshole found out Remi was still hanging out with the "fucking fag". After sticking his other leg in, he tugged his pants over his hips and grabbed the black T-shirt off the computer chair by his bed. "Start walking toward town. I'm on my way."

"But you have to stop him."

Like hell he did. What he *had* to do was get Sterling away from there, before the old man decided to start in on him. "Do what I said and start walking." Remi moved faster, putting on the T-shirt and jerking his black baseball jersey out of the closet. The hanger whizzed past him and clattered against the side of the sleigh bed. When he drew the jersey over his right arm, his phone fell from his shoulder. Juggling, he caught it before it hit the floor and put the phone back on his shoulder. "Move it, goddamnit. Hang up the phone and get away from the house." Remi winced at the bite in his voice. Snapping at Sterling wasn't something he did often, but he was scared. If anything happened to— No, he wasn't going to think that way.

"I am. I'm going now, but, Remi, what if—"

Wait a minute. Did that say—? Remi pulled the phone off his shoulder and glanced at the caller ID again. Sterling was on his cell phone. If the bastard caught Sterling with a cell phone, he'd kick both their asses. Dirk had forbidden Remi from buying Sterling a phone, saying the kid didn't need it. What a joke that was. Sterling *did* need it. Without it, how could he call Remi when he was in trouble? He damn sure couldn't use the house phone to do it. Which was the exact reason Remi had bought it and told Sterling to hide it. And sadly, he'd used the phone several times already.

Remi placed the phone on his shoulder and looked around for his boots, spotting them at the end of the bed. Socks. He needed socks. "I'm not going to go over this with you again. She doesn't want my help. I've tried to help her over and over. You can't help someone who doesn't help themselves." *Fuck the socks.* Sitting on the edge of the bed, Remi snagged his boots and forced his bare foot into one. He laced it and got the other. *Oh God, Sterling didn't—* "You didn't try to break them up, did you? Did he hit you?"

"No. I hate it when he yells. I went out my window and around back."

Remi laced the second boot and stood, securing the phone with his hand. "Good. Don't you ever try to break them apart." *Keys, keys, keys,* where the hell were his keys? Geez, his room was a mess. Ah, kitchen. He'd left them in the kitchen when he came home from the fire station last night.

"I won't. Hurry, Remi." Sterling's voice hitched like he was crying.

I'm hurrying. Grabbing his keys and helmet off the counter with one hand, Remi squeezed the phone between his shoulder and ear to close and lock the door. He brought his hand back to the phone and jogged down the apartment stairs to his bike.

He hated to get off the phone, but he had no choice. "I'm hanging up now. I'll be there in about ten minutes."

"'Kay. See you then. I'm walking."

"Good, see you in a few." Remi flipped his phone shut and stuffed it into his pocket. Starting the motorcycle, he put his helmet on. His hands were shaking so bad he could barely fasten it, but he managed. He had to get to Sterling. If the asshole happened to leave the house and see him walking— Remi's throat constricted, making it hard to breathe. No, no, it was cool, Mom would cover for Sterling and say she'd given him permission to spend the weekend with Remi, she always did. But if the old man caught Sterling walking and realized he hadn't been picked up earlier— "Fuck."

Remi backed his bike out of the parking spot under the awning and took off toward the rez.

ɷ

Sterling got off the bike, unfastened the helmet and took it from his head, leaving his short black hair sticking up on top.

Remi brushed the spiky strands down.

Sterling was getting tall, almost as tall as Remi now. The kid was growing up and becoming quite handsome too. He had the dark coloring from their Apache father, with his dark skin, hair and eyes. From their white mother, he'd inherited softer facial features and a straight, narrow nose that turned up slightly at the end. His face was less angular than most Apaches, even though he'd inherited their father's high cheekbones. No doubt about it, he'd have women falling all over him in a couple years, if he didn't already.

"Thank you." Sterling's lip trembled faintly, then he took a deep breath and handed Remi the helmet. Raking his fingers through his hair, he composed himself.

"You don't have to thank me. That's what I'm here for." Taking the helmet, Remi fastened the strap before hanging it on the handlebar. He'd completely forgotten to grab both helmets in his rush to get to his brother. Thankfully, the helmet law was only for those under eighteen. Stupid in his opinion—everyone should wear a helmet—but he'd had no choice but to go helmet-less.

Sliding his arm around his little brother's shoulders, Remi ushered him toward the restaurant. He squeezed Sterling's neck with the crook of his arm, bringing their heads together. His heart was still pounding, like it did every time he got a call from his brother.

Wrapping his arm around Remi's waist, Sterling hugged him briefly, then shrugged and lengthened his stride. "Okay, dude, you're cramping my style. I'm not six anymore."

Remi chuckled and shoved the little shit's shoulder. Some of the tension left him, seeing Sterling acting like a fourteen-year-old again. "Brat. I offer to take you to breakfast and this is the thanks I get."

Opening the door of the diner, Sterling nodded and held it for Remi. "Uh-huh."

An array of scents assaulted Remi's nose, making him wrinkle it. *God.* Was he ever going to get used to all the strong smells? Being a werewolf was hell on the senses.

Stepping out from behind the cash register, the hostess greeted them. She smiled and puffed out her chest a little as she went to the podium. Grabbing menus and napkin-covered utensils from the pockets on the side of the stand, she asked, "Two?"

"Yes," Remi answered, studying his brother and trying to block out the suffocating aromas.

Sterling seemed okay, but Remi wasn't fooled. He knew how scary the situation was. The kid was putting up a good front. He was more at ease now that he was away from the house, but shit like this didn't just go away. Remi knew that firsthand. He'd been dealing with it all his life.

Sighing, he took a seat across from his brother at the booth the hostess indicated.

She placed their menus on the table, leaning over way more than necessary to put their silverware down.

Whoa, that's where the overwhelming flowery smell was coming from. Did she bathe in perfume? What was she doing anyway? Remi glanced up and got an eyeful. Good God, the woman was about to pop out of her white dress shirt. Remi averted his attention from her boobs and met her gaze.

"Your waitress's name is Sally." She winked. "But you let me know if there is anything *I* can do for you."

Had her voice sounded that sultry when she'd first greeted them? Remi nodded and gave her a polite smile. Normally, he'd have flirted back but under the circumstances he wasn't in the mood. Besides, her scent didn't appeal to him. And that was too bizarre to think about. The weirdness that came from becoming a werewolf never ceased to amaze him.

Sterling batted his lashes at her, grinning from ear to ear. "Oh, he will, I'm sure."

Biting his lip to hold back a chuckle, Remi furrowed his brow at the brat.

The hostess smiled at Sterling before giving Remi one last look and leaving.

Remi waited until she was out of hearing range. "What was

that for?"

Sterling shrugged, but his eyes were bright with mischief. "Only trying to help you out. She was totally into you. Besides, you always used to use me as a chick magnet. I thought I'd bump up the magnetism a little. You need a girlfriend." Sterling unrolled his silverware out of the dark green cloth napkin.

"I did not use you as a chick magnet. You always seemed to attract them." Which was the absolute truth. Remi had never taken Sterling with him to entice female attention. However, he found out real quick a teen lugging around an infant did just that. Hell, even when Remi was in his early twenties and Sterling was in elementary school, Remi ended up getting phone numbers and offers that generally had him covering Sterling's ears. "And I do *not* need a girlfriend." Especially not one who doused herself in perfume.

"You haven't been dating much lately."

"And since when did you become my keeper?"

"I thought—" Sterling shrugged again. "Sorry. I was only trying to help. You seem lonely. You rarely hang out with Chay anymore and you keep to yourself lately, except when you're with me. She was pretty, wasn't she?"

Remi reached across the table and grabbed Sterling's hand. He had to nip this in the bud right now. The last thing he needed, while trying to learn to be a werewolf, was a girlfriend. "She was okay. But I'm serious, if I want a date I'll get one myself."

"You should go out with Chay's assistant. Tina's nice." Sterling grinned.

For some odd reason, Tina's brother, Jake, sprang to mind. Jake was tall, dark and handsome, in a rugged way. He was appealing to Remi's nose too. Remi's cock began to fill and he swore he could smell Jake, but it was only his imagination.

Even if Jake were in the restaurant, who could smell anything with all these people around? And why the fuck did he always get hard thinking about Jake? Jake was a guy. Remi groaned. He should be dissuading his sibling from playing matchmaker, not trying to figure out his strange reaction to another man. "Sterling..."

"Hmmm, what do I want to eat?" Sterling looked away, still smiling, and picked up his menu, flipping it open.

A purplish spot peeked out of the cuff of his long sleeve T-shirt. It looked like—

The sick feeling Remi had banished returned with a vengeance. It felt like someone twisted a knife into his heart. He seized Sterling's hand, and Sterling dropped the menu.

"What—?"

Pushing the cuff out of the way, Remi studied the bruises. They were perfectly shaped like a hand. Someone had held Sterling around the wrist, hard. Further up his arm were bigger spots. Nausea swam in Remi's throat, making him swallow hard. He gritted his teeth and his vision clouded over. If that son of a bitch hurt Sterling... "When? When did this happen? Did Dirk hit you? Where else are you hurt?" He growled, trying—but failing miserably—to keep the anger out of his voice. Some of his own past beatings filtered through his mind. The fear, the hurt and the anger had never faded with age. It was bad enough Sterling had to witness their father's cruelty toward their mother, and even to Remi on occasion, but there was no way Remi was going to allow the bastard to beat his baby brother. "Answer me."

Sterling's eyes widened, looking startled. Slowly, he shook his head. "He hasn't hit me."

Yet. Their father hadn't hit Sterling yet, but he would. Remi was going to throw up. Even now, after all this time, he was

17

terrified to face the old man and hated himself for the weakness. Somehow he'd convinced himself, by being the model son, he could make things right. He'd promised to behave as long as Sterling was not harmed, but now because of his own fear he'd failed his brother. He should have taken the kid years ago and run away. Why had he thought the asshole would stick to his end of the bargain?

Closing his eyes, Remi took a deep breath. A warm, fresh scent assailed his nose and a sense of peace overcame him. No, not peace exactly, he was anything but calm. It was strange, like a feeling of safety, a lessening of his physical tension, if not his mind.

A hand touched his shoulder. "Remi. I'm glad I ran into you. I've got something for you, can you follow me outside?"

Remi gazed up into a chiseled face and nearly black eyes. "Jake, hey, uh..." It *was* Jake he'd smelled earlier.

Glancing at Sterling, Jake dropped a hand around Remi's biceps and tugged. "Will you excuse us for a moment?"

Sterling mumbled something, but Remi was too busy trying to figure out why Jake was dragging him out of his seat to catch it. His head whirled, barely registering which end was up. That was very rare for a trained firefighter, but given the circumstance and Jake's nearness, Remi doubted anyone could blame him. Not that he was going to let anyone know how Jake affected him, of course.

Staggering to his feet, Remi was given no choice but to go as Jake continued to pull him along. *What the fuck?* Why was Jake leading him out of the diner? Halfway to the door, Remi mustered the strength to draw his arm back. "What—?"

"Your eyes. Come on."

Huh? His eyes? *Fuck.* Everything was black and white. Which was probably Jake's fault. Every time Jake was within

18

three feet of— *Oh shit.* What if Sterling saw?

Following Jake out the door and to his SUV, Remi concentrated on seeing color, like Keaton had taught him.

Jake opened the SUV's door and motioned toward the seat.

Remi sat, peering up at his...well, his friend. Jake had become a friend during the last few months, since Remi had become a werewolf. Despite his effort to steer clear of the man, Remi usually ended up hunting with Jake on the night of a full moon. "Where'd you come from?"

Leaning his arm against the door, Jake stared at Remi. He took the mirrored sunglasses off the top of his head and held them out.

Damn, Jake was big. Accepting the shades, Remi put them on, then shook his head to clear it.

"I smelled you when you walked in. I was going to come and say hi after I was done eating, but your scent changed and I figured I better try to help you get a handle on things." Frowning, Jake glanced at the diner then back to Remi. "Everything okay?"

Hell no, everything wasn't okay. He no longer had the surge of adrenaline his anger had spurred, but now he was fighting off arousal. Remi groaned, dropping his head into his hands. *Fuckin' Chay.* Turning him into a werewolf and making his life even more difficult.

Remi lifted his head. "Everything is fine."

"You always get mad then terrified in a span of seconds for no reason? Yeah, okay, pull the other leg. What's the matter, Remi?"

That wasn't what he wanted to be pulling on Jake at the moment. And where the hell had that come from?

Remi sighed, and for a second he thought of telling Jake

everything, but he didn't. He'd never talked about Dirk. Not even to his friends. No way was he going to risk anyone else, especially a friend, by dragging them into it. He looked right into Jake's dark eyes and hoped Jake would let it go. "That's my baby brother in there."

Jake turned his head, peeking back at the diner. "I kinda assumed. Cute kid. He looks like you."

Following Jake's attention, Remi saw Sterling duck out of sight of the window and scurry back to their table. He grinned. Yeah, Sterling did look just like him, well except for the eyes. Sterling had Dirk's brown eyes. No, he had the asshole's eye *color*. Sterling didn't have mean, dead eyes like the son of a bitch.

"That isn't what I asked though."

Remi sighed. *That figures.* Jake wasn't going to let it go. "I don't want to talk about it." He had to get a grip and go back inside. Telling Jake what a wuss he was about his father was out of the question. He had to live with his own failures. This was his problem and he had to fix it. And to do that, he needed to talk to Sterling. *Color. Concentrate.* "Blue."

"Huh?"

"You're wearing a blue shirt." A tight dark blue shirt which showed off Jake's pecs and—fuck, Remi was seeing black and white again. He had to focus on something other than Jake.

Jake chuckled, a low, sexy rumbling sound. The man could make a fortune in radio. "They changed back, didn't they?"

"My scent change again?"

"Yeah."

Could werewolves smell attraction? God, he hoped not. He couldn't. No, that wasn't true, he could smell all sorts of scents coming from people, but he didn't know what they meant. He was still trying to learn to scent prey and the different scents of nature when he hunted. Keaton promised to help him with people next. Until then, he was going to have to be careful. How embarrassing would it be to be caught lusting after a guy? He wasn't gay, damn it.

Remi gazed past the big man to the car parked next to the SUV. What color was it?

"Let me help you, Remi." Jake's deep voice softened into a caress. "I want to help you."

The sincerity was Remi's undoing. He closed his eyes, dipping his head. *Un-fucking-believable.* The slightest show of concern from someone and he was breaking down. No, that wasn't true, it was Jake. Remi had never had a problem putting on a good face when his friends tried to help. He'd always known their help would make it worse for not only him, but everyone involved. But with Jake...there was something about the man that made Remi feel he would always be there for him.

Jake's hand landed on his shoulder. "Deep breath. Relax. Getting worked up again isn't going to get your eyes back to normal."

Nodding, he focused his attention past Jake again and took a deep breath.

Something brushed past his cheek, startling him.

Remi sat up straight, trying to figure out what had happened.

Jake stared at him, wide-eyed, and stepped away.

Oh fuck. He'd leaned into Jake's hand, rubbing his cheek against it. What the fuck was he thinking? He glanced down, trying to act cool. "I'm sorry, I uh, I—"

"No big deal. You just surprised me. Tell me about your family. What happened to Sterling?"

My family? Remi's head jerked up. *How does he know it has something to do with Sterling?* How had he forgotten Jake was a PI? Maybe Jake *could* help. "Can you follow someone for me and gather info on them?" He knew damn well his father was a dirty cop—which was what made him dangerous—maybe if Remi could prove it he could get the information to the right people and no one would have to know he or Jake were involved.

Jake cocked his head. "I think you need to tell me more, but yeah, I can do that."

Remi relaxed, feeling better now that he had started thinking of a plan. He had no idea how he was going to come up with the dough to hire Jake, but he'd figure out something. Keeping Sterling from suffering what Remi had gone through was worth it.

He stood and Jake stepped back further, but not before Remi got a good whiff of the man. Damn, he smelled raw and masculine and—he was doing it again. If he was going to let Jake help him, he was going to have to rid himself of this infatuation.

Remi shut the door and tried to hand the glasses back to Jake, but Jake shook his head.

"Keep them, you may need to put them back on."

Nodding, Remi shoved them on top of his head. It was probably a smart idea considering Jake's nearness always made him go haywire. "Come on, I'll introduce you to my little brother. You can bring your breakfast over to our table."

Chapter Two

Remi stuffed a bite of pancake in his mouth, trying not to laugh at Jake's expression. The poor man. Sterling had taken to Jake right away. And when Sterling was comfortable around someone... Remi hadn't seen him this talkative in ages, but Jake seemed to be taking the endless chatter in stride. He wasn't the least bit annoyed at all the questions.

"Do you ever do skip tracing?" Leaning forward, Sterling put his elbows on the table.

"You mean like bounty hunting?" Already nodding, Jake took a drink of his orange juice. "On occasion. Rhys does more of the fugitive recovery than I do."

"Who's Rhys?" Remi frowned. Jake had never mentioned him before. Then again, Remi didn't know Jake all that well. He'd spent most of the last three full moons with him, but they were in wolf form. It wasn't real conducive to talking.

"My business partner. You've met him."

"I don't think so." He had? When? Rhys was an unusual name, surely he'd remember.

"Three weeks ago, while we were hunting."

"Oh." Well, duh, Rhys was a wolf. How was Remi supposed to know the name of a wolf who had met up with them a few hours before dawn? He was a big black wolf, as were Jake and

Chay, hell Remi was too for that matter. They all looked the same. Oh, now that was just bad. Remi burst out laughing, unable to help himself. For a guy who'd seen his share of racism, he should be ashamed of himself.

Sterling's head snapped around. "What?"

Jake grinned, looking confused.

"Ignore me. I thought of something funny." Still smiling, Remi shrugged.

"Uh, you know that's a sign of mental illness, right?" Sterling taunted.

Remi took a drink of his coffee, catching Jake's gaze over the cup. "Yeah, and it runs in the family."

Jake made a *hmm* sound as he chewed a bite of his omelet. "They say it's more prominent with each generation."

"Yeah, I believe it. It's characterized by excessive talking." Remi cut his focus to Sterling, who was seated next to him, and raised his mug for another drink.

Rolling his eyes, Sterling groaned and bumped Remi's shoulder with his own.

Remi laughed, juggling his sloshing coffee. Setting it on the table, he used his napkin to wipe a lukewarm drop off his forearm before flinging the cloth at Sterling.

Caught off guard, Sterling sputtered and flailed his arms. As soon as he caught the napkin, Jake's came sailing across the table and landed on his head. "Okay, not fair." Sterling yanked the green cloth off his face, trying to scowl at them. "You guys are teaming up against me. And since when do you go hunting, Remi?" He threw Jake's napkin back at him. "I wanna go."

"Uh." *Shit.* Remi blinked. How was he gonna get out of this one?

After catching the napkin, Jake put it back in his lap. "When do you want to go? We'll take you."

Remi didn't know whether to be grateful or not. Now he was going to have to dodge questions about hunting and when he was going to take Sterling.

"What do you hunt?" Sterling asked.

How the hell was Remi to know what season they were in? Was it deer season? Duck? Quail? Damn, he had no clue. He'd never gone hunting before with a rifle and stuff. "Duck."

"Rabbit," Jake answered at the exact same time.

Crap. Remi nearly groaned aloud.

"Well, which is it?" Sterling frowned.

Jake met his gaze, his eyes twinkling. "Wabbit season."

Oh, man, nice save. Remi's lip twitched. "Duck season."

"Wabbit season."

Sterling groaned. "Y'all don't really go hunting, do you?"

"Sure we do. We just don't usually shoot anything." Which was the absolute truth. They ran it down and chomped its neck. Remi grinned at Jake.

Jake grinned back.

"I can go with y'all next time, honest?" Sterling asked.

"Sure." Jake arched a brow at Remi. "But you have to be vewy, vewy quiet."

Remi couldn't help himself, he laughed. He'd figure out how he was going to answer Sterling's endless questions about hunting later. Oh wow, he liked Jake. Well, when he wasn't lusting after the man. Come to think of it, on the full moon was one of the few times he ever had fun anymore. In wolf form they seemed to have a comfortable silence with one another. It shouldn't be any surprise to him that he and Jake would get along good in human form also. He'd just never been around Jake when he wasn't trying to control his wolf nature. He decided he liked it. "Yeah, 'cause wabbits are vewy timid wittle cweatures."

Jake smiled. A full-on, happy smile. It lit up his face and made his dark brown eyes dance.

And it went straight to Remi's cock. His eyes went unfocused and his gums began to sting. *Fuck.*

Remi extracted Jake's sunglasses off his head and put them on.

෨෴෴

Laughing, Sterling shoved Remi in the back and bounded past him out the diner door. "What are we gonna do now?" He ran across the parking lot toward Remi's motorcycle. When he turned back toward Jake and Remi, Sterling had a huge grin on his face. "Can I drive?"

Jake chuckled. Sterling was everything a little brother should be, like a playful puppy, animated and full of energy. Not only was he smart and cute as he could be, he was personable. Jake suspected the kid had never met anyone he couldn't charm.

Handing Jake his sunglasses, Remi groaned and shook his head. "Not in the city." Remi walked slightly behind Jake until they reached his bike. Putting the key in the ignition, he squinted at Jake. The sunlight caught his eyes just right, showing off the unusual green color. "Maybe we can go grab a beer tomorrow sometime to discuss what we were talking about earlier?"

Damn, his eyes were fucking gorgeous. The first time Jake

had seen them, he'd thought they were contacts. They weren't. Even in wolf form, Remi's eyes were a clear peridot. He had to quit thinking like that. He put on his shades. If he got all keyed up, his arousal would trigger Remi's. And Remi wasn't near as good at hiding it as he was. Jake dragged his mind away from the piercing green long enough to answer. "Sure. You have my number?"

"Yeah, you gave it to me when you were watching after Keaton." Reaching for the helmet hanging on the handlebars, Remi threw his leg over and sat. Once Sterling was settled on the bike, Remi handed the helmet back to him.

Sterling took the helmet as his head whipped around to Jake. "You were watching Keaton? Like a bodyguard or something? That's so cool. Why did Keaton need a bodyguard? Was there trouble at the college? Did he fail a student or something? Oh." Sterling's eyes widened. "Was it because he's gay?"

Frowning, Remi pinched Sterling's leg.

"Oww." The kid yelped and scowled at his brother. "What?"

"Shh...that's rude." Remi looked back at Jake. "Sorry, Jake, just igno—"

"Why's that rude? I'm only curious. Maybe I wanna be a private detective one day. I need to know these things, in case," Sterling shot back.

Jake watched them, fascinated.

Rolling his eyes at Sterling, Remi groaned and scowled over his shoulder. When he twisted, his baseball jersey fell open and the tight black T-shirt stretched taut across his toned muscles. "You're being nosy and Jake has better things to do than answer your endless questions. Besides, I thought you were going to be a fireman."

Jake chuckled, only half listening to the friendly banter

between the siblings. He was having a hard time dragging his gaze away from Remi's chest. Even knowing what was underneath the clothes from seeing Remi shift, there was something very enticing about how those square pecs showed through the fabric. It made Jake's fingers itch to touch. He'd love to pinch those nipples and watch Remi squirm and beg for him. Remi's chest would ripple and glisten with sweat and— Jake shook himself. Remi was straight. He might never truly be Jake's mate, much less submit to Jake's more dominant tendencies.

Sterling shrugged, drawing Jake's attention. "Okay, fine, I'm nosy." Sterling put the helmet on. "I want to know because I like Keaton. I don't care what Dirk sa—"

Remi revved the engine.

Interesting. Jake wondered what that was about.

"I'll give you a call later." Tilting the bike, Remi raised the kickstand with his foot. He wasn't wearing a helmet.

Sterling looped his arms around Remi's waist. "Bye, Jake."

"Wait." Jake gripped Remi's arm. There was no way in hell he was going to let his mate go without a helmet. Werewolf or not a head injury could kill anyone. Wolves may heal faster than humans, but dead was dead.

Fuck. Remi's scent changed as soon as Jake touched him. It grew heavier—aroused—and it went straight to Jake's cock.

Remi's dark eyebrows pulled together. The green bled out into the whites of his eyes and his warm arm flexed under Jake's hand. "What's up?"

Clearing his throat, Jake released Remi's arm. "Where's your helmet?" Jake handed Remi his shades and glanced at Sterling from the corner of his eyes.

Swallowing so hard his Adam's apple bobbed, Remi blinked

and put the glasses on. He hitched his thumb over his shoulder. "I was in a hurry and forgot his helmet. So he's wearing mine."

Jake had to proceed with caution. Demanding that Remi be safe would likely piss the man off. "Why don't you let me take Sterling and follow you to your place? That way you don't have to ride without a helmet."

Remi shook his head. "I—"

"Come on, Sterling. I'll tell you more about the PI business on the way." Jake offered the kid a hand. He wasn't taking no for an answer.

Predictably, Sterling grinned and unbuckled his helmet. "Cool. You wanna hang out with us today? Hey, Remi, can we go toss a ball around?"

Remi turned his head. "Sterling..."

Throwing his leg over the bike, Sterling hopped off and handed his helmet to Remi.

Sighing, Remi took it. "Jake, are you sure this is no trouble? I mean, if you have work to do or something—"

"No trouble at all." Jake smiled. It was probably a little underhanded, but he'd just figured out the key to his mate, and he was sure as shit going to use it. He gazed at Sterling, who was bouncing up and down on his toes impatiently. If including Sterling meant getting closer to Remi...so be it. Thankfully, Jake liked the kid, therefore it wasn't as much using him as it was looking after him too. From what little Jake had heard of Remi and Sterling's conversation before he dragged Remi outside earlier, the kid needed all the protection and support he could get.

Clasping his hand on Sterling's shoulder, Jake led him toward his Chevy. "Toss a ball around?"

"Yeah, football. I want to try out for the junior varsity team next year."

Remi pulled up beside them, wearing his helmet, and pointed a finger at Sterling. "Behave." He waved at Jake. "See you at my apartment."

Oh yes, this was going to work well. Jake nodded and punched the button on his key ring to unlock his black Tahoe.

Sterling climbed in and buckled his seat belt.

When Jake opened his own door and slid in, Sterling watched him, cocking his head. He remained quiet as Jake started the engine and backed out of the parking space. That probably wasn't a good sign, considering how much the kid talked. "What's up? You're awfully quiet all of a sudden. I thought you were curious about my work?"

"Who were you protecting Keaton from?"

A deranged werewolf. "You'll have to ask Keaton that. Client confidentiality and all."

"I don't see Keaton very often. Remi doesn't take me to Chay's with him very much anymore."

"Why not?"

Sterling blinked. "Dirk, uh, I mean our dad—" He turned away.

Jake wanted to ask why Sterling called his dad Dirk, but he was anxious to hear more about Remi's father, and why the man didn't like Keaton. "Your dad what?"

"Are you gay?"

"Excuse me?" Jake hit the brakes a little harder than normal, making the SUV jerk forward.

"Are you gay?"

Okay, he hadn't expected that question. Furthermore, he didn't know how to answer it. Shifting into drive, Jake headed out of the parking lot and toward Remi's apartment. He didn't want to lie to Sterling, but he wasn't sure it was in his best interest to tell the kid either, considering how close Sterling was to Remi. According to Chay, Remi was a bit on the homophobic side. Letting Remi find out Jake was gay probably wasn't the best way to get close to him. And how seriously fucked up was it that he might never claim his mate because his mate was straight?

"You don't have to tell me." Sterling shrugged. "I'm just being nosy. I see the way you look at Remi though."

Wonderful. Chatty and observant. "And this is your way of telling me to back off?"

Sterling chuckled and shook his head. "No, if I wanted you to back off, I'd tell you. Remi is more of a dad to me than a big brother and I love him very much. I want him happy, and right now, he worries me. He needs friends."

"And what does me being gay or not have to do with me being friends with your brother?" If there were still problems between Remi and Chay, Jake hadn't noticed. "As far as I know Remi is straight."

"Remi treats you different."

Did the kid know something, or was he playing with Jake? Jake glanced over, trying to get a feel for him.

Sterling stared out the front window. He seemed composed. "He hasn't been on a date in ages."

"That still doesn't answer my question, kid. Are you saying he's still freaked out over Chay hooking up with Keaton?"

"Nah, he only freaked in the first place because he was worried about Dirk finding out. Chay is his best buddy and he didn't want Dirk to force him to stop seeing Chay. Remi even likes Keaton, even though he pretends not to at times."

Sterling was quiet for a few seconds.

Jake could sense the scrutiny. He turned, catching Sterling's gaze.

Finally, Sterling took a deep breath and nodded. "Well, all I know is you guys get along really well. He acts like himself when you're around. He lets down his guard with you. He doesn't do that with anyone but me."

Jake had thought the change had been due to Sterling's presence. Was it because no one else was around *except* Sterling, rather than *because* of Sterling? Remi *was* different this morning. Usually, he tended to be more guarded. He normally had a cocky air about him. Jake had always suspected it to be a pretense.

"Well, Remi is a grown man so I have no idea why his father's—Dirk's opinion matters when Chay is his best friend." But it was one hell of a revelation and it gave Jake hope. "And why in the hell do you call your father Dirk? He's yours and Remi's real father, right?"

"Yeah."

"Then why do you call him Dirk?"

Sterling shrugged. "He doesn't let us call him Dad."

Chapter Three

Jake shut the door to his Tahoe and went to the back to get the small cooler he'd brought with him. After closing the back door, he headed around the school building toward the playground and playing fields. He'd dropped Sterling off at Remi's, telling Sterling he'd meet them at the schoolyard, then Jake had gone home to change. Now, he had to find them.

They were easy to spot. There was a lady jogging around the field and an old guy sitting under a tree by the swings drinking out of a brown paper bag, but other than that Remi and Sterling were the only ones there.

As Jake walked closer, Remi threw the football in a perfect spiral, right to Sterling.

Jake let out a low whistle. It was an impressive pass. The kid didn't even need to break stride. The ball fell right into his hands.

Sprinting back toward Remi, Sterling tossed the ball to his brother and took a stance beside him.

Remi motioned with his empty hand for Sterling to run. Taking a few steps back, Remi threw the ball. Once again it was a tight spiral, right to Sterling.

The kid was pretty good. He appeared to have excellent hands, but Jake wasn't sure how much real practice he was going to get with someone who threw as well as Remi. Maybe

Jake would call his friends and see about putting together a team for the kid to practice with next weekend. It would do him good to have to get through a defense.

Setting the cooler about ten feet from Remi, Jake turned to watch Sterling jog back toward them. "I'm impressed. That was a hell of a pass."

Remi flinched, apparently caught off guard, his sunglasses slipping down his nose a little. "Yeah, guess I still have it."

Jake grinned. He was going to have to work with the man on using his senses. "I brought us some water." The shades on Remi's face were the Oakleys he normally wore, not mirrored Ray-Bans. Jake's glasses hung from the collar of Remi's tank top. He took them and put them on. "What do you mean, still?"

"I used to play in high school."

Panting, Sterling stopped in front of them. He also wore a tank top but bruises covered his arms. After tossing the ball to Remi, he dropped his hands to his knees. "He was quarterback the year our high school made it to state."

Jake ignored the bruises. He would ask Remi about them later. Remi played football in high school? "Holy shit. Lassiter, number twelve." How had Jake never made the connection? Tina had been a freshman and on the drill team that year. Jake had gone to most of the home games to watch his younger sister and found himself watching the sexy starting quarterback more than a few times. *No wonder.* Had he ever gotten close enough, he might have realized the man was his mate back then. "You were fuckin' awesome, man."

Remi shrugged off the praise.

If Jake hadn't been watching closely, he would have missed the brief grin.

"Where'd you play college ball?" Jake asked.

After tossing the ball into the air, Remi caught it.

"He didn't." Sterling stood and stretched his hands over his head.

What? How could he not have played in college? He was damn good. Several players on the team had gotten scholarships to big name colleges. He figured Remi would have been one of them. If Jake remembered correctly the middle linebacker was now in the NFL. "Why not? I heard guys were getting scouted left and right."

"Yeah, some were." Remi flipped the ball to Jake. "Jake, you can snap me the ball." He studied Sterling. "Ready to go again?"

Catching the ball, Jake frowned. Remi's scent had changed. *He's hiding the truth for some reason.*

"Same pattern, Sterling." Remi stepped back, motioning for Jake to get in front of him.

Jake wanted nothing more than to ask what was going on, but he had a feeling it would put Remi on the spot. He could sense Remi had been upset by the conversation.

Giving in to the need to nurture and protect his mate, Jake bent over and set the ball on the grass, and let the conversation drop. He glanced back at Remi, raising a brow, then clapped his hands together to gain Sterling's attention. "Okay, let's go. Let's play. Sterling, get over there. Remi, what count?"

Sterling jogged over to his position.

Dipping his head, Remi caught Jake's gaze. "Okay, on two."

After about three passes, Remi's pensive mood dissolved. At first, all Jake could concentrate on was Remi's unease, but after Remi relaxed and started having fun again, Jake became ultra aware of Remi's hands on his body, constantly touching him. To make matters worse, Remi was beginning to work up a sweat.

He smelled so fucking good. Jake nearly groaned the next time the strong hand touched his back, before getting into position behind him.

"Hut! Hut!"

Jake snapped the ball into Remi's hands and Remi dropped back, holding onto the ball a few seconds before releasing it. As soon as it left his hand, Remi took off running toward Sterling.

Catching the ball, Sterling looked back. His eyes widened when he spotted Remi coming toward him. Whipping his head back around, he turned on the speed. The kid was quick. A great asset if he was going to play receiver. Getting to the edge of the schoolyard, he spiked the ball and yelled, "Ha."

Remi never stopped. He dipped his shoulder, planted it into his brother's midsection and swooped Sterling up.

Sterling hollered in surprise and started beating on Remi's back. When Remi set Sterling on his feet, they both fell to the ground laughing.

Grinning from ear to ear, Jake made his way toward them. He loved seeing this side of Remi. He'd seen the man joke and cut up around Chay, but it was nothing like this. This was real...unreserved. Whatever had bothered him earlier about discussing his high school days was gone now.

"Butthead." Sterling tore grass from the ground and threw it at Remi.

Jerking his head to the side, Remi nudged Sterling's thigh with his own. "Brat." Remi licked his lips and smiled. The shiny gold surface of his Oakley lenses reflected Jake's image.

Before Jake realized his intent, Remi caught his ankle and tugged.

"Shit." Jake leaned forward to keep from landing on his ass. Catching himself, he fell with his hands on either side of

Remi's head. His face poised inches from Remi's, his glasses slipped, hanging on his ears by the earpieces.

Sterling roared with laughter, but it seemed distant. Jake couldn't focus on anything but his mate being so close.

Remi wasn't unaffected. His breath hitched and the smell of arousal filled the air. A soft sound of surprise left his lips and fanned over Jake's face.

Blood rushed to Jake's prick and his stomach tightened with anticipation. His vision went monochrome. He wanted to press himself against the lean body and claim Remi's full mouth.

Turning his face up slightly, Remi parted his lips, displaying the tips of canines. Then he shook his head and snapped out of it. He chuckled, "Gotcha," put his hands on Jake's shoulders and shoved.

Reluctantly, Jake rolled onto his back next to Remi. What would Remi have done if Jake had kissed him? "Asshole."

Sterling laughed harder, seemingly oblivious to Jake and Remi's plight, and held his hand up to Remi. "Good one."

Laughing, Remi slapped his brother's hand, but the smell of lust still surrounded him.

Jake knew damn well Remi was as hard as he was. It was both comforting and puzzling. Maybe he wasn't going to have as hard a time claiming his mate as he'd first thought. He wondered if Remi could handle him wanting to be more than a friend.

ᙀᙁ

Jake couldn't remember the last time he'd enjoyed himself so much. After playing football they'd eaten lunch and gone back to Remi's apartment and taken showers. Fortunately, Jake had brought a change of clothes with him. He got trounced at video games by Sterling and Remi, then he'd sat back and watched the brothers take turns beating each other and rubbing it in. They'd ordered pizza and dug through Remi's DVD collection. Time had flown by, as it always seemed to when you were having fun.

Now, he and Remi sat on the couch in Remi's small living room, bemoaning the fact that they'd eaten too much. They were watching the end of *The Howling* and Sterling was asleep on the floor.

"Ah, fuck. What a day." Remi leaned his head back, putting his hands over his face as the ending credits played on the TV. Dragging his hands down, he sat back up and turned toward Jake. "Thanks."

"For what?"

"For calming me this morning. For hanging out all day and helping me cheer Sterling up."

"Didn't look like Sterling needed much cheering up. Something tells me the kid could have fun at an insurance seminar." Remi had been the one who needed his mood lifted.

Remi glanced down at Sterling, and a fond grin crept across his face. "Yeah, he's a good kid."

"He is. Wanna tell me about the bruises on his arms? Does it have anything to do with the person you want me to investigate?"

Remi closed his eyes and bent forward to rest his forearms on his knees. Exhaling noisily, he nodded. "Yeah, let me put Sterling in bed before we talk." He shoved himself from the couch and walked around the battered oak coffee table.

Jake stood. "Let me. Where do you want to put him?"

"I can get him. He's not that heavy." Bending, Remi scooped Sterling into his arms. He groaned a little on the way up. "Okay, maybe he is getting a bit heavy." Remi chuckled.

Sterling never even moved, he was dead to the world. Not surprising. Anyone who had as much energy as he did awake should sleep like a rock.

Holding out his arms, Jake tried to offer help, but Remi shook his head. "Nah, I got him. Just go make sure his door is open and pull his covers back."

It didn't surprise Jake one bit that Sterling had his own room in Remi's apartment. Jake was beginning to realize his mate had hidden depths. Most bachelors would have turned the extra room into an office or storage, but not Remi. Remi wasn't the self-centered ass he tried to come across as most of the time.

Jake hurried down the hall ahead of Remi. There were only two rooms and the bathroom, so he had a fifty/fifty chance. He'd already been in the bathroom, so he knew that door was not it. Pushing open the first door he came too, Jake flipped the light next to the door and peeked inside.

The room was small. A big, dark wood sleigh bed that had seen better days, and an old, beat-up dresser with peeling white paint were the biggest pieces of furniture in the room. There was a small desk—with a laptop on it—and chair next to the bed. The one window was covered with an old quilt. A raw wooden crate, doubling for a nightstand, sat next to the bed. On it was the ugliest lamp Jake had ever seen. It looked like the vase Peter glued back together in *The Brady Bunch* crossed with the lamp from *I Dream of Jeannie*. The base was shaped like Jeannie's bottle, only it was brown. There were two different colored orange oval-shaped facets on the top of the rounded bottom part. The long stem led to a plain white cone-shaped shade. Aside from the awful lamp, it was a man's room, decorated with hand-me-downs, but not unpleasant.

"That's mine. Sterling's is the door on the left."

Flipping the light off, Jake made a mental note to buy Remi a new lamp. He opened the other door and turned on the light. Taking a brief look around, he shook his head. The kid's room was nicer than Remi's. The furniture, while not expensive, was new. The curtains and bedspread matched. There was even a small TV with a video game console opposite the bed.

Jake pulled the dark blue comforter and sheets back and stepped out of the way.

When Remi laid Sterling down and reached across him for the comforter, Jake's attention zeroed in on Remi's butt. Fuck, the man made baggy jean shorts look good. Of course, it could be because they stretched tight across his ass when he bent over.

As Sterling rolled to his side and snuggled into his pillow, Remi straightened and headed toward the door.

Leaving Remi to turn off the light and shut the door, Jake went to the living room and sat on the old plaid couch. He waited for Remi to do the same, but instead of joining Jake on the couch, Remi removed the empty pizza box and the bottles from the table and took them to the kitchen.

Jake was certain it was a delay tactic, but he let it go. Obviously, Remi needed to gather his thoughts. Talking about family issues was never easy, especially when abuse was involved.

Chay had mentioned Remi's dad had slapped him around as a kid without being too specific. Jake was beginning to suspect the abuse hadn't ended with Remi moving out.

Things just didn't add together. Sterling seemed to think Remi had kicked up a fuss over Chay and Keaton because he was afraid of their father. How the man got to Remi was not a surprise. From what Jake witnessed today, Remi would do anything to keep his brother safe.

Remi came back into the living room with two beer bottles in hand. Giving one to Jake, he sat on the couch with a leg underneath him.

"Thanks." Jake took a swig of beer and turned his body to more easily see Remi.

Dipping his head in acknowledgment without ever making eye contact, Remi fiddled with the label on his bottle. He smelled uneasy. Not upset exactly, but nervous. Why? Did he think Jake would condemn him for his father's sins?

"If you want my help, you have it, but I need to know what's going on."

Remi glanced up, his eyes solemn. "I don't even know if I can afford to pay you."

Jake started shaking his head as soon as the word *afford* left Remi's lips. "I'm not worried about it. You're my"—*mate*—"my friend. If you feel like you have to pay me, we can work something out. I'm not agreeing to help you for money. I keep getting the hint that you think Sterling is in danger of being hurt by someone and I want to help if I can." Not to mention that helping—protecting—his mate was his job and made him feel good.

"Okay." Taking a sip of his beer, Remi pulled his other foot onto the couch, bending it in front of him and resting his arm on it. He watched the beer bottle dangling between his fingers for a few moments and nodded, like he'd made up his mind. "It's Dirk. He's never hurt Sterling before. This is the first time, but..."

"But it probably won't be the last," Jake finished for him. *Fuck.* Even Remi called him Dirk. The guy was a piece of work.

What kind of man didn't want his own kids calling him dad?

"Well, that was my experience when I lived there, but I've always kept him from hurting Sterling. He pretty much ignores Sterling as long as Sterling stays out of his hair and I continue to live my life by his rules." Shaking his head, Remi snorted. "I've done that. I don't even hang around my fag best friend anymore." The venom in Remi's voice said the word fag wasn't his, but his father's. "Well, not where he would find out about it anyway. I still go to Chay and Keaton's, I just hide my bike. Pretty fucking pathetic, huh?" He took a long swig of beer, finishing it in one shot. He set it on the table and rested both his hands on his knees. He appeared far away, lost. "Simon and Bobby came with me to pick up Sterling one day and he kicked them out of the house. He told them to never come back because they're still friends with Chay. So I pretty much steer clear of them too."

Jake had the urge to pull Remi into his lap and assure him it'd be okay, but instead he sat and listened. His heart ached for Remi. Given what he'd learned throughout the day, it shouldn't come as such a shock the amount of control Remi's father had over his life, but it did. And it pissed Jake off to no end. The idea of someone threatening his mate didn't sit well with him.

Remi's eyes were watery, the scent of tears heavy in the air, but he didn't cry. He laughed, almost evilly. "The son of a bitch even told me what I was going to do for a living. One night over dinner he said, 'You need to fill out this application to the fire department, I already told the fire chief to be looking for it.' He threw the application at me and asked Sterling, 'What do you think about Remi being a fireman?' I don't know if it was a threat or not, but I didn't even argue. Besides, Sterling seemed to think it was cool. Of course, most six-year-olds do, huh? They all want to be firemen, policemen or astronauts...or a sports star. At that age, I wanted to be the quarterback of the

Dallas Cowboys."

"Ah, that explains your jersey number in high school. Roger Staubach, huh?"

Remi grinned. "Yeah."

"You were damn good. You probably could have been the Cowboy's quarterback, well a NFL quarterback at least. Tell me truthfully, how many colleges offered you football scholarships?"

"Only two. The scouts were watching other players, not me."

Jake didn't ask why Remi didn't take them up on it or seek out a scholarship to a school of his choice, when it meant he could've escaped his father. He didn't need to.

Jake came to the sudden realization that Remi's sexual orientation and getting him to accept being Jake's mate, were not the only obstacles in the way. He needed to help Remi find a way to protect and care for Sterling while getting the threat of Remi's abusive father out of their lives.

Setting his beer on the table, Jake moved a bit closer to Remi. "What about your mother? Is she still around?"

"Since I moved out, it seems like he beats Mom more. Sterling says it's because she makes sure Dirk doesn't go after him." The tears Remi had been holding back dripped down his cheek. Turning his head toward the TV, which was now a blue screen, he rested his cheek on his knee. "She's a lost cause. I've tried. I've tried so damn hard. She won't leave. Says she loves him and he needs her. At first I thought she was scared, but now..." He dashed the tears away with his hand. "Now, I think he means more to her than we do. Sterling and I have always depended on each other. That's how it's been since he was born. If it weren't for Sterling..." Remi raised his head, tears no longer on his cheeks, but his eyes were brimming with them.

"I'd have never gotten out of there alive if not for Sterling. Now, I need to get him out too before something terrible happens."

Jake swallowed the lump in his throat at what Remi implied. The thought of Remi not being around twisted Jake's insides in knots. Already, he saw a man he admired, even if Remi weren't his mate. The fact that he was made him that much more special.

Remi shook his head, and the tears ran down his cheeks. "I don't know why she didn't love us enough to leave. How could she choose him over her own kids? How can—? I should have taken him and run away a long time ago. This is my fault, I failed Sterl—"

"Shh. No, you didn't. Looks to me like you're doing a damn good job of looking out for your little brother." Jake touched his cheek, half expecting Remi to pull away. He didn't. Running his hand over Remi's face, Jake brushed away the tears. From day one, Remi's smaller size made Jake want to protect him, but now the feelings were even stronger. "It isn't your fault, Remi."

Remi leaned forward. His eyes shifted to wolf eyes as his head cocked. Finally, he closed his eyes.

Fuck, if that wasn't a turn-on Jake didn't know what was. His own eyes changed, drawing a groan from him. Blood rushed south, right to his cock.

Wrapping his hand around the back of Remi's neck, Jake tugged him forward. The smell of arousal pierced his nose before his lips covered Remi's. Jake didn't mess around. He caught his mate's chin in his other hand and pulled down as his tongue swooped into Remi's mouth.

Opening for him, Remi followed Jake's lead. His tongue slid along Jake's as his hands found their way to Jake's shoulders.

Jake ran his tongue over Remi's teeth, feeling the extended canines, and his own reciprocated. He'd never lost control over his body—his eyes and teeth—like he did with Remi around. It was both frustrating and fascinating at the same time. He wanted Remi writhing beneath him, wanting to please Jake as much as Jake wanted to please him.

His need to take over was so intense he was nearly shaking with it. He barely managed to suppress his more aggressive tendencies. Given Remi's past, Jake didn't want Remi feeling trapped.

They ended up with Jake lying on the couch and Remi on top of him.

Remi's hard cock pressed into Jake's hip and his dark hair fanned around them, concealing their faces.

Grabbing two handfuls of his mate's ass, Jake pressed against him, making sure Remi had no doubts that he was hard too.

Remi moaned and thrust his hips. He turned his head, breaking their kiss and exposing his neck as he nuzzled his face against Jake's shoulder.

Oh fuck. Jake's cock jerked, his hips bucking. The submissive action was almost his undoing. Turning Remi's head further, he brushed his hair back and licked a long line over the slim column of his throat.

Remi's pulse thundered beneath his tongue, attesting to his arousal just as strongly as the erection pressed against Jake's.

Dragging one fang down Remi's neck, Jake fought the urge to bite. He wanted to pin Remi still with his teeth and fuck him until neither of them could move. He didn't dare.

Remi shivered, spreading his legs, allowing Jake more access, and pressed his neck into Jake's teeth.

Oh fuck. It was too much. How could Jake resist such a sweet offer?

Riiiing.

Remi's whole body stiffened.

Fuck, fuck, fuck. Jake was either going to murder whoever was on the other end of the phone or buy them a fruit basket, he didn't know which.

Remi lifted his head. His eyes—still canine—widened and he pushed himself off of Jake. He opened his mouth to say something, his fangs still extended, and the phone rang again. Turning, he fled toward the kitchen.

Saved by the bell. Groaning, Jake sat up and ran his hands down his face. His fangs mashed against the inside of his lip. *Damn.* What had he been thinking? He shouldn't have taken things so far. As he adjusted himself, a movement out of the corner of his eye caught his attention. He looked in time to see Sterling's dark head pop back down the hallway.

Oh God! What had he done? Remi hung up the phone, feeling like his stomach was in his throat, and leaned forward on the counter. He rested his head between his forearms. Thank God his mom had called to make sure he had Sterling. What if the phone hadn't rung?

Remi rocked his forehead back and forth on the cool laminate, resisting the urge to bang his head into it a few times and knock some sense into himself. At the time, the fact that Jake was a man had never crossed Remi's mind. It had felt like the most natural thing in the world to do. It had been a compulsion, a deep aching need, but now... *Fuck.* He'd wanted it. What the hell was wrong with him? He wasn't gay...he couldn't be.

Shit. Was Jake gay? Or had Remi made him kiss back somehow?

"Remi?"

Remi raised his head and stood as Jake stepped into the kitchen. Jake cocked a brow, looking Remi up and down. "Everything okay?"

Remi's stomach plummeted under the scrutiny. He had to get Jake out of here so he could think. "Uh, yeah. It was just my mom calling to make sure I had Sterling." How the hell was he going to explain his actions? Remi set the cordless phone down on the counter, knowing any excuse he offered was going to sound lame as hell, but he had to try. He wanted to just forget this. "Listen, Jake, I'm so—"

Jake shook his head. "Nothing to be sorry about." He frowned and lifted his hand. For a brief moment Remi thought Jake was going to reach out to him, but Jake threaded his fingers through his hair and let out a deep breath. "You've had a hell of a day. I should probably go."

A jolt of disappointment—no, relief—rushed through Remi. Jake had just given him a way out. Discovering Sterling's bruises had fried his brain. *Yeah, that's it.* His kissing Jake was due to stress, and he was out of his mind with worry. A niggling in the back of his head said that wasn't right, that he'd been attracted to Jake from the instant he'd met him, but Remi shook it off. It was anxiety, it had to be. "Yeah."

Chapter Four

Matt Mahihkan barely let Jake get all the way in the office before he started hounding him. "Come on, Jake. Give me a chance. I'm good with a gun."

Jake growled and pushed past the pup. Matt was eighteen years old and dying to be something he considered cooler than the office manager he was.

"No. You're not getting a gun. You're here to run the office. And for the hundredth time, we don't shoot people." Jake had had this same damn conversation every morning since hiring the kid.

"Rhys shoots people," Matt whispered and darted a glance toward Rhys' office. He leaned against the doorframe between Jake's office and the reception area.

Jake sat and shuffled through the messages on his desk, trying his best to ignore the kid. The next time Rhys suggested they hire pack, he was going to fire the man, best friend or not. "Matt, go get me some coffee."

Matt threw his hands in the air, let out a long suffering sigh and stalked off.

For the first time Jake noticed the pup's clothes, a pale pink polo shirt with thin yellow stripes, a pair of khakis, pink socks and black leather loafers. Jake cocked his head and blinked, not sure he was seeing correctly.

48

Rhys came around the corner with a coffee cup in hand, grumbling under his breath. "I haven't shot anyone...this week." He scowled, showing off the small scar on his forehead, and glanced back at Matt. Shaking his head, he continued into Jake's office. His limp was more pronounced than usual. "We need to come up with a fucking dress code now?"

"Apparently." Jake knew better than to question the man about his leg, but he wondered what Rhys had done to make it act up. He resigned himself to keeping an eye on Rhys. If it seemed like the old injury was bothering Rhys too much, Jake would browbeat his friend into taking something for the pain.

"Wait until I see Gadget. I'm going to give him all sorts of shit. Does he know his oldest boy is dressing like a fucking yuppie?" Setting his cup on Jake's desk, Rhys eased into the chair opposite Jake. His leg was stiff enough that he ended up more or less falling into the seat. Picking his coffee back up, he took a sip. "You been up all night or something?"

Jake shrugged. He'd tossed and turned all night but hell if he would tell Rhys. At around two in the morning he'd gotten up to do some work on a case, though he couldn't think of anything but Remi's blushing apology. Jake never should have let Remi off so easily, except it'd been hard not to when Remi had reeked of unease. The man had so much to deal with Jake hadn't felt right about pressuring him. Now he was beginning to wonder if he'd made the right decision.

Then there was Sterling ducking back around the corner. Had Sterling seen them kissing on the couch? How was Remi going to react when he found out what Sterling saw?

Jake wavered between wanting the phone to ring and praying it wouldn't. He was pretty sure Remi would try to act like the kiss hadn't happened, and that was the last thing Jake wanted to do.

"Hey, you still with me?" Rhys waved his hand back and forth.

"Yeah, what's up?"

"I remembered where I had heard that name you mentioned last night."

"And?" Jake had called Rhys on his way home from Remi's apartment and given him Remi's dad's name. He knew Rhys well enough to know if he had a name, he'd start investigating first thing in the morning. Rhys lived to solve crimes, chase bad guys and raise hell.

Rhys nodded. "Lassiter is a fucking reservation cop. I came across him when I worked for the FBI. He's a real ass."

Fuck. Jake sat back in his chair, stunned. *Un-fucking-believable.* Why hadn't Remi told him his dad was a rez cop?

"There was a murder out at the reservation about fifteen years ago. It was before I was in the agency but I've heard stories and I don't doubt them from my own run-ins with the man." Rhys took a drink, watching Jake over the brim of the cup.

"Like what? What did you hear?"

"Here's your coffee." Matt came in carrying Jake's steaming cup. "I still don't see why you won't hire someone else to run the office and let me investigate. I'd be good at it." He set Jake's mug down, sloshing a little bit onto the desk. "Oops. Sorry."

Before Jake could roll his chair over and get the tissues off the bookcase to his right, Matt squeezed past Rhys and the desk and tripped over Rhys' outstretched legs.

"Watch it." Rhys growled and his hand shot out, quick as lightning, catching the kid before he went down. Rhys didn't even spill the contents of his mug.

Damn, the man had amazing reflexes. Jake got up and

grabbed the box of tissues.

"Sorry, Rhys." Matt darted a glance at Jake and back to Rhys. "Uh..."

"It's all right. Go—" Jake waved his hand around, "—do something."

Matt was a good kid, but the boy had two left feet. Especially in Rhys' presence. The kid was terrified of Rhys. It amused Jake to no end. It shouldn't, since lots of people were afraid of Rhys, but it seemed irrational. Rhys may be big, dark and intimidating, but the man did what he did very well because he honestly cared and wanted to help others.

Jake blotted the mess up and tossed the tissue in the trash next to his desk.

As soon as Matt left, closing the door behind him, Rhys grimaced and rubbed his bad thigh. His tanned face was a little pale.

Jake raised a brow, asking without asking.

"I'm fine."

Jake nodded. "You were telling me about Lassiter?"

"That murder case went cold, but there were all sorts of things that didn't add together. The asshole's own kid got beaten badly. The kid was in ICU, internal bleeding, and a whole bunch of other shit. He was in critical condition. According to agents who worked the case, Lassiter was more pissed his son didn't stand up for himself than he was worried. Didn't even treat it like it was connected to the other boy's death."

What? Jake growled, feeling like someone had slapped him. *The scars on Remi's back and legs.* Jake had wondered what they were from, but he'd never— He'd assumed it was some sort of accident, but knowing Remi had nearly died...

His jaw clenched and a chill raced up Jake's spine. Nothing like that would ever happen to Remi again. Anyone who laid a hand on him would answer to Jake.

"Jake, you okay? What are you pissed off about all of a sudden?"

"No, I'm not fine." He wanted to hit something, preferably Dirk Lassiter. "See what else you can dig up. I want to know everything about this fucker."

Rhys nodded. "I've already got a call in to my ex boss. He's still with the FBI and he worked that case. What are you not telling me?"

"Dirk Lassiter is Remi's dad."

Rhys shook his head, letting out a long whistle.

"Exactly. And that kid who nearly died is my mate."

ৎৡৡৡ

Is that Jake? It's blac—no it's not a Tahoe.

"Yo, Remi. Hello? Throw the ball." Sterling waved his arms back and forth over his head.

Huh? Oh, right. Sterling. Remi tossed the ball, being careful not to overthrow it because they were in the empty lot behind Remi's apartment. If Sterling missed, the football would end up in the street.

Remi glanced beyond Sterling at the road, looking for a certain black SUV and hating himself for the weakness. He told himself it was because Jake was helping him and that he needed to apologize for last night, but he couldn't deny the thought of seeing Jake was appealing. But then why wouldn't it be? Jake was a great guy...a good friend.

"Remi!"

Remi looked up in time for the football to hit him right smack-dab in the middle of the forehead. *Oww.* His sunglasses fell off his nose with the impact. Staggering back a little, he rubbed his head with one hand and adjusted his shades with the other. Oh man, maybe Sterling had his heart set on the wrong position. If he threw that hard all the time—

"Oh my God. Are you okay?" Sterling jogged toward him, already reaching for Remi's head. "Let me see. Are you hurt?"

"Cut it out. I'm fine." Remi batted his brother's hands away. "It was a good, hard throw."

Sterling groaned. "You have a big red spot in the middle of your forehead."

"I bet. Maybe you should play quarterback."

"What are you doing? I thought we were going to play ball."

"We are playing ball." Was that a—nope, it was a minivan.

"Since when did you start catching with your head?" Sterling stepped into his line of sight, cutting off the view of the road.

"Don't be a smartass." He shoved Sterling's shoulder lightly.

Sterling shoved back. "What's bugging you?" He grinned and arched a brow.

"What?" Remi frowned.

The kid's smirk was downright evil. "Thinking about Jake?"

"Wha—uh. Whata you mean?" Good God, when did Sterling start reading minds? How the fuck was Remi supposed to answer? "Why in the world would I be thinking about Jake?"

"Other than the fact he's a really great guy?"

Ugh, like he needed a reminder. Remi cringed and picked

up the ball, shaking his head. When he straightened, ball in hand, Sterling was beaming at him.

"Jake's hot."

What? Remi got a funny feeling in his stomach. *Damn, it's really warm out today.* He ran his hand over the back of his neck. Sterling shouldn't be looking at other guys. Especially when the guy in question was Remi's. Wait. Where had that thought come from?

"Don't you think so?" Sterling's brow wrinkled.

"No. I guess. Why?" The image of Jake grabbing a handful of Remi's hair, jerking his head back and biting his neck, popped into Remi's mind. He could practically feel Jake's fangs pressed against his neck, like last night. *Fuck.* He was getting hard. Right before Remi's eyes Sterling's blue shirt turned gray. *Damnit.* He was losing his mind. Remi took a deep breath, trying to clear his head.

"Are you sure you're okay? You're blushing."

"No, I'm not blushing. Don't be ridiculous. I mean—he's a guy. You aren't supposed to think other guys are hot." Remi didn't sound convincing, even to himself.

Sterling sighed and gave him a look from under his lashes as if to say, "Yeah sure."

What the fuck is that about? Remi glared, his vision returning to normal. "Just—go out for a pass already." Jesus, all he needed was for Sterling to start checking out guys. Remi pointed toward the far end of the lot. "Go."

Sterling took off.

Remi threw the ball in a beautiful spiral, right into his brother's hands.

This time after Sterling caught the ball, he ran it back instead of throwing it. He came to a halt, panting and sweaty, in front of Remi. After giving Remi the ball, he dropped his hands to his knees. "You know, there's nothing wrong with being gay. Jake's gay. Chay and Keaton are gay. I mean..."

Remi sputtered before finding his voice. "What? How do you know Jake's gay?" Of course, Remi had come to the same conclusion last night. It made sense, Jake had kissed Remi. However, Remi wasn't gay and he'd kissed Jake. It had been a hell of a kiss, though. And it would have gone much further if— *Fuck*, there went his eyes again. Remi groaned and rubbed his forehead. He was beginning to get a headache. Funny, Sterling hitting him in the head hadn't done it, but all the talk about who's gay and who's not. And God, if Sterling slipped and said something... "Sterling, can we just play ball? Not everyone's gay, all right?"

The kid shrugged. "Okay, well, bi then." He turned and ran toward the street.

Remi let his eyes adjust once more then tossed the ball and waited. If the kid kept on like this, Remi was going to be grateful for summer vacation to be over.

Sterling caught it and trotted back toward Remi. As soon as he was within talking distance, he flipped the ball to Remi. "You know I don't care. I mean if you and Jake—"

"Sterling..."

"It's perfectly fine with me. You guys looked good together last ni—"

Oh fuck! What had he seen? "Sterling, I don't care what you saw, drop it." Remi shook his head and pointed for Sterling to go out for a pass. *Damn.* He himself didn't understand his attraction to Jake.

"Okay, okay." Sterling held his hands up and took off again.

Remi stepped back and passed the ball. He threw it harder

this time, making Sterling have to hustle for it. Maybe it would wear him out and he'd stop with the uncomfortable questions.

The ball was high, but Sterling didn't hesitate, he jumped for it, snagging it out of midair.

It was a hell of a catch. Remi smiled.

Sterling tripped over his own feet as soon as he landed. Tucking his head, he rolled and ended up flat on his back. He lay there for a few seconds, then his hand shot straight up, ball still clutched in it. "I freakin' rock." Sterling hopped to his feet, grinning from ear to ear.

Please throw the damn thing back. I can't take any more of Sterling's endless questions. Remi groaned, seeing Sterling head toward him.

Halfway back, Sterling hesitated and the happy expression slipped from his face.

What the—? Something hit the back of Remi's head, hard. "Ow. Fuck." Remi rubbed it.

"Watch your mouth, Remington. Is that any way to greet me?"

Bile rose in Remi's throat. *Shit.* He swallowed hard, turning toward his father. "No. I'm sorry, Dirk."

Dirk Lassiter stood two feet away with his arms crossed over his massive chest. He appeared to be looking down his hawk-like nose at Remi, even though his brown eyes were hidden behind his mirrored sunglasses.

He wasn't much taller than Remi, but he was bigger, more intimidating. The years had not diminished the lean, hard muscle he'd worked hard to build. His long black hair was tied back in a braid. He was in his tan uniform with the gun belt around his waist.

God, Remi hated that fucking belt. It was a standard law

enforcement utility belt, essentially two leather straps velcroed together, making it thick. Getting hit with it hurt like a son of a bitch. Remi shivered.

"You need a haircut." Dirk's breath was surprisingly liquor free today.

Remi didn't know what to say. His hair wasn't at all longer than Dirk's. But any response would get him smacked, so he just nodded.

"How's work? Put out any fires lately?"

Out of habit, Remi fidgeted, shifting from foot to foot, and managed to get himself out of striking distance. *Okay, this is good. A safe subject. I can do this.* "Work is good. Thankfully, we haven't had any fires lately. I'm thinking about applying for the open EMT position."

Dirk's brow furrowed.

Oh fuck. Remi winced.

Stepping closer, Dirk glowered. "That's the thanks I get for getting you that great job? You want to be a fucking nurse? Why not tell everyone you want to be a faggot while you're at it. It's a faggot job."

Remi flinched, inching backward, not even caring if it appeared like he was retreating.

Sterling finally came up beside them. His hand touched the small of Remi's back briefly and slid away. "Hey, Dirk, is it time for me to go?"

"Yeah. Get your shit. It's hot out here." He glanced at Sterling, then grinned, looking back at Remi. "You don't honestly want to be a pansy-ass EMT, do you?"

"No." Remi chuckled, hoping it didn't sound nervous. "I was joking around."

"Well, quit joking and take your goddamn job more

seriously and maybe you'll make something of your worthless ass." He looked back at Sterling. "What are you doing standing there? I said I was ready to leave."

"I'm ready. I didn't bring anything with me." Handing Remi the ball, Sterling gave him a wobbly smile.

Taking the ball, Remi ruffled the kid's hair. It was the most affection he was allowed to show in front of his father. "I'll come get you tomorrow and we can practice again. We'll have you ready for football season in no time."

"Bunch of horseshit. He ain't gonna make the team. 'Sides, who the hell is going to pay for it if he does?" Dirk glared at Remi.

Fuck. If the bastard denied Sterling the opportunity to play... "It's not a problem. I'll pay—"

"You saying I don't have enough money to take care of my family?" Dirk came closer, bumping Remi with his chest.

Remi backed away, out of reach again. "No, Dirk. I didn't want you to be bothered with it. Honest. I was only trying to help." If Sterling enjoyed it and he got a scholarship, he could go to college and get away. Not that it mattered. Remi would scrounge up the money to pay for Sterling's college.

"I don't need your money, Remington." Dirk's cool tone never changed, but the snarl he made was downright nasty, letting Remi know he'd been insulted.

"No, of course not, I—I'm sorry."

Grinning, Dirk nodded. "That's what I thought." He lifted his hand toward Remi's face.

It was a mean, nasty grin and Remi recoiled, waiting for the blow.

Dirk patted his cheek, hard, making it sting a little. "Nevertheless, if you wanna pay for the brat to play ball, I'll let you. It's a waste of money in my opinion. I wasted enough letting you play. And we all see how well that turned out."

Remi nearly sighed in relief. God, he hated the son of a bitch. The man got some perverse pleasure out of making Remi squirm.

Sterling's attention darted back and forth between them, all the while inching his way closer to Remi.

Dirk cleared his throat. "Let's go, boy. Your mother has dinner going." He walked away.

Bending close to Sterling's ear, Remi whispered, "Do not mention football to him again. Just let it go. I'll take care of it, okay?"

Nodding, Sterling squeezed Remi's arm. "See you tomorrow." He ran to catch up with their father.

Dirk turned around, coming back.

Damn, damn, damn. What did he want? Remi tried not to fidget. His heart was racing, and his palms were so sweaty the ball kept slipping. He pressed it against his leg.

"Who's the new friend of yours?" Dirk cocked a brow.

"Excuse me?" Remi stiffened. "What friend?"

"The big guy. Drives a black Tahoe."

How did he know about Jake? He couldn't possibly know about the other night. No, of course not. Chill bumps raised on Remi's arms.

"Jake?" Sterling asked.

Dirk looked toward Sterling. "Jake, huh? What's he do for a living?"

"He's a security guard or something," Sterling answered without missing a beat.

Remi didn't know whether to kiss him or kill him. If Dirk

found out Sterling had lied— Fuck, Remi's hands were shaking.

Apparently satisfied for now, Dirk nodded. Moving back around, he walked off.

Sterling shrugged, his eyes wide, then followed their father to the car.

Remi tried to breathe normally. Even though Dirk was leaving, the panic was still there. He hated himself for letting the man affect him like this. When would he outgrow the feeling of helplessness?

A sense of peace overcame Remi, his lungs taking in air again. His hands stopped quivering and suddenly everything felt all right. It was the same calm that came over him at the diner the other morning.

"Remi?" A hand touched his shoulder.

Chapter Five

As Dirk Lassiter drove off, Jake rubbed Remi's back with one hand and tried not to let his anger show. Watching his normally cocky, self-assured mate cower gave Jake a real uneasy feeling. It took every ounce of energy he possessed to stand back until Dirk left. What had Remi endured when he lived at home?

Amazingly, when Jake had showed up, the fear dissipated from Remi's scent in seconds. He was beginning to suspect that Remi was reacting to his presence. It must be a mate thing, their bodies responding to one another, although he'd never heard of such a thing. Lust? Sure, it was pretty common for mates to react to one another's arousal, but this... Jake knew darn well Remi's mind was still in turmoil, he could see it on his face. "You okay?"

Remi leaned into Jake's touch a little, not quite enough to bring their bodies in contact. "Yeah. I hate letting Sterling go with him, knowing there's a chance something bad might happen."

"We're going to fix that."

Remi's head whipped around, his gaze meeting Jake's. "We are?"

"Yes, but we need to talk."

J. L. Langley

Remi looked skeptical, but dipped his head toward the apartments. "You want a beer?"

"Yeah."

Flipping the football to Jake, Remi walked to the buildings.

Jake caught the ball and followed. "You didn't tell me he was a rez cop."

"I didn't?" Remi's steps faltered.

Staying quiet until they were inside, Jake shut the door and leaned against it. "You know you didn't. Why?"

Remi groaned and his shoulders slumped before he turned around. "I was afraid you wouldn't help me. Most people are intimidated when they find out what Dirk does for a living. Being a rez cop has a lot more leeway than a city cop. The feds only get involved when there's a murder. There are supposed to be checks and balances, but..." His gaze was cast downward.

Fuck, Jake hated that look. It was the same look Remi had the other night when he'd admitted to being abused by his dad. It was shame. "You have to trust me, Remi. If I'm going to help I have to be able to prove he's a dirty cop or a danger to Sterling. He is, right? Both of those?" Tossing the ball onto the couch, Jake pushed off of the door. He knew damn well he shouldn't but he went to Remi, catching his chin and making him look up.

Remi closed his eyes and nuzzled his face into Jake's hand.

Jake stared, mesmerized. It was such a subservient reaction. He had never seen a werewolf react this way. Only his human lovers had ever been this submissive. He sort of understood how mating worked, but it still baffled him. Remi was straight, yet here he stood once again showing a willingness to physically surrender to Jake. And damned if it didn't make Jake harder than a fucking rock. Of course, the smell of Remi all sweaty from playing ball didn't hurt either.

Remi blinked. His eyes turned canine and the scent of arousal grew strong.

It took every ounce of willpower he had, but Jake stepped back. He wanted nothing more than to take what his mate offered, but he needed information to try and protect Sterling *and* Remi. "Tell me about the murder."

"What?" Remi's voice cracked. A blush tinged his face before he abruptly moved away and began pacing. The scent of lust turned to unease and Remi's shoulders stiffened. "How'd you know about that? You started looking into it already?"

Interesting. Once again Jake had to wonder if Remi had even realized he'd nestled into the touch until after Jake had drawn attention to it by pulling away. "Yes, I've started looking into it already, I told you I would. Now, I need you to tell me what you know."

"There isn't much to tell."

"According to my source there's a lot to tell."

Shrugging, Remi walked off toward the kitchen. "Not really. It didn't have anything to do with Dirk." He opened the refrigerator, withdrew two beers and tossed one to Jake.

Jake caught it and set it on the coffee table. "Remi."

Remi sprawled on the couch, propping his feet on the table.

Jake hadn't seen the posturing in the last two days. The smug air was back. Whatever happened, Remi had no intention of letting on that it bothered him. Jake knew damn well this was Remi's way of keeping his friends at bay, but it pissed Jake off anyway. Maybe Remi's distance was due to the kiss last night.

Remi didn't say a word.

When Remi finally looked at him, Jake sat there, holding Remi's gaze. Jake was not going to let Remi hide from him.

Maybe it was selfish but he wanted everything, the bad and the good.

Fidgeting a little, Remi turned away. He set the beer on the table so hard some sloshed out, and he ran his hands over his face. "Billy and I were on our way back home from the movies. We got jumped crossing a field. That's all there was to it."

"By who? Did you see who attacked you?"

"Don't know."

"You didn't know them? Or they didn't catch them?"

"I don't remember. I got the shit beat out of me. All I remember is waking in the hospital, with Simon, Bobby and Chay around me. Dirk had work to do like he always did and my mom was taking care of Sterling, who had just been born."

Jake closed his eyes, getting his emotions under control. He couldn't imagine not having a family to count on. Before his parents died, they'd been wonderful. They'd been strict at times, sure, but there was never a doubt they'd loved Jake and Tina. It was amazing that Remi had the relationship he did with Sterling since he certainly had nothing to compare it to.

Opening his eyes, Jake found Remi staring at him, bottom lip held between his teeth. "Did your father even try to find out who did it?"

Remi shook his head. "I don't know. Dirk never had me questioned. I was in the hospital for most of the investigation. Not that it would have mattered, I didn't remember the attack. Still don't." He looked down. "I just remember..." Taking several deep breaths, he rolled his eyes toward the ceiling, keeping the tears at bay. He finally turned back to Jake and smiled. It was a sad smile, full of sorrow.

It made Jake's heart hurt. He wanted to haul Remi into his arms and comfort him, but he didn't dare. Remi wasn't telling him something and Jake needed to find out what that something was. He had a feeling it was very important. "What do you remember?"

"Doesn't matter. I don't recall anything useful. I can't even remember the movie we went to see, or why we were in the field."

Standing, Jake caught Remi's arm and pulled him up. "I need you to trust me."

"I do trust you. I trust you so much it scares the hell outta me." Remi's voice was soft, awed.

The honesty and faith went straight to Jake's head and his cock, which had never fully softened. He stared into Remi's beautiful eyes, watching as they shifted. "I've been needing to kiss you since the moment I got here."

Remi's eyes widened, then he sighed and closed his eyes.

It was all the invitation Jake needed. He never even stopped to think what he was doing. He just took what his mate offered, tugging Remi forward and slanting his mouth over Remi's. Without wasting any time, his tongue traced the seam of Remi's lips.

Remi opened, kissing back. He let Jake explore his mouth, following Jake's lead. Panting, he pulled away and held Jake's gaze as he slid to the floor. Resting his head against Jake's thigh, he closed his eyes again. "Jake." His voice was strangled, a raspy plea. The war he waged in his mind was written all over his face.

Running his hand over Remi's head, Jake tried to soothe him. "Remi." Why was he doing this?

A hand snaked up the inside of his leg, stroking his calf through the denim. Remi rubbed his cheek against Jake's leg and his pale green eyes fluttered open, already shifted into wolf eyes. He lifted his nose in the air and sniffed. His fangs peeked out from under his top lip. Moving his face closer to Jake's crotch, he scrunched his nose and snuggled his face against Jake's jeans.

Fuck. Jake hissed out a breath and his cock jerked. His vision blurred, no longer seeing color, making him blink several times to focus.

He brushed his fingers through Remi's hair. He wanted desperately to draw Remi's head forward and demand Remi take out his cock and suck it. But he didn't dare.

His hand clenched and unclenched in the silky dark hair. He should stop this, yet he hadn't started it in the first place.

Remi blinked and unbuttoned Jake's jeans without ever looking away. Slowly, he tugged down the waistband, licking his lips as he bared the head of Jake's cock.

Oh God. The sight of him licking his lips— Jake moaned.

As Remi pulled the pants down further, Jake's prick slapped against his lower abdomen, leaving a wet spot. His conscience screamed at him to make certain this was what Remi really wanted, yet at the same time he found himself reluctant to break the spell. Maybe Remi needed this...maybe they both did.

Remi leaned forward and buried his nose in Jake's balls. A soft drawn-out satisfied sound left his throat. It wasn't the sound of a reluctant man. It was like music to Jake's ears.

Something warm and wet slid across his balls. Startled, he caught Remi's hair in his fist and tilted his head back slightly. As good as it felt, Jake was still being cautious. Had he somehow made Remi feel pressured?

Remi shook off Jake's hold and licked a long line up Jake's balls to the base of his cock. His eyes were glazed over as he concentrated on what he was doing. The look of sheer bliss on his face was all Jake needed to see to make him give in and enjoy the moment. It was also the prettiest fucking sight he had ever seen. His stomach muscles clenched and unclenched. His prick jerked.

Using Remi's hair to pull him away, Jake grabbed his dick with his other hand and tapped Remi on the cheek with it. And damned if Remi didn't open his mouth, trying to catch it. Jake tightened his hold on Remi and tugged him back.

Remi licked his lips, focused on Jake's cock. After a few seconds, Remi's canine gaze met Jake's, then his lips parted and he whimpered. Closing his mouth over Jake's cock, Remi slipped all the way down in one movement. No gagging. Nothing. He drew back up and did it again. His hands slid to knead Jake's thighs.

Jake's head swam and his whole body tingled. Remi was like a whirlwind. He alternated between licking and running his mouth over the shaft of Jake's cock. He found a rhythm, using suction every time he went up. Happy little moaning noises vibrated along Jake's prick and wet slurping sounds echoed in the quiet apartment.

Holy shit. Remi knew exactly what the fuck he was doing. This couldn't be the first time he'd ever sucked cock, could it? He was just too damn good at it. Even his newly acquired fangs didn't seem to hamper the apparent talent he was showing Jake. And he seemed to love doing it. Jake could barely wrap his mind around what his brain was telling him. How? When? He couldn't think with Remi on his knees, driving him insane.

Panting, Jake fought to keep from driving deep into Remi's sweet mouth. His gums stung and his own teeth dropped. Remi's saliva ran over his balls. Fuck, he was so close.

Sliding a hand down, Remi cupped Jake's balls, then used the spit that had dripped and smeared it around. Remi groaned around his prick, and the smell of Remi's come reached Jake's nose.

"Oh, fuck." With his whole body tingling, Jake arched his back. When he came, Remi's nose was buried in his pubes.

Instead of gagging, Remi purred.

When Jake could finally think again he realized he had Remi's hair in a death grip. *Shit.* He let go, but Remi didn't. He kept sucking lightly.

It was beginning to tickle. Jake ran his fingers over Remi's cheek. Remi leaned into the caress, as was becoming his habit, then he stiffened and let go of Jake's cock.

"Oh God." Remi's eyes were once again human and all the color had drained from his face. His hand flew to his mouth and he fell back on his butt. Scuttling backward, he began shaking his head.

Shit. Jake hitched his pants up and dropped to his knees. He reached out, but Remi moved further away. When he hit the wall, he pushed himself up, coming to his feet. He looked like he'd seen a ghost.

Jake wasn't sure what to do to ease Remi's mind. He wasn't about to let Remi pretend it didn't happen, nor would he let his mate distance himself from him. "Remi?"

"No." Remi held up a hand, warding Jake off. "Don't touch me." Oh God, what had he done? He'd actually— He shook his head harder, trying to make it go away. No, he hadn't. He couldn't. It wasn't him. But he *had* done it. He could still taste Jake in his mouth. His teeth itched, threatening to lengthen again at the thought.

"Remi..." Jake acted as though he was trying to gentle a scared animal.

Remi watched the hand coming toward him. It was like slow motion. He argued with himself. Should he let Jake touch him? Why was he even considering it? He batted Jake's hand aside and walked backward toward the front door. He had to get Jake to leave. "Out!"

"Let's talk about this." Jake spoke softly, sounding steady and sure.

It pissed Remi off even further. Why wasn't he upset? Remi had lost his fucking mind and here Jake was trying to act like this wasn't a big fucking deal, when it was. What had Remi been thinking? Why had he done that? Damn it, his chest hurt and he couldn't fucking breathe. It felt like someone had slugged him and knocked the air out of him. "Get out!" The doorknob hit him in the back and his elbow banged against the door, but he barely felt it.

Jake's face flushed, his jaw clenching. "We *both* wanted that."

"No."

Groaning, Jake dragged his hand through his hair. He took a deep breath and lowered his voice again. "This is a natural reaction. We're werewolves. We're mates— Shit, I've been trying not to tell you that but, damn it... Don't pull away from me now, Remi."

Remi snapped.

"What? Mates? You did this to me? It's some werewolf bullshit?" That was it. He was possessed or something. Jake had done something to him to make Remi want him. Remi jerked the door open. He was losing it, he knew he was but he couldn't seem to stop himself. "Get the fuck out!"

Growling, Jake shook his head and closed his eyes for a moment then headed toward the door. He stopped right before he walked out, keeping his back to Remi. "We aren't done with this. I won't pressure you, but I'm not going to let you ignore what's between us." He turned his head, his gaze boring into

Remi's. He looked...sad. "You know where I am when you're ready to talk."

Remi closed his eyes, fighting the tears, and shut the door. Why did Jake have to look so hurt? "Goddamn it!" Remi punched the wall beside the door. It hurt like a son of a bitch and didn't solve a damn thing. Now he was going to have to patch the hole he'd left.

Looking down at the wet spot on his shorts, Remi remembered how Jake had felt and tasted. He shivered, then banged the back of his head into the wall, trying to forget. Sinking to the floor, Remi finally let the tears fall.

Chapter Six

"You should get him a dog."

Remi considered it for a minute as he watched Sterling roll around in the grass with Pita, his best friend's golden retriever puppy. "What in the world would I do with a dog while I was at work? You know there's no way in hell Dirk would let Sterling keep it at home."

Chay shrugged and leaned on the railing of his redwood deck. "You've never had a pet, have you?"

"Nope."

Keaton, Chay's mate—there was that word again, whatever the hell it was supposed to mean—came out of the back door with a yellow tennis ball in hand.

Spotting Keaton, Remi grinned. "You could just give me Pita. You have Keaton now, what do you need with two—?"

Keaton flipped Remi off on his way down the steps.

Remi chuckled. After last night it felt good to get back some normalcy. Keaton was so much fun to pick on. Over the past several months he and Keaton had become good friends, but when they'd first met, he was ashamed to admit, the insults had been real. Now it was a game they both continued. "It's not nice to give me the finger in front of my little brother."

"Yeah, and it's not nice to call me a dog either, dipshit." Smiling, Keaton kept walking toward where Sterling and Pita were playing, obviously not in the least upset by Remi's teasing.

Chay groaned, shaking his head, but he too was grinning as he watched Keaton throw the tennis ball.

Abandoning Sterling, Pita gave chase. Keaton reached out a hand and helped Sterling up. Within seconds the puppy brought the ball back and dropped it at Sterling's feet. Sterling tossed it.

His laughter made Remi rethink getting him a puppy of his own, but Remi had other things to get under control first.

He'd done a lot of thinking about what Jake had said last night. He wanted to ask Chay about it, but didn't know how to bring it up. Remi turned his attention back to Chay.

The look on Chay's face when he watched his mate—like now—was very tender, loving. It made Remi even more curious about mates. Chay had never looked at any girl like that, as though they were the center of his world. He'd always been a happy-go-lucky kind of guy and the one in the group who picked everyone else's spirits up. Looking on the bright side of things was a habit of his. But now, it was as if he had this inner peace and he was where he wanted to be. It was really strange, but somehow right.

The corner of Chay's lip turned up, his eyes sparkling.

Remi switched his focus back to the yard.

Keaton, Sterling and Pita were all digging under a bush next to the fence. Trying to get the ball, Remi assumed. Sterling was on his belly, his cheek pressed to the ground, peering under the shrub. The only visible part of Pita was his wagging tail. Keaton was on his butt with one leg under the bush and a look of total concentration on his face.

Remi found himself grinning too. "You'd think they'd be

smart enough to get a broom or something. Or at the very least get Sterling to try and kick it out. He's got longer legs."

Chay laughed. "Shh... Bit has a Napoleon complex as it is, don't go pointing out to him that your fourteen-year-old brother is taller."

"Well, Sterling *is* almost fifteen," Remi teased.

"Sometimes I'm not sure Bit isn't." He turned to Remi and chuckled. "Fifteen, I mean. He's very playful when you get him around the pups. Guess that's why he makes a good teacher. I keep trying to convince him he should teach elementary school rather than college."

Chay had always liked kids himself. It had never occurred to Remi until now that by being with Keaton, his friend would likely miss out on kids of his own.

"Why are you frowning?" Chay bumped Remi's shoulder. "You've looked distracted since you got here."

"Yeah?"

"Yeah. What's up?"

What wasn't? "Why did you pick Keaton as a mate?"

Turning his body toward Remi, Chay furrowed his brow.

Remi held up his hand, stalling Chay. "Don't blow a gasket. I like Keaton and I want you to be happy. But you have to admit, it's pretty damn weird. You never liked men before."

Chay jerked his head toward the back door. "Come on, let's get a beer." After opening the door for Remi, Chay followed him in. When they reached the kitchen, Chay got them both a beer and hopped onto the counter.

Spinning one of the kitchen chairs around, Remi sat too and took a swig from his can. He tried to think of a way to rephrase his question. He wanted to know about mates, yet at the same time he didn't. *Fuck*, his hands were shaking. "Why

Keaton? Why not a woman?"

Chay cocked his head. "You wanna tell me what happened? Why you're this unnerved?"

"Not really, no."

Chay frowned. "I think you need to anyway."

Setting his beer on the table, Remi clutched his hands together, stuffed them between his knees and squeezed. As he stared up at the ceiling, his stomach cramped and sweat trickled down his temple.

The back door opened and Keaton came in, sniffed and darted a glance at Remi, then Chay. His eyebrows shot up. "Umm, okay. Uh, how about I take Sterling and go get some pizza?"

Sterling came in behind Keaton, grinning from ear to ear, and shut the door behind him. "Can I have a dog?"

"No." Remi flinched. That hadn't come out right. He'd sort of snapped. "We'll see. Not right now, though."

Wrinkling his nose, Sterling looked like he was going to argue but he shrugged instead. "Okay."

Keaton stepped up to Chay, rested his hand on Chay's chest and raised up on his toes. He kissed Chay's cheek and whispered something in his ear. Catching the words "okay" and "Remi", Remi realized Keaton was asking about him.

Chay nodded and kissed Keaton back. "There's money in my wallet. Make certain Sterling stays in the car and not visible. If his father finds out he was with you, there will be hell to pay."

Remi groaned. How fucked up was it that Remi hadn't even considered Sterling being seen?

Sterling ducked his head, a blush staining his cheeks. "Y'all know it has nothing to do with what Remi and I think, right?"

"Of course we do." Keaton slung his arm over Sterling's shoulder, escorting him out of the kitchen. "Come on, let's go get pizza."

The front door opened and closed. Remi picked up his beer.

Chay walked over and sat in the chair next to Remi. "Now tell me what happened. Why the unease and the sudden interest in mates?"

"I don't know where to start." The queasy feeling crawled up his chest and his pulse pounded in his ears. He debated telling Chay what had happened for several minutes before finally deciding he was probably the only person who would understand. If anyone could help Remi figure things out, it was Chay.

Remi told Chay everything—the kiss, the blowjob, Jake's confirmation that they were mates—and waited, half expecting Chay to laugh at him. It would have been no less than he deserved, considering the amount of shit he'd given Chay over Keaton, but Chay didn't laugh.

"You don't pick your mate. Everything about them calls to you."

So it *was* an instinctual response? Like he had to Jake? "You mean you lose control over your eyes and your teeth."

Taking another taste of his beer, Chay nodded. "Arousal, and all that... Exactly. But there's more to it. Your mate is your other half. Take Keaton and myself for example. He knows what I'm thinking before I do. He gets all my jokes. We have opposite strengths and weaknesses. Sounds corny I know, but it's like he's part of me. Sometimes I think he knows me better than I know myself. And I always know what he's feeling and thinking. I can tell you how he's going to react to any given situation." He grew quiet for a moment, sipping his drink. "And then there's the physical response. If you ask Keaton he'll tell you it's our screwed up pheromones."

"You like how they smell."

Chay nodded. "Yeah. Which is exactly what Keaton means by pheromones."

Damn, damn, damn. "But didn't it bother you that he's a guy?"

"It wasn't what I expected. But I've wanted to find my mate for so long, I wasn't about to give Keaton up when I found him. So I dealt with it. Which wasn't easy given Bit's sparkling personality." Chay snorted. "The smallest hint that I was uncomfortable would set him off on a tangent about how we should forget we were mates."

Wow. Keaton had been opposed to the relationship? Remi had thought Keaton latched onto Chay immediately without question. Did that mean the attraction could be ignored? Remi wished he knew how to ignore what Jake made him feel. "Why didn't you?"

Chay cocked his head to the side. He looked pensive. "Because he's the only mate I'll ever have. Some wolves never find their mate." He got a faraway look on his face then he shook it off and took a sip of his beer. "Besides, the connection is too strong. It's not very easy to ignore."

Staring at the ceramic tile, Remi put the pieces together. This couldn't be happening. He was in real trouble. Not only was his body responding to Jake, but his mind was too. What the fuck was he going to do?

Something wet fell on his wrist. He glanced down and noticed his hands shaking so much the beer was sloshing out. He tried to put his beer on the table, but Chay grabbed his wrist.

Chay gave him a sad smile. "How do you feel about it?"

"I don't know... And if Dirk finds out—"

"I didn't ask what Dirk thinks about it or what society in general thinks. You need to decide what *you* think. How *you* feel."

That was just it, Remi didn't know how he felt. He liked Jake...a lot. Tugging his hand away from Chay, Remi set his can down. He couldn't imagine not ever seeing Jake again. His breath hitched. The thought of never seeing Jake again made his chest hurt.

He dropped his head to his hands. "I didn't even think about the fact that he was a guy at the time. It felt like the most natural thing in the world to do. Like I was in a trance or something, where nothing mattered but the two of us. All I could think about was needing him and—" *pleasing him.* "Fuck!" Groaning, Remi sat up, pulling at his hair. "What the hell am I going to do?"

"What can you do?" Chay shrugged. "You have to ask yourself what's important. If you don't have a problem with it, you can deal with the rest. Trust me, it's not impossible, I know."

Remi felt raw, open, like a bug under a microscope. His shoulders slumped. Instead of feeling better about the situation, it seemed even more hopeless. "What happens if you do ignore it?"

Chay closed his eyes for a minute and let out a breath. When he opened them, his eyes were haunted. "You mean *if* you can? Then you learn to live with only half your soul."

❧

Jake motioned for the bartender to pour him another one.

How could he have screwed up so badly? He should have stopped Remi from blowing him.

"You look like shit." Rhys sat on the barstool next to him and waved down the bartender.

"Thanks." Jake groaned. So much for drinking alone to clear his mind. "What are you doing here?"

The bartender came back, poured Jake another scotch and wiped down the bar in front of Rhys. "What'll it be?"

"Bud Light." Rhys turned to Jake. "I'm meeting Dago and Gadget for a couple games of pool and some beer. What are you doing here? I thought you'd be with Remi."

Snorting, Jake took a sip of his scotch. "Fucked up."

Rhys arched a brow.

"He freaked after giving me a blowjob."

"Giving you a blowjob is fucked up? Shit, if that has you fucked up, hand him over."

Jake growled. He knew Rhys was pulling his chain, but the thought of giving Remi up didn't sit well. "The blowjob wasn't what was fucked up. Him freaking out afterward was. You aren't helping, smartass."

"Fine, I'm all ears, tell me what happened."

"I rushed things. I even blurted out that we were mates." Jake was still shocked he'd done that. He'd done so well, keeping that from Remi, not wanting to scare him off. Shit, maybe that was the problem. Maybe he should have told Remi upfront. Remi could have been getting used to the idea. *Oh hell*, Jake didn't know anymore. The constant what if's and should I's where Remi was concerned were all starting to run together.

"So back off. Let him come to you. Keep working on the case, but keep it professional." Rhys took his beer from the bartender. "Thanks."

"Spoken like a man without a mate."

"Just trying to help, asshole. If you're gonna be pissy, I'll go wait for the guys somewhere else."

"Sorry. You're probably right. What else can I do? But it sucks. The whole situation sucks."

"Hey, Jake. Rhys."

Jake turned as Dago clapped him on the back and slid onto the barstool beside him.

"Hey, man. How's it going?" Jake slugged his friend's shoulder.

Diego, or Dago as his friends called him, was part Italian, part Latino. He was also pack. Dago and Jake had been friends in school and hunted together since they'd both shifted for the first time. Dago was normally a happy, outgoing guy, unless you got that Latino temper riled.

Dago's brown eyes twinkled and a smile crept across his face, making the dimple in his right cheek pop out. "Not bad. So tell me, when are we going to get to meet him? He's important enough to ditch us for, we should meet him, huh, Rhys?" He glanced around Jake, meeting Rhys' gaze.

Jake groaned. "No clue. He's not speaking to me at the moment."

Dago hissed out a breath. "Shit. Sorry, man."

Jake shrugged. "How about you? What have you been up to? You still seeing that guy?" He'd been so busy hanging out with Remi, he hadn't seen his friends in over a week. Which was pretty uncommon. Not only did they all hunt together on the night of a full moon, but they usually raised hell together on the weekends too. He wondered what Remi would think of his friends.

Rhys' phone rang, drawing their attention. He snagged it

from his belt and flipped it open. "Hello?"

Jake turned back to Dago.

Motioning to the bartender, Dago smiled. "Coors," he told the bartender before focusing on Jake. "Yeah. I've seen him four times in the past week."

Ah damn. The guy in question was human. Jake frowned. "You gotta be careful with that shit, man. What if you get carried away? Or shift during a scene?"

"Yeah, I know, I know." Dago sighed. "I've been careful. So far, I've kept control over myself. I haven't even stayed all night." He didn't sound exactly happy about it.

Frankly, Jake couldn't blame him. He'd never much cared about spending an entire night with any lover, but with Remi... Jake wondered briefly if Dago's new top could be his mate. Nah, probably not, Dago would know. Jake had known the instant he'd gotten close to Remi.

"Well shit. That was Gadget, he's not going to make it." Rhys flipped his phone shut with a snap. "You gonna hang around, Jake?"

What else did he have to do? Sit and brood over Remi? The situation wasn't going to change anytime soon. Then again, he wasn't likely to quit thinking about Remi anytime soon either. "Yeah. Go get us a table. I'll kick your ass at nine ball before I head out."

Dago bumped his side. "Cheer up, man. Things will work out. Why don't you meet us here tomorrow night? The whole gang will be here. It will take your mind off things."

Jake got up, taking his scotch with him. He'd been neglecting his friends. "Yeah, I'll come tomorrow. You think about what I said though. Lots of bad shit can happen if someone finds out what you are."

"Yeah, I know, man." Dago walked next to him, headed toward the pool table Rhys had confiscated.

Jake knew the feeling, his own love life wasn't exactly looking very promising lately.

ᖆᎧᏒ

After dropping off Sterling at home, Remi pulled into his apartment complex and parked under the awning. He climbed from his bike with his mind still whirling over Jake being his mate. If he really thought about it, like Chay said, it didn't bother him all that much. That got to him most.

Remi took off his helmet on the way up the stairs and fumbled with his keys. Emotion and common sense still warred within him, but he found himself pushing it aside much quicker and with a lot more ease. Jake made him feel safe—the man was so in control. Remi believed in him and he couldn't say that about a lot of people.

He wanted something like Chay and Keaton had. If Chay could deal with having a male mate and being happy, why couldn't Remi? The other day, before reality sank in, he'd felt alive. He'd done something he'd wanted to do. He'd given in to *his* desires.

Remi unlocked the door and shut it behind him. He didn't need the light, so he left it off. Seeing in the dark was one advantage of being a werewolf. Of course, it had disadvantages too. The biggest was that he'd given up hope that his body would ever behave around Jake.

Remi locked the front door and headed to his room. He sat on the edge of the bed and took his boots off, then removed the rest of his clothes. It was too hot for covers so he climbed into bed on top of them. Laying there staring at the ceiling, he realized he was going to have to talk to Jake. They were going to have to work something out, because Remi knew he couldn't just walk away.

For whatever reason—whether a curse or a blessing, Remi hadn't totally decided yet—Jake was his. His cock perked up at the thought.

Jake called to him, his size, his looks, even his voice. Remi grabbed his prick and squeezed. He could get off just listening to that voice. It was deep and sultry. The way Jake had groaned out "oh fuck" when he came... Remi moaned.

After spitting in his hand, he wrapped it around his prick and pumped slowly. His thigh muscles contracted. His cock was so engorged and red, it throbbed. Closing his eyes, he lazily slid his hand over his prick.

He thought back to last night. Oh God, being at Jake's feet had felt right. Remi shivered, stroking a little faster. Jake had tasted incredible. Remi couldn't remember the last time he'd come in his jeans with no stimulation whatsoever. He let his mind go, imagining Jake.

Jake stood over him, naked, sweat dripping down the planes of his wide chest. His legs were braced apart, so his cock was nearly even with Remi's lips. "Suck me."

Shuddering, Remi went with it. His balls drew tighter and he stroked faster. His prick was incredibly hard.

"Suck me, open your mouth and suck my cock." Jake's knuckles brushed across Remi's cheek and he guided his dick into Remi's mouth with his free hand. Jake's cock slid through his lips.

Remi's whole body tensed, his cock feeling hot in his hand as he pumped.

Spit dribbled down his chin as Jake thrust into his mouth

82

over and over. He told Remi how good he was, how special. Jake pulled out from between Remi's lips, grabbed a handful of his hair and tilted his head back. With a deep moan, he came. Semen hit Remi on the cheek.

Remi lapped at it, moving his face as much as he could, trying to taste.

"You're mine now," Jake growled.

"Uhh." Remi came, his eyes snapping open. He could barely drag air into his lungs. His back arched off the bed as come hit his stomach. His legs shook and his stomach muscles quivered. His orgasm seemed to last forever.

After what felt like an eternity, he stopped shaking and relaxed back on the bed.

Something dripped onto his chin. He wiped his face and held his hand in front of him. *Dark.* He couldn't see the color because his eyes had shifted. So had his teeth. He'd bit his lip.

He got up and went to the bathroom then grabbed a washcloth, wet it in the sink and glanced at the mirror. Green eyes stared back at him, and a red drop of blood trailed down his chin and into the white sink. "What are you doing, Remi? What if Dirk finds out?"

His reflection didn't answer, he didn't expect it to, but he knew the answer. Somehow or another, this was meant to be. He'd just have to trust Jake to take care of him and help him protect his brother. Aside from his fear of Dirk, Remi couldn't come up with a good reason to ditch his mate.

Chapter Seven

Come on, Remi, get it together, you're fighting the inevitable. He was nervous before he ever got off his bike, but damn it, he didn't want only half a soul.

There were enough regrets in his life, he didn't need another. He could do this. At least he damn sure wanted to try. Battling his feelings and instincts where Jake was concerned was a losing effort. Remi didn't want to fight anymore.

Climbing from his bike, Remi took off his helmet and put it under his arm.

Jake's house was in a new subdivision that wasn't complete. It was one of the nice, simple, cream-colored adobes that were popular throughout New Mexico, with a heavy wood arched door. The only other completed residence in this small cul-de-sac was two lots over to the left.

There was a frame of a structure half finished a lot down and to the right of Jake's, but other than that, the place was undeveloped. Somehow the raw feel of the place fit Jake.

Pulling the rubber band out of his hair as he went, Remi made his way up the cobblestone walk.

Rocks, cacti and yuccas dominated the arid landscaping. It gave the place a really masculine and solitary sort of feel.

Taking a deep breath, he lifted his fist to knock. Normally, things just fell into place and felt right—natural—with Jake, but with what happened the other night... Remi hoped he hadn't ruined the comfort level they shared.

Jake opened the door before Remi knocked. "Hey." Smiling, he let his gaze rake over Remi like it always did. Only today, Remi felt every bit of Jake's interest. The attention was like a lingering caress. It took his breath away and made his body tingle.

Standing there with his hand in the air and helmet under his arm, he stared.

Jake was an incredible looking man. He had the dark Apache coloring, broad shoulders and towering height. Even the way he walked with smooth purposeful strides was appealing. Chay was right. Everything about his mate called to Remi. It was terrifying and comforting at the same time. He had never had the urge to give in so completely.

Allowing the instant arousal to wash over him, and not trying to suppress it as he normally did, made it even more intense. His cock was already on its way to hard. "We're mates." Oh shit, had he said that out loud?

Jake grabbed Remi's raised hand and pulled him inside before shutting the door. He didn't let go of Remi's hand. Instead, he backed Remi against the closed door and placed his hand on Jake's chest. "Yes, we are. Are you okay with that?" For once, it was Jake's eyes that shifted first, but it didn't take Remi's long to follow.

The hard thump of Jake's heart pulsed against Remi's palm. His teeth dropped and his hand clenched against the thin cotton of Jake's shirt. The helmet thudded to the ground, followed by the elastic band Remi had taken out of his hair, and he clutched at Jake with his other hand. It was now or never.

"Yes."

Groaning, Jake leaned forward and slanted his mouth over Remi's. His tongue demanded entrance while he ran his hands over Remi's chest and down his arms.

"Mmm..." It was like drowning, scary but at the same time there was no use struggling. His own feelings made it hopeless to resist. Arching into the touch felt like the most natural thing in the world to do.

Catching Remi's hands, Jake placed them by Remi's sides against the door. He pulled away from Remi's lips, his breath coming faster. "Keep them there."

A jolt of desire shot through Remi. The command brought back the memory of last night's fantasy. Closing his eyes, Remi waited...anticipating. His stomach tautened, making his jeans gap open a little. His hard cock strained against his jock and jeans.

Kissing his way down Remi's neck, Jake palmed Remi's erection, making it grow even harder.

Remi moaned and opened his eyes, surprised at how great it felt to give in.

The heat of Jake's lips raised goose bumps on his arms. A shiver raced down his spine, nearly buckling his knees. Not only *could* he do this, he was damn close to begging for it.

"You like that?" Jake mumbled against his throat.

Nodding, Remi pressed his neck closer. He wanted Jake to bite him. He had no idea where the strange urge came from but it shocked him. Pain had never been his thing, but his senses argued with him that it would be more pleasurable than painful. But much to Remi's regret, with one last kiss, Jake drew back.

"I don't want to hurt you, Remi." Jake squeezed Remi's

cock through his jeans.

"You would never hurt me." It was the one thing Remi had a hundred percent confidence in.

"Mmm..." Jake unfastened and parted Remi's jeans. When he got the denim past Remi's thighs, he dropped to his knees and buried his face against Remi's dark green jock. Opening his mouth, Jake sucked the shaft of Remi's cock through the cotton.

Remi's hip bucked and he moaned. He barely wrapped his brain around what was happening before Jake tugged the jock aside, baring his balls and prick.

After licking up to the tip of Remi's cock, Jake closed his mouth over the head. God, had anything ever felt so good? Remi's hands dug for purchase on the wood door, but he didn't move them. Jake had told him not to. And why did the idea of Jake commanding him not to move his hands make Remi's cock flex and leak precome?

Slipping down further, Jake caressed Remi's shaft with his tongue and sucked softly.

Remi gasped and clenched his ass cheeks together. "Jake..."

"Be still, pup, and don't come." Jake held Remi's hips against the door in an almost bruising grip. His gaze darted back up to Remi then he took Remi's cock between his lips again.

"Okay." Staying motionless, Remi fought the urge to squirm. Only his thighs tensed occasionally. He wanted to please Jake as much as Jake was pleasing him. Remi's stomach muscles contracted and he whimpered, making mewling sounds in his throat. The urge to thrust overwhelmed him. It was like trying not to breathe.

Jake stopped pressing Remi's hips against the smooth

J. L. Langley

wood and one hand disappeared entirely.

When Remi felt the finger slide into Jake's mouth alongside Remi's cock, he knew what was coming and was a little intimidated. His faith in Jake, accompanied with his curiosity and his heightened arousal, outweighed the hesitancy though.

Slipping a finger behind Remi's balls, Jake pressed against his hole. He sucked harder as he pushed inside.

Even with the resolve to let it happen, Remi tensed up. It stung a bit.

Jake kept swallowing his cock and kept his finger stationary, barely inside. It didn't take long for Remi to get used to the feeling. In no time he was pushing himself back on that finger. It was incredible. At first, the finger fucking his ass pulled him back from the brink of orgasm that Jake's talented mouth was edging him closer to, but eventually it added to the sensation. Once Remi got used to it and started to enjoy himself, Jake added a finger, throwing him off balance.

He was nearly out of his head with pleasure by the time Jake had three fingers inside him. Then Jake found his prostate.

It was like nothing Remi had ever felt. The closest he could come to describing it was like a jolt of lightning—it was shocking and tingly and—fucking hell, he was going to come. "No, stop, please. I want you to fuck me." Voicing his need felt like a weight was lifted off his shoulders.

Jake withdrew his fingers and mouth. Standing, he kissed Remi hard on the mouth. "Come on." He walked down the hall, and the smell of his arousal drifted back toward Remi.

Mmm, musky male and a fresh woodsy essence. That was becoming Remi's favorite scent in a hurry.

Grabbing his pants, Remi hitched them up enough to walk and followed. In his haste to catch his mate, he barely registered the rustic surroundings, but the breeze caressing his saliva-soaked prick had his undivided attention. His cock was so damn hard he was beginning to ache.

When he reached the bedroom, Jake sat on the edge of the bed and pulled off his shoes. Joining him, Remi sat and took his off as well. Neither of them said a word, but the tension and arousal was so heavy it was nearly suffocating.

Standing, Jake shucked his pants and ripped his shirt over his head. When he turned Remi saw the gleaming drop of precome on the tip of his cock and got the sudden overwhelming urge to lick it off. His mouth watered, remembering how good Jake tasted. That had surprised him, he'd sampled his own come before but it was nothing like Jake's.

Kneeling between Remi's thighs, Jake caught the back of Remi's neck with one hand and his own cock with the other. He covered Remi's mouth and stroked his own prick.

Remi whimpered into his mouth, mashing their fangs against their lips, and covered Jake's hand with his own. "Please, fuck me..."

Growling, Jake let go and stood. Together they got Remi's pants and jock the rest of the way off, then his shirt. For several seconds Jake stared into Remi's eyes. "Are you sure?"

Remi nodded, biting back a moan. He was positive. He had to know what it felt like to have sex with a man.

Jake dug into the nightstand beside the bed and took out a bottle of lube. He coated his cock with the lube and stroked up and down. "Get in the middle of the bed. On your back."

Remi shivered at the deep commanding voice and moved to do Jake's bidding. He was dying to feel his mate inside him. Jake's fingers had felt so good stroking over his prostate.

His ass actually clenched and unclenched, begging for

Jake's cock. He wanted this so bad, he couldn't deny it any longer.

Jake climbed onto the bed between his legs. He fumbled with the bottle, and lube slid down the crack of Remi's ass. It was cold, but Jake's finger followed the trail, circled Remi's hole and warmed it up.

"Please." He quivered with anticipation. God, he was going to lose his mind if he didn't come soon.

Jake's finger retreated then the head of his cock pressed against Remi's hole.

After hesitating for a second, Jake slowly pressed in.

Oh, that was different. Really, really different. It burned. Remi bit his lip, his cock still hard as a fucking rock, but his teeth shrank and his eyes switched back to human vision for the first time in what felt like hours.

"Shhh, relax." Jake's other hand rubbed his stomach, before gripping Remi's cock and squeezing.

Riiight. That was way bigger than any goddamned finger! Remi blinked, trying to get his eyes to focus. Making himself loosen up, he pushed out. If he could just relax it would be good.

Jake pulled back a little, making the pain ease, and he continued to stroke Remi's cock, distracting him from the foreign feeling.

Oh fuck yeah, that's it. Still damn big and not quite comfortable, but it didn't hurt much now. Remi's eyes shifted back, his teeth extended. Yeah, that was—

Jake thrust all the way in until his balls rested against Remi's ass. When he drew back the next time, Remi came unglued. *Fuck*, out felt good. His balls grew even tighter and his cock felt like it was going to burst. Then Jake nailed his

90

prostate.

"Oh my fucking God!"

Gripping his hips with both hands, Jake shoved into him again, his balls slapping against Remi. Jake didn't stop. He kept pounding into Remi. Sweat dripped down his temples and his chest and arm muscles flexed with each movement.

Remi moaned, trying to push forward. The slap of skin was loud in the quiet room, or maybe it was his wolf hearing, he didn't know but it sounded so fucking hot. His whole body quivered, threatening to explode.

Dropping forward, Jake braced himself on one hand beside Remi and reached for Remi's cock with the other. He nuzzled his face against Remi's cheek and matched the rhythm of his hips to his hand pumping Remi's prick.

Oddly, the only thing Remi could think of was Jake's face close to his neck. His skin tingled, almost itching. The hair on the back of his neck rose and he shivered. It was just like the night they kissed on the couch, but stronger. This time he was too far gone to hold back. "Bite me, oh fuck, please bite me." He wanted Jake's teeth on his neck, needed it.

Jake gasped and stiffened. Raising up, he gripped Remi's hips again and thrust into him over and over, harder and harder. Letting out a deep rumbling groan, Jake shoved forward and came in Remi's ass.

Every muscle in Remi's body tensed. The prickle on the back of his neck raced down his spine. "Oh fuck." Jake's hand wrapped around his prick and tugged.

Remi writhed, his whole body on fire. He arched off the bed and came with his eyes wide open, staring into his mate's.

"Mine." Jake held Remi's gaze.

Remi nodded. "Yes." Dropping his head back to the

mattress, Remi felt like his whole world had tilted on its axis.

ᢐᢤᢢᡒᢦ

Jake hadn't meant to fall asleep, but since the argument with Remi the other night he hadn't been sleeping well. He'd only been awake now for a few minutes, but he couldn't go back to sleep. It felt like his stomach was trying to chew its way out to look for food on its own.

Damn, Jake really didn't want to get up. Remi was pressed up against him, snoring softly into his neck. The faint breath was both comforting and oddly arousing, but his stomach was beginning to growl louder than Remi's snore.

Jake slid out of bed, being careful not to wake Remi, and grabbed his jeans. Tugging his pants on, Jake watched Remi roll over into the middle of the bed and get comfortable again. Apparently, Jake hadn't been the only one not sleeping the last few nights if Remi's state of unconsciousness was anything to go by.

Remi lay on his side, his hands pressed under his face and his right leg hiked up just enough to expose part of his muscled belly and the tip of his cock. He looked sexy as hell with his hair half covering his face. It gave him a just-fucked look. Jake's cock twitched, threatening to get hard. Holy shit, he couldn't believe he'd actually fucked Remi. More to the point, Remi had pretty much initiated it by showing up here announcing they were mates.

Jake's stomach rumbled again. He really didn't want to leave the room. As ridiculous as it seemed, he was half afraid if he left, Remi might disappear. Jake groaned at himself, grasped the blanket at the foot of his bed and covered his mate with it.

Remi would likely be hungry when he woke, so Jake got out the stuff to make spaghetti and started cooking. He wanted to know what had happened to change Remi's mind.

If he were honest with himself, he also felt a bit of apprehension. What if Remi woke up and freaked out again? Not like Jake could do much about it he supposed, but damn that would suck. After having Remi, it would be pure torture to go back to a platonic relationship and pretending they were only friends.

Jake took a deep breath and let it out as he turned the burner on under the hamburger meat. Underneath the smell of cooking meat, boiling noodles and tomato, the scent of Remi clung to his skin. *Mmmm, Remi and sex.* Damned if Jake's eyes didn't shift. It made him wonder if having made love to Remi was also going to make his body harder to control. Jake sure as hell hoped not. Judging from the mates he knew, it should make the attraction wane a bit, or at least make it easier to control. But if this afternoon was any indication, he might be in trouble.

He'd wanted so badly to bite into Remi's neck and pin him in place with his teeth while he fucked him. He wanted to dominate Remi. It was overwhelming. Sheer willpower alone, which thankfully he had a ton of, let him pull away. The thought of how Remi would probably react to being bitten was sobering. It made his eyes shift back to normal.

"Mmm... What are you making?"

Oh, that was a good sign. Remi didn't sound shaken up in the least, only a little sleepy. Jake smiled and glanced toward the kitchen door. "Spaghetti. You hungry?"

Remi shrugged and stretched, showing off lean muscles. He had only put on his jeans and the enticing trail of dark hair below his bellybutton came into view with his action. "I could eat. I gotta leave at three though. I promised Sterling I'd take him to see the new Harry Potter movie and it starts at three thirty."

Jake grinned. "You've got time, it's only two. This will be done in a minute. How do you feel? Are you sore?"

Redness seeped into Remi's cheeks and he looked away. The blush was refreshing and Jake had to bite back a laugh. Remi was going to have to get use to the bluntness in regards to sex. It wasn't something Jake could turn off.

"I'm fine. You need me to help with anything?"

"It's almost ready, but why don't you get us something to drink. Glasses are in there"—he used the spatula to point at the cabinet to his left—"and there's water, beer, tea and cokes in the fridge. I want water." Jake grabbed a strainer from the cabinet, put it in the sink and dumped the noodles into it. Remi went to work behind him, getting them drinks while Jake took the skillet of meat off the fire. Neither of them said a thing for several minutes while Jake put their food on plates.

"Jake?" Remi's voice was so soft Jake barely heard it over the clatter of dishes.

He set the sauce aside and turned.

Remi stood right behind him, close enough it would have been simple to reach out and bring their bodies together. Jake wanted to do so, but he waited. The look on Remi's face was almost sad, but Jake didn't smell grief, just a bit of nervousness. *Oh please no.* His stomach plummeted, wondering if this was when Remi told him it was all a mistake.

"I'm sorry. I'm sorry about the other night, I was...scared. Still am actually." He glanced up, making eye contact. "If Dirk found out, there would be trouble, but I want to try and make this work. We have a connecti—"

Jake cupped his face and pulled him forward, slanting his

mouth down over Remi's.

Arousal scented the air.

Moaning into Jake's mouth, Remi opened up. He let Jake take the lead for a few seconds then started kissing back. Hands wrapping around Jake's waist, Remi pressed closer and rubbed himself against Jake's bare chest.

The amazing feel of bare skin reminded Jake of earlier. He trailed kisses down Remi's jaw to his neck. His teeth exploded in his mouth, making him gasp. The tips of his canines itched. He could practically feel Remi's smooth, warm flesh under his teeth, the blood rolling over his tongue. *Fuck.* Jake jerked back. He kept his eyes closed and took a breath, trying to ignore the scent of Remi's arousal, and got himself under control.

When Jake opened his eyes, Remi also appeared to be struggling for restraint. His eyes were screwed shut and he was inhaling deeply. He blinked his eyes open and rolled his shoulders, tilting his head side to side. His green irises had bled out to the edges of his eyes and his fangs peeked out from behind his top lip. "Sorry."

"What?" Jake shook his head to clear it. "No, I just don't want you to be late for your movie." *Nor do I want you to pull away from me again 'cause I can't keep my teeth to myself.* "I want to make it work too. We won't let Dirk find out. Okay?" He traced Remi's cheek with the back of his fingers.

Damned if Remi didn't close his eyes and lean into the caress for a second, before his eyes shot wide and he stepped back. He groaned then chuckled, shaking his head and smiling up at Jake. "Okay."

Jake turned back to the food. Not only did he have to hide their relationship, but he had to suppress his darker side to keep from scaring Remi away. This may prove harder than he thought.

Chapter Eight

It was a little chilly out, but Remi enjoyed the long ride to the bar. Riding his bike always helped clear his head and give him a sense of freedom.

After this afternoon, he felt great—better than he had in a long time. Jake had invited him to meet up with him tonight, and he'd jumped at the chance. He was still wary of someone finding out about them, but he wasn't going to stop seeing Jake.

Pulling into the parking lot of Hell's Kitchen, Remi was surprised at all the motorcycles. It was without a doubt a biker bar. *Weird.* He wouldn't have thought it Jake's kind of hangout.

Looking around, he saw Jake in the neon glow of the bar's sign and all other thoughts fled.

Jake was sitting on a Harley. A beautiful new Fat Boy with a red and white tank and fenders that made Remi's fifteen-year-old Vulcan seemed pretty shabby in comparison.

Remi's cock hardened right up, and his sight went colorless and grew much more acute. *Damn eyes.* Instinctively he tried to fight it then remembered his resolve to let it go.

He drove up next to Jake and cut the engine, unable to decide what was more drool worthy—the bike or the man on it. Jake had on a pair of faded black jeans, black motorcycle boots and a black leather motorcycle jacket. Sterling was right, the man was hot, and it was getting easier and easier to think so. "Whose bike?"

Jake lifted his head and grinned as he caught Remi's gaze. "Mine."

What? He'd had no idea Jake had a bike, much less a Hog. Apparently motorcycles were another thing they had in common. "Fucking sweet."

"Thanks." Jake stood and came closer. His wide shoulders captured Remi's attention and wouldn't let go.

Oh hell yeah, the man was more drool worthy than the machine. *Damn, look at those tight jeans.* They might as well have been painted on. Every little muscle was visible and even the not-so-little bulge in the front—

"Remi?" Jake chuckled. The sound, low and husky, slid right down Remi's spine.

Remi shivered. His mouth watered. He'd turned into Pavlov's dog, er wolf, whatever, except there was no bell, it was Jake's laugh. "Huh?"

"I asked if you had any problems finding the place."

"No."

"Are you cold?" Jake turned toward his bike, his boots crunching on the gravel.

I'd be a lot warmer if you threw me over that bike seat and... Damn, it felt good to let go of the guilt and just appreciate his mate.

Swiveling around, Jake held out something leather toward Remi. "Hey, Remi."

"Yeah?"

"You okay? Here." He handed Remi a black motorcycle jacket. "You need one, right? Yours got tore up in that fight at Chay and Keaton's place."

97

Oh man, Jake was giving him a new biker jacket to replace the one he'd lost the night he'd become a werewolf. Well, no, not new, but it was in nice shape with thick leather, and the padded lining was still good. There was a patch on the back. *Cool.* Remi tried it on over his long-sleeved black shirt. He held his arms out, trying to look over his shoulder. Ah damn, it smelled like Jake. He inhaled deeply. Mmmm, Jake and leather. "Are you sure? I don't want to take your jacket, Jake. It's got your club patch on it. I mean if—"

Jake touched his shoulder and squeezed. "Take it, I have a new one." He presented his back to show Remi his coat. It had a patch identical to the one on the jacket Remi wore. It was square with a yellow moon and a black wolf. There were gray mountains and a starry midnight sky in the background.

Remi blinked, not realizing his eyes had gone back to normal until right then. "Thanks."

Jake nodded. "Come on, let's introduce you to the guys."

Guys? What guys? "Uh, okay." He followed Jake into the seedy little wood-shack-looking bar with its colorful neon beer signs hanging in the windows. It was smoky as hell and loud. The smells almost knocked Remi on his ass. Shrugging it off, he tuned them out and took in the clientele. It was a good thing Jake was big, this crowd looked rougher than the ones at Remi's normal hangouts. Remi had only been to a place like this one other time with Simon, Chay and Bobby and thanks to Simon they'd almost gotten their asses kicked. Not that that would be an issue tonight, Remi had no intention of hustling pool.

Jake led him to the end of the bar close to the pool tables. "Men, this is Remi Lassiter." Grabbing Remi's shoulder, Jake pulled him forward.

A giant unfolded himself from the barstool in front of the

scarred wood bar and offered Remi a hand nearly the size of a damn dinner plate.

Holy shit. Remi's eyes widened.

"Rhys Waya, we've met before." The giant spoke deeply, like low rumbling thunder, without the slightest hint of a smile. Remi was sure he'd never have heard Rhys over the loud buzz of conversation and the jukebox if not for his wolf hearing.

Rhys was huge. Well, no, he wasn't much bigger than Jake, but something about Rhys instantly put Remi on alert. Rhys wasn't a bad-looking man, in fact, he was rather handsome, but everything about him screamed danger. No one in their right mind would screw with this guy. He appeared to be Native American, with the typical dark coloring, but he had a neatly trimmed beard and mustache. Remi had never seen an Apache with facial hair. He was only half and couldn't grow a mustache to save his life. Rhys had a faint vertical scar about an inch long at the outside corner of his right eyebrow. Remi had no clue why, but he immediately thought knife wound.

Stepping back, Remi bumped right into Jake. *Shit.*

Jake's other hand landed on his shoulder, gripping a little, showing support.

It was comforting in a weird way, but then so was having Jake at his back touching him. Not that Remi thought Rhys was going to beat the hell out of him or anything, but for some reason Remi understood meeting these men meant a lot to Jake. Rhys was important to Jake, his business partner, so Remi wanted to make a good impression. When Remi tried to step forward and offer his hand to Rhys, Jake held Remi in place, keeping them close together, so he had to extend his arm further than normal. "Nice to officially meet you. My friends call me Remi."

Giving Remi's hand a quick squeeze, Rhys dipped his head.

Jake turned him slightly to the right and pointed at another dark-skinned man. "This is Diego, but we all call him Dago."

Diego was about Remi's size, with short dark hair. Taking Remi's hand, he smiled brightly. He was a wolf. Remi wasn't sure how he knew it, it damn sure wasn't smell—who could smell anything over the smoke?—but he recognized Diego as pack.

"Dago?" Wasn't that a racial slur? "That doesn't bother you?" Remi asked.

Diego shook his head. "Nah, I'm part Italian. They're just jealous because I got the best parts."

Remi liked the guy, he seemed good-natured and able to handle himself. Which was a good thing in this place.

After that the introductions came pretty quickly. There were four other men, all Native American. Tank was a big guy, like Jake and Rhys, but not nearly as intimidating. He had very bright, almost sparkling eyes, complete with laugh lines at the corners. Gadget was a short, stout man who seemed preoccupied. According to Jake, Gadget was a hell of a mechanic and fixed all their bikes when the need arose. Nick had waist-length hair and was tall and lean. Zack was the loud, outgoing type. All the men welcomed Remi and he was fairly certain all of them were wolves. He'd have to ask Jake about it later.

Jake's friends dispersed, some getting pitchers of beer and others claiming a pool table. Jake was hailed, leaving Remi alone with Rhys. Unsure what to say to the man, Remi instead soaked in his surroundings.

There were more men than women, and most everyone appeared to be wearing denim and leather, specifically black leather. Most of the women were either skimpily clad or dressed like the men. Neon beer signs decorated the place along with a jukebox and a stage. And no chicken wire enclosed the stage. Remi took that as a good sign. Maybe this place wasn't quite as rough as he first suspected.

Someone stepped right next to Remi. "Jesus, is that what I think it is?"

"Excuse me?" Remi asked.

"That jacket." The man was a little shorter than Remi, with light brown hair. He was a mousy-looking guy. "I'm Chance, by the way. What did you do to get it?"

"Remi." Remi offered his hand and Chance shook it. "And what do you mean? It was given to me."

Chance's mouth dropped open then snapped shut. "Oh, come on, man. Jake does *not* hand out leather to wannabe submissives. Him giving you a jacket of his means you impressed him."

Submissive? Remi blinked.

Chance focused on something over Remi's left shoulder, then shook his head. "Jake and I were good together but he never allowed me to earn my leathers." A wistful look crossed his face, and he made eye contact with Remi again. "Good luck. You're one lucky son of a bitch."

Remi suppressed a growl, but didn't quite rein in his snarl. The image of Jake with this guy, in whatever capacity, did not sit well with Remi. And how crazy was that? The relationship was likely before he and Jake had even met.

Glancing over his shoulder, Remi spotted Jake, a little further away but still in conversation with the man who'd stopped him earlier. Remi turned back to Chance. He could barely get his mouth to work, so he settled for, "Thanks."

Chance started to say something else but another guy

pulled him away toward the back of the bar. "It was nice to meet you."

Remi waved.

Rhys turned from the bar and crooked his finger at Remi. "Remi, what do you want to drink?"

Jake came over and touched Remi's arm. He leaned close, his breath fanning across Remi's cheek. "Get me a scotch?" Then Jake went back to talking.

He was just getting used to being Jake's mate and now this? Did Jake expect him to be a submissive? He didn't know if he could. He stared at Jake's back, feeling like he'd been punched in the stomach. He should be mad or something, but he wasn't...only confused. Why hadn't Jake said anything? Remi rolled his eyes at himself. Oh yeah, that would have gone over well. Like Remi hadn't freaked enough over the mate thing. But still...

Rhys called him again. "Remi."

In a daze, Remi stepped up to the battered old bar, next to Rhys.

"What will it be?" the bartender asked Remi.

"I'll have a Jake and Coke—uh, Jack and Cock, uh—" Oh fuck. Remi stopped talking. He could actually feel his face heat with a blush. *Someone shoot me.*

Rhys burst out laughing. "Get him a Jack and Coke. I'll take a Crown and Coke and a scotch for Jake." Rhys smiled at Remi and reached toward his face. "Talk about your Freudian sl—"

Remi stiffened, flinching away, and waited for the blow.

It never came.

Goddamn, he was batting a thousand tonight. What else could he do to embarrass himself?

Rhys dropped his hand and the grin melted from his face. "Sorry." He came across even more grim.

"No, I'm sorry. Bad habit."

The bartender came back, setting all three drinks on the bar.

Rhys took the glasses and handed Remi's his and Jake's.

"Thanks. How much do I owe you for these?"

"You don't. Jake's uncle runs the place."

Well, shit, how many more surprises was he going to get tonight? Remi nodded, looking around for Jake. Jake had gone and joined the guys at the pool table. He was now talking to Tank and Gadget. He seemed so commanding, with his wide shoulders and straight, confident posture.

The image of Jake standing over Remi sprang to mind and he shivered. His cock got hard instantly. *No!* Wanting to please Jake was another mate thing. That was all it was. He had enough to deal with. He was certain he had a problem with being a submissive...didn't he?

The overwhelming urge to give in to Jake had been there from nearly the beginning. It felt natural to lean into Jake's touch, to trust Jake. That was another thing, he trusted Jake...really and truly trusted him. Remi couldn't think of one other person he felt he could depend on like that, except for maybe his brother.

As if he knew Remi was thinking about him, Jake walked up to Remi and Rhys as they reached the table and took the scotch from Remi. "Thanks."

"Hey, Remi, you play?" Nick asked, holding up a cue stick.

"Yeah. What are you playing?"

"Nine ball." Nick tossed him the cue.

Crap. Remi wasn't expecting it and he had his drink in the

wrong hand. He opened his left hand in an attempt to catch it, but Jake snagged it from midair then handed it to him.

Jake pointed his finger at Nick. "Watch it."

"Sorry, Remi. Wasn't thinking." Nick grimaced.

Whoa, Jake had actually sounded angry with Nick. What was that about? Remi handed his drink to Jake before addressing Nick. "No problem. Warn me next time."

Dago, who was seated on a tall chair near the table, extended his leg and shoved Nick's leg with his foot. "Kind of hard to hustle pool if you knock out your opponent before the game starts, asshole."

Remi laughed, forgetting about his latest dilemma for now. "Well, if you're hustling me, I get to break."

"What the fuck kinda rule is that?" Nick grinned and stepped back, motioning to the cue ball.

Remi lined up his shot, aiming for the one ball. Please let him hit the one ball hard enough to get a ball in the pocket. *Here goes nothing.* Remi took the shot, satisfied with the loud crack and the way the balls scattered. How many had to hit the rail for a legal break? Four? He couldn't remember, but several did, so he was probably okay. Six ball in the corner pocket. Two ball in the side. Nine ball in the corner... *Holy shit.* He'd sank the nine ball on the break. He'd only ever done that once before and just like this time it had been completely accidental, not that he was going to tell Nick of course. A refrain of holy shits, goddamns and fuck mes went around the table, followed by laughter.

Excitement bubbled inside Remi, making it impossible not to smile. Turning to find Nick standing with his mouth open, Remi raised a brow.

Tank laughed so hard he grew red in the face. Dago was nearly rolling on the floor. Even the somber Rhys was grinning.

Gadget held out his hand for a high five.

Remi slapped it and doubled up his fist and bumped knuckles with Gadget like they'd been friends for years rather than new acquaintances.

Jake was leaning against the wall, a smirk on his face. He caught Remi's gaze, raised his glass and winked before taking a drink.

Remi got a fluttery feeling in his stomach. His chest felt a little tight.

Nick bowed to Remi and threw his hands in the air. "Okay, we gotta talk. You're supposed to throw a couple games first."

"Oh no, last time I had anything to do with hustling pool I damn near got my ass kicked, and it wasn't even me doing the hustling."

Tank frowned. "Yeah? Man, you gotta be careful with shit like that. Next time you go, let me know. I'll watch your back."

Whoa. The offer puzzled and pleased Remi. Something told him he was going to get along well with Jake's friends. "Cool. Who wants to play?"

"I'll play if you let me break." Zack stood.

Dago shook his head. "Hey, no fucking around with the rules, Zack. Winner breaks."

Zack pointed his cue at Dago. "Bullshit. He's the one hustling, I get to break, he said so himself."

Remi gave them his best innocent look. "What if I said it was accidental?" No way was he admitting it really was accidental.

Dago laughed at Remi. "Smug bastard." He called out to Zack. "By all means, Remi says it's a rule, it must be."

Remi started out playing the second game pretty well, but halfway through the game he got distracted watching Jake talk

105

to everyone. His mind kept conjuring Jake standing over him, protecting him and taking care of him. Somehow the image fit. It also gave Remi an uneasy feeling.

As the game progressed, Jake's friends made Remi feel welcome, including him in their conversations, yelling out encouragement for him to, "Whip Zack's ass," and telling jokes. They were a great group of guys. Even Rhys, although he remained quiet.

By the time Zack sank the nine ball, Remi was ready for another drink.

Jake took the cue from Remi and tossed back the last of his scotch. He started to set the empty tumbler down, but Remi grabbed the glass and picked up his own as well.

"I'll get you another."

Dipping his head, Jake started to step around Remi, then hesitated. He held Remi's gaze for several seconds. "You having fun?"

"Yes, I am. Thank you." And he was, he couldn't remember the last time he'd actually had so much fun he hadn't worried about stuff.

"You're welcome. You know, I have a pair of leather chaps at home that might fit you, if you're interested."

"Yes, sir. I'm definitely interested." Remi licked his lips, wanting Jake to kiss him again.

Jake's eyes widened and his eyebrows shot up.

Remi frowned. What the— Then it dawned on him what he'd said and how Jake would've taken the "sir".

Chapter Nine

Outside of Remi's apartment, Gadget handed Jake Remi's helmet and keys. "You gonna stay with him? He's pretty messed up."

Taking the keys and helmet, Jake peeked over his shoulder to where Rhys and Remi waited in Rhys' car behind the bikes. "Yeah, I'll get him settled before I go. Thanks for bringing his bike home. I think this is the first time he's drunk hard liquor since he was changed."

Gadget laughed. "Yeah that new metabolism will fuck you up. Although the advantage to that is the drunkenness will wear off faster too." Gadget scrunched his face and headed toward Rhys' car. "Maybe that's not an advantage."

"I never get dis drunk." Remi tried to get out of the passenger side of Rhys' car but got tangled in the seat belt and fell back into the seat.

Jake jogged over to the car and reached inside to unbuckle him. He glanced over at Rhys. "Thanks."

Rhys dipped his head. "No problem."

After moving back to let Remi out and Gadget in, Jake then shut the door and ducked his head to see in the open window. "You two got plans tomorrow?"

Gadget shrugged. "When? We have a pack meeting tomorrow evening."

Shit. He'd forgotten about that. Oh well, it was at nine, that left the day open. "Around noon."

Buckling his seat belt, Gadget shook his head. "Not that I'm aware of. I'm fixing Rhys' bike day after tomorrow."

"Why? What's up, Jake?" Looking past Jake, Rhys frowned and pointed.

Jake turned around to see what Rhys was trying to show him and noticed Remi staggering off in the opposite direction of his apartment. *Well damn.* Jake whistled.

Remi stopped, faced him and waved.

Gadget and Rhys laughed.

Jake groaned, but he couldn't hold back a chuckle. Motioning with his hand for Remi to return, Jake kept his attention on his mate but spoke to Gadget and Rhys. "If you guys aren't doing anything, I thought we'd play ball."

"Play ball?" Gadget asked.

Remi started wandering off again.

Shit. "Remi, come here. Yeah, with Remi's little brother. I figured it'd be fun and help the kid out."

Remi obeyed immediately, coming back toward the car.

"Sure, just give me a call," Rhys said.

Jake peeked back at Gadget and Rhys, who were both staring out the window toward Remi with smiles on their faces.

Gadget nodded. "Yeah, I'm game. I can see if my oldest two boys wanna come too." He was quiet for a few seconds then jerked his head toward Remi. "I like him. He's good for you. Fits in with the rest of us too."

"He does." Jake grinned. Yeah, Remi did fit in with Jake's

friends. Remi's inebriated state was testament to that. Remi wasn't the type to get hammered unless he had complete confidence in who he was with. That he trusted Jake enough to drink made Jake feel good. "All right, then I'll call you tomorrow. I better go before he takes off again." Jake patted the side of Rhys' car. "Later." He grabbed one of the helmets from under his arm and held it out to Remi as he approached.

Remi took it and waved at Rhys and Gadget. "Bye."

Both men waved, called out goodbyes and Rhys drove off.

Heading toward the apartment, Jake watched his mate from his peripheral vision, making sure he was coming along. "Where were you going?"

"Going?" Remi started up the stairs, only wobbling a little.

Jake hurried after him, getting close enough to lend him a hand if he needed it. "Yeah, awhile ago. You were going the wrong way."

Remi shrugged, stepped up the last step and leaned against the wall next to his apartment door. "Don't know."

How fucking cute was that? Remi was pretty out of it. Chuckling, Jake unlocked the door and opened it. He waited for Remi to go in before shutting and locking it. As he set down his helmet and keys on the coffee table something brushed across his ass. Jake looked over his shoulder.

Remi stood with his helmet held in one hand, hanging from one strap, and his other hand on Jake's butt. "You 'ave a nice ass. You 'ave a nice ever'thing." Remi nodded.

Jake didn't know whether to groan or cry. His body, however, had no qualms about what to do. His cock stiffened right up. "Come on, let's get you to bed." He ushered his drunk mate down the hall, catching a whiff of Remi's arousal. Great.

"Have I earned my jacket?"

"What are you talking about?"

Remi continued into the bedroom. "Your old sub, Chance, said I'd impress'd you, 'at's why you gave me the jacket."

Fuck. Jake hadn't even seen Chance at the bar. "Chance was never my sub. And I gave you the jacket because yours got tore up." *And because it was a small harmless way to stake my claim.* Giving Remi the jacket was only supposed to be significant to Jake.

Remi sat on the bed. "You don't want me?" His brow furrowed.

"Of course I do. Didn't I prove that this afternoon?" Jake followed and knelt to take Remi's boots off of him. He wanted nothing more than to make Remi his sub, but he couldn't ask Remi for that. Remi's upbringing didn't lend itself to the lifestyle Jake had led before Remi came along. Jake could live without it, he needed his mate more than he needed to dominate, but there was no denying the sense of loss. He'd been a Top for over fifteen years. He'd never dated anyone who wasn't into the scene.

"Mmm... Yeah, that was nice. I was nerve'us at first, but I couldn't let you go, ya know? I didn't want only half." Remi flopped back on the bed and stared up at the ceiling.

Tossing Remi's boot aside and starting on the other, Jake frowned. Half? Half what?

"Whad kinda relationship did ya have with Chance? He said you were good together."

"He bottomed for me a couple of times. That's it. It was nothing serious." Jake pulled off both of Remi's socks and stood.

"Why?"

Why? Jake groaned. He couldn't believe he was having this

conversation. Furthermore, he knew damn well he wouldn't be in this uncomfortable predicament if Remi were sober. "Because he wasn't my mate."

Nodding, Remi smiled but never made eye contact. "He wasn't me."

Jake grinned and pulled Remi up so he could take off his jacket and shirt. "Not even close."

Remi chuckled and wrapped his arms around Jake's neck. With a smug smirk on his face, he kissed Jake.

Oh, Jake could get used to this uninhibited show of affection. It was nice. Jake kissed Remi back, then unwrapped Remi's arms from his neck and tugged the jacket free. He placed it on the back of Remi's desk chair and drew Remi's T-shirt over his head.

Remi fell back on the bed and ran his hand over his chest.

Reaching to unbutton Remi's jeans, he almost swallowed his tongue. Remi was so fucking hard his cock was outlined perfectly in the thick denim.

Remi's hand snaked down, dipping into the waistband of his jeans.

Jake didn't wait to see what Remi would do. He unfastened Remi's pants and took them and his jock off. After tossing them on the floor, he pulled back Remi's covers. "Into bed." He tapped Remi's hip, trying to ignore Remi's hand once again edging closer to Remi's prick.

Moaning, Remi gripped his cock and squeezed. "This is what you do to me. You make me want to please you." He held Jake's gaze as his hand stroked up and back down, then his eyes closed.

Jake groaned. Shutting his eyes, he tried to get the image of Remi touching himself out of his head. But instead of banishing the thought, it turned more vivid. *He leaned over Remi, fucking him as Remi stroked himself. He kissed Remi and his mouth slid down Remi's throat and—* Fuck. Jake's fangs dropped so quickly it took his breath away.

Goddamn, he had to get out of here. He wanted to bite Remi and make him submit, so badly. If he didn't put distance between them, he was liable to do just that.

Jake opened his eyes and found Remi passed out, his hand still on his cock, his head turned to the side and his mouth hanging open.

Well damn. Jake supposed he shouldn't complain, he really didn't want to think about this right now. He picked Remi up and deposited him in bed the right way. He covered Remi with the comforter and kissed his forehead. "See you tomorrow, pup."

"I fucking love your mouth." Remi dropped his head back to the pillow, his eyes closed, taking in every little sensation.

The suction on his cock increased as the clever tongue danced along the shaft.

"Oh, fuck. Gonna come. Stop. Not yet..." Winding his fingers through his lover's hair, Remi fought the growing sensation. He tried to slow the inevitable by pulling those delectable lips off him.

A soft, seductive kiss tickled his stomach, making him loosen his grip. As soon as his hand fell to the mattress, his prick was once again engulfed.

Ass muscles clenching tight, he shivered. His balls drew closer to his body and his legs tensed. It was absolute torture. A tingle raced up his spine. No, not yet. "Oh God, oh—"

The wonderful warmth left his cock.

Remi half growled, half laughed. "You fucking tease."

A snort answered him, then his dick was gripped, held upright and laved from tip to balls.

Fisting his hand in the thick hair again, Remi pulled his lover's face closer to his groin. "Yesssss, that feels good."

His legs were shoved higher, exposing him more, and that wicked tongue laved his crease, snaking down.

Remi tried concentrating on the slick caress over his perineum and the breath across his balls. Suddenly, it stopped and saliva dripped through his crease.

Then more spit landed on Remi's hole. A finger circled his anus, spreading it around.

"Tease!"

The finger pressed inside.

Remi moaned. "God..."

Bang, bang, bang. "Remi, open up."

Remi bolted upright in bed so quickly a wave of dizziness hit him.

The knock came again. "Remi, let me in already. Are you still asleep? You better not still be asleep."

Sterling? Remi blinked, trying to focus. "Coming." He jumped out of bed, looking around. What the fuck was he looking for? *Oh, pants.*

The knock came again.

"I'm coming." He yanked his pants on over his boner. He groaned and tucked his boner in his pants and zipped them. He ran to the door and flung it open.

Sterling strolled inside. "You *were* still asleep."

Remi stood there for a minute, the sunlight feeling like it was stabbing him in the head. There didn't seem to be an emergency. *Damn*, he was wobbly from getting up so fast.

His mom waved from her car.

After waving back, Remi shut the door. What the fuck? He glanced at Sterling, who stood in the middle of the living room frowning. "What?"

"Do you realize it's ten o'clock?"

Remi walked back into his bedroom and flopped on the bed. Holy shit. His heart was pounding. Remi buried his face in the mattress then turned his head to the side and took a deep breath. Damn, how much had he had to drink last night? He remembered Rhys bringing him home in his car and Jake—

"You forgot me." Sterling came in and crawled onto the bed beside him. He lay on his side facing Remi.

"I didn't forget you. I didn't realize you were coming here. I was planning on going to get you when I got up."

Sterling shrugged, flopping onto his back. "Mom was going to the store, I had her bring me. Why are you still asleep at this time a day?"

"I went out last night."

Sterling rolled back onto his side. "You did? With Jake?" He smiled.

Remi groaned, turned over and sat up. Climbing off the bed, he headed to the bathroom. It was way too fucking early for this. He couldn't remember all of what he'd said to Jake last night. Then there was that dream... He kept having it. Why?

"Hey. Where are you going?"

Crazy. I'm going crazy. "To take a piss."

ೋ∞৵

Sterling snagged his helmet off Remi's white laminate kitchen counter and, with the football under his arm, took off out the door.

Remi followed at a much slower pace. Goddamn he didn't have the energy to keep up with Sterling today.

What all had he said to Jake last night? Remi winced thinking about it. When he was drunk he didn't hold anything back, everything he thought just flew right out his mouth. It was why he never got drunk unless he was with someone he trusted completely. And while he did trust Jake, he hadn't planned on getting drunk.

What the fuck happened? Oddly, he wasn't really hung over. He'd had a bit of a headache when he first got up, but it was gone now.

He tucked his helmet under his arm, put his sunglasses on, turned the lock on the front door and shut it. He checked to make sure it locked and descended the steps. No telling what Sterling was getting into while he was up here trying to figure out what all he'd said and done last night.

The apartment door downstairs and across from Remi's opened. Mr. Morris stuck his head out. "Morning, Remi." Mr. Morris dipped his gray head toward the parking lot, where Sterling was already sitting on Remi's bike. "Looks like you have a big day planned."

"Yeah, he's going to make the team next year or kill us both trying."

Mr. Morris chuckled. "Well, he's a good kid. If anyone can teach him how to play, it's you."

"I'm sure going to try."

Mr. Morris nodded. "You'll do fine. Listen, have you noticed any bums hanging around here lately?"

Remi shook his head. "No, I haven't really noticed."

"Well, I'm going to talk to the super this morning. I swear the neighborhood is going to hell."

"Remi," Sterling called from the parking lot.

"Thanks, Mr. Morris. I better get before the kid takes off without me."

"Have fun playing ball." He waved and went back in his apartment.

Bums? Remi surveyed the lot, but didn't notice anything out of the ordinary. Wait. There was a homeless person, across the sidewalk where the next apartment building began. Interesting.

"What's up?"

Remi jumped at Sterling's voice. "Nothing." He glanced at his brother and put his own helmet on and fastened it. "Let's go."

ঙ৯৵

Smiling, Sterling ran the ball back. "Did you go home alone?"

Remi snagged the ball and growled. "Would you stop?"

"No. I wanna know."

"You are too young to know."

Sterling's eyes widened. "Holy shit, something happened."

Remi groaned. "Nothing happened. We went out for a few drinks and I met Jake's friends there." Jesus, the kid had a one-track mind. And why the hell did he seem to want something to happen? *"Where did you go? Was Jake there? Did you have fun?"* And why did his questions sound so...suspicious?

"Hi, Jake." Sterling waved, looking over Remi's shoulder.

Jake? Remi turned and, sure enough, there was Jake. Not only Jake, but Tank, Dago, Gadget, Zack, Nick and Rhys. Remi smiled, feeling a warmth spread through him that had nothing to do with the heat of the summer day.

A gasp sounded from beside him. Sterling's mouth was hanging open, his eyes wide. Then he whispered, "Oh. My. God."

Remi followed Sterling's gaze all the way to Rhys.

Rhys stood right behind Jake, in a pair of cutoffs and a tank top. He had a cooler on his shoulder, carrying it like it weighed nothing. He was limping slightly.

"I know, scary as hell, ain't he?" Remi asked.

Mute for the first time in his life, Sterling simply nodded.

Remi knew how the kid felt since he'd had the same reaction.

Stepping up to them, Jake furrowed his brow at Sterling, then met Remi's gaze.

Remi shrugged. "Rhys."

Jake nodded. "Ah."

Gadget walked up to Remi holding out his hand. "Hey, man, how's it going?"

"Good." Remi slapped Gadget's hand, then made a fist and hit Gadget's.

Nick did the same thing. Tank and Zack slapped him on the back.

Dago looked a little green as he grabbed Remi's hand and

pounded him on the back. "Hey." His voice sounded rusty.

Remi'd had as much alcohol as Dago, but apparently he'd fared better this morning. "Hey." Remi squeezed Dago's hand and slapped his arm. "How's your head?"

Dago groaned. "Oh fuck. Hurts like a son of a bitch. How's yours?"

"Actually, it's fine."

"Lucky bastard," Dago grumbled.

Remi chuckled.

"Jake, where the fuck do you want this?" Rhys asked, dipping his head toward the ice chest on his shoulder.

"Bend over and we'll show ya, Rhys," Gadget murmured.

Jake pointed to a tree. "Stick it over there in the shade."

"Fuck you, Gadget. Just for that, you stay the fuck outta the ice chest." Rhys walked past. "Hey, Remi."

Remi grinned. "Hey, Rhys." He turned around and raised a brow at Gadget. "You got a death wish?"

"Shit, Gadget would do anything to get away from all those damn kids of his." Zack flopped onto the grass and stretched his legs out.

Dago laughed, then clutched his head and groaned.

Remi fought back a laugh. He could imagine. He'd learned last night that Gadget was married and had nine kids. "All right, guys, play nice."

Tank went to Sterling, who was standing next to Remi with a blank look on his face, and offered his hand. "Hey, pup. Sterling, right? Remi's told us a lot about you. Nice to meet you."

"Nice to meet you too." Sterling shook Nick's hand and became his normal chatty self, introducing himself to the rest of the gang. If Remi wasn't mistaken he heard the little shit mention his name a couple of times, asking about last night.

Jake sidled up next to Remi and bumped his shoulder. "Kid is as protective over you as you are him. How do you feel this morning?"

"Good. No hangover. What the fuck did I do last night? And what are all of you doing here?" Not that Remi was complaining. He and Jake were beginning to get back the easy camaraderie they'd shared before the night Remi'd discovered they were mates. Actually, now it was better. Remi didn't have to try and hide his attraction.

Jake took the ball from him, answering the second question and ignoring the first. "Thought the kid could use some group practice." He glanced at his friends. "We're almost a team, only two short."

"We're like thirteen short, Jake," Sterling corrected.

"I said *a* team, not two teams," Jake countered.

"A team is one whole side. Did you mean we're all going to play offense?" Sterling raised a brow.

"Well, I meant—"

"Okay, okay." Remi intervened to keep Jake from strangling Sterling. The kid questioned *everything*...to death. "How about two teams, one of four the other five?"

They wound up playing Remi, Sterling, Jake and Rhys against Dago, Gadget, Tank, Zack and Nick. It went pretty smoothly until the guys realized how good Sterling was and Zack tried to tackle him. Rhys planted Zack on his ass and winced before hobbling away.

Remi leaned into Jake. "He gonna be all right?"

Jake nodded. "Shhh... Don't mention it."

Sterling ran back after his second touchdown. He took one

look at Rhys, who was trying to walk the pain off, and went right to him, grabbing his arm. "You okay? Will your leg be all right?"

It got eerily quiet. Remi couldn't hear anything but the traffic a block away and a dog barking somewhere nearby.

After a few seconds Rhys stared at Sterling's hand on his arm, then back at Sterling's face and smiled. "It's an old wound. I got into a shootout with a Mexican drug lord. I got wounded pretty bad...leg ain't never been the same since."

Remi walked over, knelt in front of Rhys and tapped his calf. "Off with the shoe."

"It's fine." Rhys glared down at him.

"Fuck that. You're as bad as Sterling. Lose the goddamned shoe." Remi had seen his share of injuries, first in football and now as a fireman. Regardless what Dirk said, he'd make a good EMT.

Rhys grumbled and started cussing under his breath, but he didn't say a thing when Remi untied his shoe and eased it and his sock off. He checked for mobility, moving Rhys' ankle side to side, then watched for tenderness, massaging the leg. Rhys' ankle was a little swollen, but there was no bruising.

Remi stood and tossed Rhys his shoe and sock. "Go put ice on it."

Remi noticed all of the other guys staring at them. "What?"

No one said anything.

Sterling caught Rhys' arm. "Come on, I'll go with you. So, tell me about the shootout and how you caught them."

Rhys grumbled some more, but let Sterling pull him along.

Jake's hand landed on Remi's shoulder. "I swear. Leave it to Sterling to be the only person ballsy enough to ask about the limp. It's a sore subject. Rhys punched out the last guy who asked."

Remi jerked his head around, looking at Jake. "What?" Remi spared his brother—who was chattering away to a very bewildered-looking Rhys—one last glance then leaned closer to Jake. "Umm, is he dangerous?"

Jake's attention focused on Rhys and Sterling. "Very. But not to any of us."

Chapter Ten

After pulling the SUV into a clearing near the woods, Jake turned off the headlights and the ignition and looked over at Remi. "You ready?"

"Yeah. Ready when you are."

Jake gave a crisp nod and opened the door. "Let's go."

The buzz of several different conversations hit them at once. Quite a few pack members were here already. He shut the door and met Remi at the front of the Tahoe.

When they stepped into the clearing, the talking stopped. About thirty pack members stood near a big campfire in the middle of the small area, which was surrounded by trees. All of them were focused on Remi.

Jake got an eerie feeling, then dismissed it. This was Remi's first time meeting most of the pack. Keaton and Chay had kept him sheltered, only introducing him to the pack alpha, while they taught him how to be a wolf. It made sense the members would be curious about him.

Remi stepped closer, brushing Jake's arm with his shoulder. As though that were a sign, everyone turned back to their conversations.

Putting his hand in the middle of Remi's back to let his mate know he was there, Jake kept walking.

Chay, a strange look on his face, waved from across the fire and immediately strode forward. He met Jake and Remi halfway with Keaton hurrying after him.

"Hey." Keaton nodded to Jake.

Jake tipped his chin. "Hey."

Chay didn't say anything. He leaned close to Remi and sniffed.

"Cut it out, asshole." Remi flicked Chay's ear. The unease surrounding Remi seconds before had vanished. "God, this werewolf shit is hard to get used to."

"Ow." Chay slapped a hand to the side of his head and flicked Remi's ear back.

"Ow." Remi clutched his ear, glaring at Chay.

Shaking his head, Jake chuckled. At least Remi was no longer nervous.

Standing over near a group of trees, Rhys jerked his head, indicating he wanted Jake to come to him. Rhys' glower was more pronounced than usual. Something must be up.

Jake nodded and turned to Remi. "When you and Chay are done assaulting one another, come find me. I'm going to see what Rhys wants."

"Okay." Remi glanced out past the fire and dipped his chin in greeting to Rhys.

Rhys returned the action.

As Jake walked off he heard Keaton say to Remi, "You smell different."

Exchanging hellos here and there, Jake made his way to Rhys. "'Sup?"

Rhys' brow furrowed. "Something strange is going on."

Jake's lip quirked, but he didn't dare laugh. Rhys was

serious. "How so?"

"I know damn well I sprained my ankle tackling Zack's ass today, now it's good as new. More to the point, my fucked-up leg isn't aching. I can't remember the last time this son of a bitch didn't ache, especially after doing something stupid like trying to play football."

Jake frowned. He'd noticed this afternoon after Remi examined Rhys' foot that he was walking more evenly. How could Remi handling Rhys' leg make it better? Remi hadn't done anything but massage it a little. Jake stared back at Remi. He was still talking to his friends. Fuck, the man looked good. The firelight made his skin glow. He was something else, but he wasn't a miracle worker.

Rhys inhaled audibly next to him. "What did you do to him? He smells fucking great." Rhys shook his head as if to clear it.

"Man, I will kick your ass. You know that, right?"

The corner of Rhys' mouth turned up. "You can try. But you know damn well you don't have anything to worry about from me. It's just weird as hell though. It's strong. I noticed it as soon as y'all got here. Everyone did. Think it has something to do with him fixing my leg?"

Jake opened his mouth to tell Rhys that Remi could not have possibly healed his leg and all hell broke loose.

Men started yelling at once.

Tank, Dago, Gadget, Zack, Nick and Chay were in a circle, damn near fighting with several of the pack's alpha wolves. They heaved people back, exchanging blows every few shoves. Fangs flashed and eyes glowed. The smell of blood, anger, arousal and sweat filled the air. Remi wasn't in sight.

Heart racing, Jake ran toward the commotion. His fangs dropped and his hands balled into fists, preparing to defend his

124

mate. He inhaled deeply, trying to find Remi. He was somewhere in the crowd, the smell of his fear was everywhere, but Jake couldn't see him. "Where the fuck is Remi?"

Rhys kept pace beside him, his gait more even than normal. "He's in the middle with Keaton."

"Halt," John Carter, the pack leader, yelled in a deep, booming voice that didn't sound like his own. Everyone froze, except Jake, Rhys and Joe Winston.

Joe Winston, Chay's father and the pack Beta, rushed forward, pushing through the crowd.

Jake shoved past Tank and Gadget, ignoring John Carter's demand for everyone to stay back. He had to get to Remi and make certain he was all right. If it meant having to take on his own pack alpha to do it, he damn sure would.

Remi had his back to Jake, talking to Joe and Keaton.

Keaton argued with his mate's father about something, his hands were claws—thanks to his ability to shift into a third wolf form—by his sides.

"Remi." Jake touched Remi's shoulder.

Remi turned and crouched into a fighting stance.

Claws raised, Keaton swung around and put himself in front of Remi.

Growling, Jake bared his teeth. *Mine.*

"Sorry, Jake." Keaton stepped out of the way.

"Fuck. I thought this was only supposed to be a get together. No big deal. What the fuck is going on?" Remi's voice climbed with each word he spoke until he was shouting at Jake.

Trying to keep it together, Jake took a deep breath. Remi was fine, pissed as hell, but unscathed. Jake grabbed Remi's shoulder, pulling him close and wrapping his arms around his mate. "What happened?"

Remi shrugged his arms away, still madder than hell, and pointed through the crowd to a man standing in front of Gadget. "That fuckhead tried to bite me." He looked around then pointed at Miles Crawford, who stood in front of Dago. "So did that asshole."

"Whoa, whoa, whoa. Let's calm down now." Joe came forward and put his hand on Remi's shoulder. "Jake, we need to talk."

At that moment John Carter shoved through the crowd into the circle, and the members who'd been fighting with Jake's friends all stepped back. "Jake, Keaton, Chay. Over there, now." He pointed to a stand of trees about ten yards away.

Grabbing Remi's hand, Jake began to follow.

John shook his head, glowering at Jake. "Not him. You. Do you trust your friends to protect him?"

Jake frowned and started to tell the alpha to go to hell, his mate was coming with him, but caught Rhys' gaze. His best friend nodded and faced outward like the rest of the gang. They positioned themselves to defend Remi and Jake.

John, Joe, Chay and Keaton stood outside the circle waiting for them.

Remi tugged Jake's hand, making him turn. "What the fuck, Jake?" Remi's eyes widened and darted around.

It took everything Jake had not to pull Remi into his arms. "I don't know. Stay here and let me go find out. I'll be right back." He tried his damnedest not to let Remi see how uneasy he felt, but he had no idea if he was successful. Then he remembered the calming effect he seemed to have over Remi. He took a deep breath and willed himself to relax. He knew the guys wouldn't let anything happen to Remi.

Jake was relieved to see Remi's fear had receded a little with Jake's anger. He touched Remi's cheek and as usual Remi nuzzled in, closing his eyes.

Jake kissed his forehead. "Let me go talk to John and see what's going on and I'll come right back." Dropping his head, he stepped away from his mate and out of the loose circle his friends had made.

John led the way to the spot he'd indicated. Jake followed, listening intently for the slightest sound of distress from behind him. When he got to the trees, he turned so he could keep Remi in sight.

"First off. You"—John pointed a finger at Chay then Keaton—"and you, stay out of this. You're part of my pack and as your alpha I'm telling you that you cannot help in this challenge."

Chay started to protest, but Keaton caught Chay's arm and pulled him back.

Jake bristled, stepping next to Chay. Chay and Keaton were defending Remi. Jake had no clue what the fuck John's problem was, but Jake had no problem deciding whose side he was on. And what challenge? "Somebody better start talking. What the hell is going on?"

John pinched the bridge of his nose, looking down for a moment, then gave Jake his undivided attention. "Let's take a walk, Jake."

Jake shook his head, trying to find Remi in the crowd. So far everyone was behaving and no one had come near the circle, but—

"Go. We're watching him," Chay said.

Jake followed John. It was a tough thing to do, but he trusted his friends to protect Remi.

Once they were out of sight of the others, John spoke. "Remi is an omega."

"Excuse me?" Jake frowned.

"He's a true omega wolf. They are very rare and precious. You probably haven't noticed because he's also your mate."

Jake felt like someone had slapped him. He had been a werewolf all his life and he'd never known an omega. But he had heard of them. Omegas were submissive by nature. Was that why Remi seemed to bring out all of Jake's dominate tendencies? "Are you sure?" Omegas were the backbone of the pack, they enhanced an alpha's power and had powers themselves.

John Carter nodded.

"What in the hell does Remi being one have to do with everyone losing their fucking minds and resorting to violence? How the hell does everyone else know when I didn't?"

"They don't know. It's Remi's scent. He didn't smell this way before. He had to grow into it. It takes a couple shifts for turned wolves to mature into their powers. They're just reacting to his scent."

"Which is why I didn't notice it, because of our mate bond?" Maybe Jake should have seen it. He had thought it odd that Remi acted so differently than other wolves.

"Yes." John sighed. "Yet you haven't claimed him, and this is why things are fucked up right now."

But he *had* claimed Remi. He'd fucked Remi within an inch of both their lives.

"Listen, Jake, part of an omega's power is his ability to calm his pack. Each individual omega has a different gift. Some can make things grow, some can put the pack in a trance, some can speak telepathically to their alpha. It's very individual to the omega. In addition, you will develop new strengths due to his presence. It's why they are very valuable and kept secret. But before they are claimed, their presence is easily detected

128

and can start riots. All the alphas go on instinct, trying to make them submit and make them theirs. Even though they don't realize why." He hesitated and studied Jake for a moment. "Daniel is my omega. Only my betas know that."

Daniel Eagle? Jake thought about it for a second. Daniel was the pack peacemaker and the coordinator, he was as recognizable as any of the betas. He and John were best friends, as were their mates. Jake could remember as a pup it was nearly impossible to get into a fight with the other pups without Daniel breaking them apart.

"He is not, however, my mate like Remi is yours. Lucky you, you don't have to explain to your jealous mate about claiming your omega." John patted his shoulder.

They walked further, Jake still concerned about letting Remi out of his sight. "What's all this mean, John? Just give it to me straight."

"It is time for you to form your own pack. When you claim your mate, you will be a pack alpha, Jake."

"My own pack?"

"Think about it. You've always been a strong leader. Many of those men in that circle have been following you since you were kids. Your mate being an omega is no accident."

"You're asking me to leave the pack?"

"Essentially, yes. This isn't punishment, Jake, it's an honor. You shouldn't think of it as exile, it's not."

Fuck, fuck, fuck. He could not leave the pack. If he left the pack, he'd have to leave the territory. Remi and Jake couldn't leave Sterling. More to the point, Remi would not leave him. "I can't, John. Remi can't leave the area...not yet."

John held up a hand. "Relax, I'll give you some time if you need it. You and your pack can hunt on unmarked land. But given that the rest of the pack will eventually figure out why they're reacting like this, it's not going to be easy. Your pack is liable to have several fights on their hands. I'll do my best, but I can't promise anything. Which is why you and your pack must defend him tonight. Because these men have scented him, you have to make it clear that he is yours and you and your pack will defend him. I don't expect trouble, but it needs to be made clear what the consequences will be should they decide to mess with Remi."

Pack? Fuck, Jake's heart felt like it was in his throat. "John, I don't have a pack."

"Don't you? Those men back there protecting your claim to Remi, even though you have not marked him yet? Jake, they're defending you and yours against the rest of their own pack."

"They're my friends."

"You will discover that you do not get to choose who will follow you. They choose you, just as your omega has obviously chosen you." John arched a brow. "You aren't denying them, are you?"

"No, of course not. I don't have any choice in this, do I?"

"As with most good men who come to lead, I'm afraid not. Remi being your mate takes that choice away. Unless you are prepared to let another alpha claim your omega as his?"

"Fuck no!"

John laughed. "I didn't think so."

"What do I have to do?"

John stopped walking and turned, looking him in the eye, his expression suddenly somber.

Goddamn it. Why did Jake get the feeling he wasn't going to like what John had to say? Jake frowned.

"You have to claim your omega, as you will have to every

now and again so that others do not. Which shouldn't be too difficult, since he's also your mate. It's why none of you know what Daniel is. As long as an omega has been and continues to be claimed by their alpha, no one, even in the pack, can sense that they are omegas. Which is essential. Otherwise you'd have alphas coming out of the woodwork trying to stake their own claim to your omega."

"Claim him how?"

"He has to submit to you sexually and you must claim him with a bite."

"I've claimed him as my mate." *Sexually.* "Can't I just go bite him?"

John shook his head. "I'm afraid not. The hormones released during sex interact with the ones released during the bite, which is what triggers their scent change. They must also physically submit."

Jake closed his eyes, feeling damn near sick. Rough sex with others nearby? He could not do this to Remi. This would make him a monster in Remi's eyes. "And if I don't?"

"Someone else will."

Un-fucking-believable. Remi'd suddenly inherited his own pack and Jake was now his alpha. And Remi was now an omega...whatever the hell that meant. He didn't feel any different. Remi groaned and did his damnedest to not start yelling. How could they possibly fight all those men? What if...?

Gadget paced past Remi, shaking his head. "Carter's holding them off now. Why can't he tell them to fuck off and leave Remi alone, he's ours?"

Tank nodded. "They have their own omega, don't they?"

"Yeah." Jake nodded.

Remi stood there amazed. They were arguing over him. He'd started feeling a connection to all of them when they'd first met, but it was getting stronger. It was hard to explain, and given how few people Remi actually considered friends, it made him feel better about the situation.

This whole thing was something right out of a movie. Gadget was right, John Carter was holding the rest of the pack off, or was he? Maybe it was their pack omega. Jake had said omegas could calm a pack. Remi glanced out over the pack, trying to figure out who the omega was. No one appeared to be doing anything to control them, yet they were definitely more composed than earlier. Then John Carter had shouted a command in a strange tone and everyone had frozen instantly, like they were under a spell or something. Now they all waited patiently, talking, almost like nothing had happened. It was eerie as hell and unnerving, since Remi now knew they were waiting for John Carter to allow them to challenge Jake.

"He's giving us time to talk." Rhys stood a few feet away from Jake, being his typical calm, cool and collected self.

Jake had been reluctant to tell them what was going on. The look on his face was pinched, uptight. He didn't want to do this. Hell, neither did Remi, but they really didn't have a choice.

Dago groaned, his fist clenching and unclenching. Tank kept fidgeting, and Gadget was about to wear a groove in the hard-packed dirt from pacing. Nick could not stop staring and growling at the crowd.

Remi went to Jake, needing his strength.

Placing his hands on Remi's shoulders, Jake stared into Remi's eyes. Like always, the muscles in Remi's shoulders eased without his permission. His body was Jake's to command. How did Jake do that? Remi was mad and scared, but it was like he could suddenly think clearly. He knew what he had to do. "It will be okay."

Jake touched his cheek.

Remi stared into the big brown eyes and melted. Whenever Jake touched him his whole body came alive, sensitized. Remi had no choice but to follow willingly or be swept away. Changing into a wolf was similar, but not nearly as exciting. He closed his eyes, leaning into Jake's hand, taking what he needed, willing Jake to do the same.

"Amazing." Jake's tone was soft, barely a whisper.

At the awe in Jake's voice, Remi opened his eyes.

Jake stared past Remi. Running his thumb over Remi's cheek, he jerked his head.

Remi turned.

Gadget had stopped pacing and was glaring out toward the other pack. Dago's hands were no longer fisted. Zack, Nick and Tank were watching Remi and Jake. All of them were alert, but at ease. Like they were awaiting a command. How? Why?

"We're theirs as much as they are ours."

Remi didn't quite understand it, but the sense of belonging was there nonetheless. They had a bond, all of them.

Jake kissed Remi, acting more like himself. When Jake pulled back, his brown eyes had shifted. He stared at Remi for several seconds, caressing his cheek, then abruptly stepped away. "Everyone, get rid of your clothes." His voice had that same weird cadence to it that John Carter's had earlier. Remi noticed the others seemed compelled to act. Instantly, their pack began to strip.

Remi stood frozen, amazed at this new development. "Jake?"

"Trust me. If they shift in clothes, they'll get tangled and not be able to defend themselves." Jake tossed his shirt away

133

and reached for Remi again.

Damn it, Remi really hated this werewolf-culture shit. Glancing around, he noticed the guys were naked and fanning out around them, prepared to defend them, to fight for them.

Taking a deep breath, Remi let Jake's scent invade his senses. A feeling of warmth filled him. His gums stung, his cock hardened. He could do this.

As the men talked, Jake undressed Remi. When Remi opened his eyes, his vision had changed. He watched in a daze as the other pack fought his friends. Some of them had already shifted.

Jake pulled Remi back into the trees, concealing them from view. His mouth slammed over Remi's and his hot strong body melded against him.

Remi forgot about everything else. Need coursed through him, making him moan into Jake's mouth. God, he needed Jake. It was like this every time he got close to Jake. Every time they touched or kissed. Remi couldn't think beyond Jake, he wanted Jake.

Jake drew back until only the wet tip of his cock touched Remi's stomach. "On your hands and knees, pup."

Remi wanted to feel the soft skin of Jake's balls on his nose, his cheek. He wanted that smell, the weight of Jake in his mouth, but he did as he was told. "Yes, sir." Remi dropped to all fours, the title slipping easily from his lips. Remi's ass clenched and unclenched as he thought back to the other day. The cool night breeze blew over his skin. His belly contracted. Damn, had he ever been this turned on? It was like waking from a wet dream in the middle of climax—it took his breath away. His cock throbbed in anticipation and his balls were so tight they were nearing pain. He could feel Jake's heat behind him. Why wasn't Jake hurrying? Remi whimpered, pushing back toward his mate. "Please..."

Jake growled, his hand touching the middle of Remi's back.

Remi obeyed the unspoken command to be still. A chill ran down his spine and his neck began to itch. He wanted Jake's cock inside him very badly.

Now that Remi knew what awaited him, he could almost imagine the feeling. He moaned and shivered, remembering how it felt when Jake pulled almost all the way out and then pushed in.

Suddenly, Jake's fingers were in his crease, wet and slippery. Jake speared two fingers into him.

"Oh fuck." Remi moved back, his ass squeezing those fingers. His cock felt like it was about to burst. His stomach tensed and he could think of nothing but getting Jake inside of him.

Groaning, Jake lined his prick up and pushed right in.

Remi gasped for air, his ass swallowing Jake and milking his cock. The burning feeling shot through him. A tingle raced over his spine, making his arms and legs feel almost heavy. Within seconds the twinge of pain was gone. Panting and pushing, Remi fucked himself on Jake's prick.

After a few seconds, Jake drew back. Then, gripping Remi's hips, Jake pounded into him over and over, making his balls slap hard against Remi's ass.

The sound of men fighting just beyond the trees seemed miles away. Remi let out a low keening sound, dropped his head and further exposed his nape. It felt so good, the cool air on the tip of his prick, Jake's cock sliding in and out of his hole. He didn't want it to ever stop.

Jake fell forward on one hand, his fingers digging into Remi's hip with the other. Rooting his face against Remi's neck,

Jake growled. The sound was low, deep and possessive, stating better than words that Remi was his.

The skin on the back of Remi's neck crawled, feeling hot and itchy, just as it had this afternoon. Remi whimpered. "Bite me. Please bite me." He needed Jake's teeth. If Jake would claim him, mark him, Remi could come. He didn't know how he knew that but he did. Oh God, he wanted to come.

If Jake didn't bite him soon, he was going to go crazy.

Jake's teeth clamped down on Remi's neck where it met his shoulder. The fangs pierced his flesh and Remi yelled. His body stiffened, his ass clenched around Jake's cock and he came. The pain morphed into pleasure, racking his body.

Jake thrust forward once again. "Mine!" He came, filling Remi's ass.

Remi's hands and knees hurt, rocks and twigs digging into them. Funny he hadn't felt that before. His muscles were so loose...tired.

Jake let go of Remi's neck and Remi collapsed. He gasped as his body gave out, unable to even hold his head up.

Jake slid his hand off Remi's hip and wrapped an arm around Remi's chest, tugging Remi backward against his chest. "Mmm..." Jake's nose tickled Remi's neck, nuzzling.

Remi sighed and snuggled into his mate's warm body. Something tickled, trailing over his shoulder, making him open his eyes. Blood. The red drop trickled down his chest, pooling in the crease of his leg where it joined his body.

Swiping the wound with his tongue, Jake held Remi closer.

Remi moaned. The feeling of Jake's tongue radiated out, making his cock threaten to rise again. Oh he could so get used to submitting. If this was what it felt like to give in, to please his mate... He wanted to do it again.

"Holy shit," someone murmured.

Remi realized they had an audience. How had he forgotten?

Every one of their gang stood just inside the tree line watching them, bloody and bruised with shifted eyes and teeth. The clearing was nearly empty. Only their family remained.

"Our pack." Jake's breath caressed Remi's neck.

"What now?" Remi asked.

Dago stepped closer, wincing and clutching his side.

Remi stood, going to him without even considering what he'd do when he got there. Behind him he heard Jake say, "We accept them."

Chapter Eleven

"You worry too much, Jake." Rhys shoved away from the wall of his garage and walked up behind Gadget, who was working on Rhys' bike. "Is that supposed to be like that?" Rhys pointed at something on the engine.

Gadget knocked his hand out of the way. "Fuck off. Who's the mechanic around here?"

Dago came through the door from the house with three beers in hand. He passed them out to Jake and Rhys, before sitting on the cement floor by Gadget. "I agree I think you're worrying for nothing. I don't know Remi as well as you do, but he doesn't seem to do things he doesn't want to do."

"Where the hell is my beer?" Gadget held his hand out, glaring at Dago, who muttered, "Get your own."

Jake ignored his friends' bickering and hefted himself off the top of the washing machine. Taking a swig from his bottle, he grimaced. The smell of laundry detergent didn't really go with the flavor of his beer. "That's just it, Dago, he seems to always be taking care of others and not himself. Like last night after the fight. Did you notice how he tried to take care of everyone when I was taking your oaths?"

Rhys took one of the folding metal chairs from against the wall and sat in it. "What does that have to do with Remi being your mate?"

It had everything to do with Remi being his mate. What if he couldn't control his urge to dominate Remi? Remi would submit just to please Jake. Hell, Remi'd loved being claimed in front of the whole pack, he couldn't fake that. Jake's senses didn't lie. Maybe Jake was worrying too much, but with Remi's background it was kind of hard not to.

Gadget's hand slipped off the wrench and it went clanking to the ground. "Son of a bitch."

Rhys arched a brow.

"Jake, you'd never hurt him. If he says he wants it, then trust him to know what he wants. He obviously trusts you. Shouldn't you give him the same respect?" Dago took a sip of his beer, then set it next to him and leaned back on his hands.

Jake walked around Rhys' bike. They were right. Remi did trust him, so much so that it made Jake crazy with wanting Remi. Which was part of the problem. "What if it's instinct? What if he only trusts me like that because of our bond? Because he's an omega?"

Rhys shrugged. "Hell, Jake, if you don't want him, I'll take him."

He knew Rhys was fucking with him, but damned if it didn't irritate the shit out of Jake anyway. Walking right to Rhys' chair, Jake crowded him and growled.

Rhys stood, snarling right back.

"Whoa hey, guys, chill the fuck out." Dago shoved his way in between them then turned toward Jake. "Who cares what the reason is. As long as you never break that trust, and Remi doesn't freak about it, then it doesn't matter."

"Are you so caught up in instinct that you can't think for yourself?" Rhys grumbled as he sat.

Jake snagged another one of the gray folding chairs away

from the unfinished garage wall. "No, not usually." *Only when assholes say they'll take my mate.* He swung it around backward and straddled it.

"Well, then why do you think Remi would be different?" Rhys took a drink.

There was that little thing Remi did, where he was always rubbing the side of his face on Jake's hand, but that was because he was an omega, wasn't it? Jake scowled at his beer bottle, dangling it between his fingers. Rhys might be correct about need and instinct being the same thing.

Who was Jake kidding? Even he questioned denying Remi the chance to submit or he'd have never packed those clamps in his saddlebags. He'd brought them with every intention of playing with his mate tonight.

Jake took a sip. "Yeah, I guess you're right. I need to be making sure he adapts rather than fighting him over it, huh?"

"Yes. 'Cause him turning out to be an omega just means it's ingrained." Gadget's wrench slipped again. "Goddamn it. Dago, hand me a five sixteenths."

Going to the big red Craftsman toolbox along the wall, Dago opened a drawer and retrieved a wrench. He brought it to Gadget, holding it over Gadget's shoulder until he took it. "You know, speaking of Remi being an omega. I was certain my ribs were broke last night, then after he touched them asking me if it hurt and all that doctoring shit, they felt better. Today—" He lifted his gray T-shirt and turned to the side, showing off his torso. It looked fine to Jake. "It's completely healed, no bruises or anything. I'm pretty damn sure they were broken. It took days for them to heal last time I was in a bad fight."

Gadget raised his gaze from Rhys' bike, giving the conversation his undivided attention, and grabbed Dago's beer, taking a drink.

Snagging his bottle back, Dago scowled at Gadget.

Rhys nodded. "Yeah, like I was telling you yesterday, my leg is better too."

"Jake, can you and Remi come to my house for dinner this week, have him take a look at my youngest?" Gadget rubbed the back of his hand over his forehead, wiping away sweat and leaving a big grease smudge behind, before going back to Rhys' engine.

Gadget's youngest had juvenile arthritis. Jake didn't want to get the man's hopes up. The healing could all be coincidence. No one knew yet what all Remi's being an Omega entailed. "Yeah, I'll ask Remi about it."

Jake glanced at Rhys. "You find out any more about Dirk Lassiter?"

"What you see is what you get, the guy is a first-rate asshole. I asked around a little, but my source at the bureau hasn't gotten back to me yet. I got a name to check into though. Apparently, the kid who was killed still has family in this area. An older brother. I'm going to drop in on him tomorrow."

Dago lay back on the cement, rolling his head toward Jake and Rhys. "We could arrange for Remi's dad to find himself on the wrong end of an angry wolf."

Jake glared at him, nipping that in the bud before it started, although he had considered it himself. "We aren't going to go breaking pack laws. We'll handle this legally." Jake used the tone he'd used last night, making sure they realized it was a command. Werewolves did not go around murdering people. All Jake needed was for one of his men to be labeled a rogue. But, if worse came to worse, Jake would seriously consider it. Dirk Lassiter had to go.

Jake's cell phone rang.

Setting his beer on the garage floor, he snagged the phone

off his belt and read the Caller ID. *R. Lassiter.* But it wasn't Remi's number. Jake flipped the phone open. "Hello?"

"Jake?"

Sterling. Jake had forgotten about giving the kid his business card. Every sense suddenly on alert, Jake stood. "Yeah, Sterling, what's wrong? Are you okay?"

Rhys jumped out of his chair so fast it clattered and the legs skidded on the ground behind him.

"Yeah, I'm okay. Do you know where Remi is?" Sterling's voice was shaky, not his usual fast, excited pace.

"Did you try his cell?"

"I did, he isn't answering."

Getting right in Jake's face, Rhys started to say something.

Jake brushed him off and stepped past him. Remi was probably on the motorcycle. He needed to get an earpiece for his phone so he could answer it even on his bike. "Where are you? Do you need me to come get you, Sterling?"

"Can you? I'm walking toward town. I don't want Dirk to catch me."

"You bet. Tell me how to get to you, kid." Jake looked over at Rhys. "I need another helmet."

Rhys took off toward the house.

Going to his bike, Jake started it as Sterling gave him directions.

Rhys was back in no time, fastening an extra helmet on Jake's backrest.

"Okay, kid, I'm on my way." Jake clipped his phone on his belt and put his helmet on.

"Is he okay? What happened?" Rhys asked.

"He's fine. I'll call you when I get him. Do me a favor and

call around and see if you can find Remi." Jake turned his bike and headed out of the drive toward the rez. Thank God he'd thought to give Sterling his number.

౷౿

Remi pulled his bike up close to Keaton's car, trying to block it from view. He'd left his stupid cell phone at home to charge it so he couldn't stay long. He'd have to get his phone before he went to Jake's house.

Looking around out of habit, Remi spotted a guy walking down the street. The guy appeared a little rugged, but he seemed familiar. Must be a neighbor or something. Remi shrugged it off and hurried to the front door of the small ranch-style house, hoping he wasn't seen.

Barking greeted him before he even knocked and made him smile.

The door swung open and Pita jumped on him, wagging his tail.

"Hey, Pita. Let me inside, huh?" Remi petted his head and walked in. The door closed behind him and he turned to find Keaton frowning at him. "What?"

"You okay?" Keaton had a knife in one hand and a dishtowel in the other.

"Yeah, I'm good."

Arching a brow, Keaton jerked his head to the side and walked past Remi into the kitchen.

Remi groaned, following. He knew Keaton well enough to suspect the man wasn't going to let the events of the pack meeting drop. Oh well, maybe talking to Keaton about being an omega wasn't such a bad idea.

143

Pita pounced into the kitchen in front of Remi.

When Remi got into the kitchen, Keaton was standing at the sink peeling potatoes. "Holy shit. Will miracles never cease? You're cooking?"

Keaton pointed the knife at him. "Don't make me beat your ass, dickhead. Get a knife out of the drawer and help me."

Going to the silverware drawer, Remi rummaged through it. "Don't you have a potato peeler?"

"A what?"

"You know it's like a knife with a slit in the middle of the blade." He rifled through the drawer, not finding one.

"Why the fuck would we have that?" Keaton blinked and blew a curl off his forehead. "Quit stalling and get over here and talk to me. Are you sure you're okay?"

Taking out a paring knife, Remi went to the sink and grabbed a potato. He turned on the water and began helping Keaton. "I'm fine. What are you making?"

"French fries. I'm trying to learn to cook. I'm sick of pizza and hamburgers." Keaton stopped peeling for a second and looked over at Remi. "Chay says you seem okay with Jake. You finally accept it?"

"What, the mate part or the new pack leader part?"

Snorting, Keaton went back to peeling.

Remi started cutting off the skin on the spud. "Yeah, I'm okay with it. Not like I got much of a choice, is there?"

"No, but...well, I've been worried about how you'd react when you found out your mate was a guy. Made me wonder if saving your ass was a good idea."

"Gee, thanks a lot, Bit." Remi nudged the shorter man with his shoulder.

Keaton grinned and nudged back. "You know damn well I

don't want you dead, asshole. It pains me to admit it, but if I'd have known you then as well as I do now, I'd have probably beat Jake to the punch when he changed you. I only meant I wondered if it was like a fate worse than death for you."

Remi froze, staring at Keaton. Jake changed him? Remi had thought Chay had turned him into a werewolf.

"What?" Keaton's big blue eyes widened. "What'd I say?"

"Jake changed me? But why? He didn't even know—" Jake had realized even then that Remi was his mate. "Why didn't y'all tell me Jake was my mate from the beginning?"

"Jake thought it'd be better off if we let you discover it on your own. You had a lot to take in, in a short time." Sighing, Keaton went back to peeling. "I'm sorry, Remi. We should have told you, but..."

"There was the whole gay thing and how I reacted to you?"

"Well yeah. After your shouting match with Chay, we *all* felt like Jake had a good idea."

In a way Remi was glad they'd given him time to get used to some of the weirder werewolf crap, but it would have been nice to know why he was attracted to Jake. He might not have fought it so hard if he'd known. Then it occurred to him, Jake had cared for him from the very beginning.

"What about the omega thing?" Keaton finished, set the knife down and turned and pointed past Remi. There was a bowl on the counter.

"It's weird. The whole werewolf thing is strange, but I like my pack, they're good men. I still don't understand it though. I feel like I've known all of them forever, but I've only known most of them a couple of days. I don't get it. There isn't anything special about me."

Keaton lifted one light brown eyebrow, then the little demon got an evil smirk on his face. "Just remember you said it, not me."

Remi narrowed his eyes at Keaton.

"There is something special, you just haven't figured out what it is yet. Aside from uniting their packs, omegas usually have some sort of talent that also strengthens a pack. It's part of the reason it's kept a secret. I doubt most people realize what omegas do. I guess I'm only sensitive to it 'cause of my third form. I know one who has this inner calm thing. Being around him makes the pack less aggressive when things go bad, like last night. All omegas have that to some extent, but his is way more powerful."

"What about the pack you came from? What did your omega do?"

Keaton shook his head. "We didn't have an omega. They are rare, which is why everyone started running at you. If allowed, they would have tried to force you to submit. The omega should choose the alpha, not the other way around. But alpha wolves don't realize it or they think they can change an omega's mind. Their hormones get the better of them when they catch scent of an omega. You are going to have to be on your guard from now on."

Lifting his arm, Remi sniffed. "Do I still smell funny?"

Keaton rolled his eyes. "No, and you couldn't smell yourself even if you did. Or more to the point, the smell wouldn't have the same effect on you it does others. Your scent changed when Jake claimed you. Or rather when you allowed Jake to claim you."

Allowed? "If I hadn't wanted Jake, my scent wouldn't have changed?"

Keaton faced Remi with the potato held out in one hand and the knife in the other. "Right. And to keep your scent normal, where no one realizes you're an omega, he'll have to reclaim you every so often."

"Well, thankfully he's my mate, huh?"

"I've never heard of an omega whose alpha was also his mate." Keaton scrunched his face in thought. "Well no, that's not true, John Carter mentioned a couple when Chay and I got together. But I don't know them personally."

Pita jumped, snagged the potato out of Keaton's hand and took off running.

"Son of a bitch. Pita, you little shit, you are in so much trouble." Keaton started after the puppy, stopping at the kitchen door when he heard the dog door open and close. Running over to the window, Keaton stood on tiptoe and peeked outside. "Oh. That dog is dead."

Remi chuckled, studying the bowl. It had potato slices in it in all different sizes. "Hey, Bit. Why didn't you cut these with a slicer?"

"A slicer?" Coming back to the sink, Keaton picked up his knife and another spud.

"Yeah, it's a little circular grid thing, cuts it into squares."

Still cutting, Keaton looked at him. "How the hell do you know so much about cooking?"

Remi shrugged. "We take turns cooking dinner at the firehouse. What are you making to go with the fries?"

"Hamburgers."

"Ham—" Remi shook his head. "Thought you were tired of burgers and pizza."

"I am," Keaton grumbled. "But those are the only two things I know how to make. I have to start somewhere."

After chopping his potato into chunks, Remi added them to the bowl. "Where's Chay?"

Keaton shook his head and turned to look at Remi. "The offi— Ow. Fuck." The knife clattered to the sink, followed by the thud of the potato. Blood welled up on his palm.

Remi snagged Keaton's wrist. "Let me see." Pulling it under the running water, he used his thumb to rub the blood off. Grabbing the dishtowel over Keaton's shoulder, Remi removed Keaton's hand from the water, intent on putting pressure on it, but there wasn't a cut. What the fuck? He brought Keaton's arm up, convinced he was seeing things wrong. "Where did it go?"

Keaton tugged his hand free, looking at it. His brows drew together. "I know I cut it. You saw the blood too, right? I mean we heal fast, but not instantly. That is just fucking— Oh my God! That's it, that is your gift. You're a healer."

The phone rang.

Keaton's mouth dropped open while he stared at Remi. Then he reached around Remi and got the cordless off the counter. "Hello?" He continued to talk, but Remi tuned it out.

What was going on? Last night after he'd touched the guys, they'd started feeling better. Dago had been favoring his ribs. Remi had been positive from seeing them they were broken, at least one or two of them. But almost immediately Dago had been less sore and barely bruised. Remi had looked again and realized he'd made a mistake, but now...

"Remi, that was Rhys. He told me to tell you that Sterling—"

Oh my God. Sterling. Remi started for the door, digging in his pocket for his keys. Goddamn, what if he was hurt? Why hadn't Remi waited until his phone was charged before coming here?

"Remi, wait." Catching his arm, Keaton halted him. "Jake was there and went to get Sterling."

Sterling is okay. He's with Jake. Jake won't let anyone hurt him. Remi kept repeating it to himself, trying to calm his racing heart. "Mind if I use your phone?"

Keaton handed it to him. "Here."

He dialed Jake's cell phone.

Jake answered it on the first ring. "He's fine. We're on the way to your apartment."

Remi heard Sterling laughing in the background. Oh fuck. Smacking the kitchen counter with his fist, Remi let out the breath he'd been holding.

ॐ∂৶

"He hit Mom because I went to Hell's Kitchen to have a few drinks?" Remi asked, only half believing what he'd heard, and leaned back on his couch. Dirk was a psychopath. Why did his mom put up with that? Why did she subject Sterling to it?

Nodding, Sterling reclined on his hands in the middle of Remi's living room floor. "He asked her what you were up to and why you were hanging out at a dive like that. That's how the whole thing started, then he started going on about how worthless she was." Sterling darted a glance at Jake then back to Remi before looking down, embarrassed.

Jake bent forward on the couch, resting his forearms on his knees. "How did he know you went to the bar?"

Remi shrugged. That he didn't want to think about. He was going to have to be more careful. He'd been sure no one at the bar would know him. He'd been wrong.

Chapter Twelve

"Sterling is right. You're more like a father to him."

Remi blinked. Father? He'd never thought about it, but he supposed he was, more than Dirk ever was to either of them. He hadn't purposely tried to do that, it just sort of came natural.

Shrugging, he finished covering Sterling and looked across the bed at Jake. "He said that?"

Jake brushed the hair off Sterling's forehead and grinned. "Yeah, he did. He's right, too, you take very good care of him." He jerked his head to the side, indicating the door. "Come on."

Remi closed the door behind them and followed Jake into the living room. "Thanks for getting him away from that mess."

"You don't have to thank me. I would have gone and gotten him regardless." Jake cleared away the plates from the coffee table where they'd eaten dinner and took them to the kitchen.

Remi smiled. That much was true. Jake seemed to make a habit of protecting those weaker than him. Grabbing the empty coke and beer cans, Remi trailed behind his mate. "Well, thank you anyway. You helped me take his mind off Dirk and my mom fighting."

"I didn't actually *let* him kick my ass at video games for his amusement."

"Yeah, the kid is a shark. I never actually *let* him beat me either." After tossing the cans in the trash, Remi turned, intent on helping Jake wash dishes, but he got sidetracked by the breadth of Jake's shoulders. He appeared so damn big in Remi's tiny kitchen. God, it was sexy how big he was, how powerful. It felt great to finally give in to his attraction.

Remi trailed his fingers across Jake's back, feeling the muscles tense and relax under the black T-shirt. He laid his cheek between Jake's shoulder blades and wrapped his arms around Jake's waist. He inhaled deeply, taking in his mate's soft, musky scent.

"Jesus, Remi, don't start that yet."

"Start what, I was just—"

"Moaning and nuzzling?"

He'd moaned? Remi grinned and let go. "Yeah." He got a dishtowel and dried the plates as Jake handed them to him, then put them in the cabinet. When he put the last plate away, Jake drew him close, kissing him.

Remi's brain melted. How could he have ever fought this? The connection between them felt as natural as breathing.

Without breaking their kiss, Jake maneuvered them toward the living room. With his hands on Remi's ass, he walked backward, pulling Remi along. They ended up bumping into the kitchen counter and the wall and an end table before they broke apart laughing.

From the end of the couch Jake retrieved the throw-over saddlebags he'd brought in off his motorcycle. "Get your ass in the bedroom before we kill each other or demolish the furniture."

"You started it that time." Remi jumped out of the way of the swat aimed at his butt and hightailed it into the bedroom. He loved the sexy growl Jake got when he was playing.

Sitting in his computer chair, Remi took off his shoes and socks, while Jake closed the door and sat on the edge of the bed to do the same.

After Jake got his boots off, he opened the motorcycle side bags he'd brought in with him. He set his cell phone on the nightstand and laid the bags next to the bed. "Come here."

Remi walked over to the bed and started to kneel, but Jake stopped him, pulling Remi to stand between his legs. Slowly, Jake unbuttoned Remi's blue shirt. "You really do want this, don't you?"

"Yes." Oh God, yes. He'd been longing for Jake the entire day. Over and over he replayed last night at the pack meeting in his head. The way Jake had taken him, demanding Remi give in, made him hard just thinking about it.

Jake pushed Remi's shirt off his shoulders, then lifted Remi's undershirt and kissed the skin he'd bared. "Take it off."

As Remi grabbed the hem and pulled the undershirt up, Jake's tongue traced the center line of his abdomen.

Hissing out a breath, Remi lifted the shirt over his head and dropped it to the floor. His abs tensed at the soft tickle of Jake's tongue and his heart raced in anticipation. He wanted Jake so badly. His cock was already hard, straining at the material of his black jockstrap and jeans.

Jake looked up at Remi, reaching for his pants. "You will tell me if you want me to stop."

Whether it was the command or the voice, Remi didn't know, but it made his insides flutter. "Yes, sir."

Making a low purring sound of approval, Jake smiled. He set to work on Remi's pants, leaving Remi in only his jock, then leaned forward, covering Remi's erection with his mouth. The heat of his lips seared through the cotton as he mouthed the length of Remi's cock.

"Oh fuck...sir." Remi drove his hips forward without thought. Jake's touch felt incredible.

Jake hooked his fingers through the elastic waistband and tugged the jock off. "Lay down on the bed, pup."

Remi hurried and did as he was told, watching as Jake stripped.

Jake had an amazing body. He was a big man to begin with but he had to work out or something in order to get that kind of muscle tone. He wasn't sinewy like Remi. Jake's chest, arms and thighs were thick, more dense. His abs were defined, but not overly. Black hair covered the area above his cock, under his arms and on his legs, but there was very little on his chest, attesting—along with the striking tanned skin—to his Apache heritage. His cock was wide, long and cut. Remi's mouth watered just looking at it. *Fuck,* he couldn't believe he'd had that huge thing in his ass.

Right before Remi's eyes, the thick prick started getting hard, reaching for him.

"Goddamn, the way you look at me." Jake's voice was nearly a growl.

Remi licked his lips.

Straddling his hips, Jake lowered himself on top of Remi, giving him no choice but to spread his legs and accommodate Jake's body. Once they were face to face, he bent forward and touched his finger to Remi's lip. "Not a sound, pup." Sliding his finger across Remi's chin and over his neck, Jake caressed the spot he'd bitten last night.

Remi nodded as Jake made his way down his body.

"Put your hands over your head and don't move or say a word until I tell you." Jake licked a long line from Remi's throat to his nipple. The air blowing over the wet trail raised chill bumps on his skin, but it felt good.

Jake circled one nipple, then the other, before meeting Remi's gaze and continuing toward Remi's cock. Their legs tangled together and Jake's prick brushed across Remi's thigh. It could have been the only thing in the room for all the attention Remi gave it.

Jake's mouth hovered above his dick, so close Remi could feel the warm breath fan over him. His thigh muscles flexed and his cock twitched, anticipating the moist heat on his prick. It didn't come. Instead, Jake nudged Remi's thighs wide and licked the inside of his thigh all the way to his foot. After trailing his tongue around Remi's anklebone and over his arch, he released the leg and started back up the other one. He took forever dragging it out, tormenting Remi.

Evil bastard. Jake was trying to kill him, Remi was convinced of it.

By the time Jake got to his hipbone, Remi's eyes had shifted and his fangs had lengthened.

"Mmm... You smell good, pup." Jake buried his nose against Remi's balls.

Remi bit his lip to keep from whimpering. A fine sheen of sweat broke out on his forehead and chest. His hands clenched and unclenched, wanting to reach for Jake and beg him to suck his cock. His legs shook with the effort to remain still and quiet.

Finally, Jake lapped at his balls, but before Remi could even enjoy it, he stopped. Leaning over the edge of the bed, he dug around, through his saddlebags Remi assumed, looking for something. "I brought something for you." He held up a length of chain for Remi to see. With his canine vision, Remi couldn't tell whether it was gold or silver, but it was definitely metal. It had an odd oval thing at each end. They resembled misshapen peace signs, like a kind of—

Oh fuck, they were nipple clamps. Remi's nipples tingled,

getting hard at the thought of Jake putting the clamps on him. He hefted his hips up and his prick skimmed along Jake's chin.

Jake nipped his thigh. "Be still, pup." He laid the clamps on Remi's stomach.

Oh, man, he loved that commanding tone. He wanted to please Jake, to surrender and do whatever Jake asked of him.

The metal felt cool against his heated skin. His prick throbbed and seeped precome. Remi opened his mouth to say, "Yes, sir," surprised at how easily the words were coming to him, but caught himself in time.

Jake reached toward the floor again. His chest lay heavy against Remi's thigh, making Remi's body list to the side. Nostrils flaring, Jake set a bottle on the bed beside Remi and caught Remi's dick in his palm. Swiping the tip with his tongue, Jake closed his mouth over the head and sucked. When he raised his head, his teeth and eyes had shifted to match Remi's. "No coming until I say, pup. Bend your knees."

Closing his eyes, Remi raised his knees. A cool breeze caressed his balls, then a warmth covered them. Jake's mouth. The skin over Remi's balls drew tighter and his whole body trembled. A snick sounded in the quiet room and something warm and slippery touched beneath his balls, over his perineum to his hole.

Jake's finger probed, sliding inch by inch inside Remi, as his tongue laved Remi's shaft.

Oh fuck me. Sweat dripped down Remi's temple. His legs shook and blinding pleasure started in his groin and spread outward.

Adding another finger, Jake eased it into his ass, pushing until he brushed over Remi's prostate. It felt good, so intense it was nearly painful. Remi didn't know whether he wanted to push toward Jake or move away.

Gripping Remi's cock, Jake held it for his mouth and started sucking.

Remi lost it and moaned aloud.

Pulling his fingers free, Jake nipped Remi's hip in reprimand, hard enough to sting.

The bed shifted and he opened his eyes.

Jake knelt between his legs. He snagged the chain off Remi's stomach and clamped one hard nipple then the other. One side of his lip turned up and he tugged the chain.

Remi squirmed. They pinched a bit, but not too hard. The slight sting added to his mounting pleasure instead of dulling it.

He couldn't take any more, he was close to begging. He actually had tears in his eyes. His whole body was one big trembling mass.

Grinning a full-out sadistic grin, Jake grabbed the bottle of lube and coated his cock nice and slow. He stroked the thick length, teasing Remi with it. "You want this, pup? Want my cock?"

Remi jerked his head up and down. *Oh God, please, sir, please...*

After agonizing seconds, Jake greased Remi's hole with the lube before tossing the bottle aside. He tugged the chain between Remi's nipples and circled his hole with his prick.

The pressure against his ass and on his nipples had him nearly screaming.

When Jake finally pushed in, Remi was so turned on he felt nothing but mind-numbing pleasure. And God, if Jake didn't hurry, he was going to go fucking crazy. He bit his lip, trying not to moan as Jake thrust forward. When his balls rested against Remi's ass, he stopped. Just stopped. The gleam in his eyes said he knew exactly what he was doing to Remi. "You feel real fucking good, so damn tight."

Remi whimpered.

Hooking his arms under Remi's knees, Jake lifted his legs and thrust. He fucked Remi hard and fast, slamming into him over and over, grunting low in his throat.

Remi's cock slapped against his lower abdomen with every powerful shove. Drops of precome dotted the line of dark hair below his navel. He kept himself from driving toward Jake's thrusts only because the position made it difficult for him to do so.

By the time Jake let go of his legs and leaned over him, they were both out of breath and coated with sweat. It dripped off Jake's forehead and chest onto Remi.

Jake pulled on the chain as his mouth covered Remi's.

Remi's back arched into the tingling sensation stabbing his nipples. It hurt and felt good at the same time. He couldn't hold back any longer. Moving with his mate, he moaned as Jake's tongue speared into his. He managed to angle his hips just right for Jake's cock to graze his gland.

Jake's mouth slid to Remi's neck.

The delicious pain and drag on his nipples and the cock in Remi's ass was too much. Remi groaned. "Oh God, please. Please, sir..."

Jake bit his shoulder where it met his neck and tugged the nipple clamps so hard they snapped off Remi's chest, flying to the sheets.

He saw stars. His whole body stiffened and he came. As hot semen shot over Remi's stomach and chest, Jake stilled, letting out a guttural yell. Then heat filled Remi's ass.

The next thing he knew, Jake was sitting on the edge of the bed with a glass of water in hand.

He sat up and Jake helped him drink. Damn, his throat
was sore, and his hair was sticking to his face and his neck.
Why was his throat so—? Oh God, he'd not only failed to be
quiet, he fucking yelled his head off. Thank God Sterling slept
like the dead.

Jake moved the glass away. "More?"

He shook his head. "I'm sorry. I wasn't very quiet."

Smiling, Jake cupped his cheek and kissed him. His tongue
traced Remi's lips lovingly before slipping inside. It wasn't long
before he drew back and caressed his cheek. "You'll make up
for it next time I'm sure."

ॐ

*"I fucking love your mouth." Remi dropped his head back to
the pillow, his eyes closed, taking in every little sensation.*

*The suction on his cock increased as that clever tongue
danced along the shaft.*

*"Oh, fuck. Gonna come. Stop. Not yet..." Winding his fingers
through his lover's hair, Remi fought the growing sensation. He
tried to slow the inevitable by pulling those delectable lips off
him.*

*A soft, seductive kiss tickled his stomach, making him loosen
his grip. As soon as his hand fell to the mattress, his prick was
once again engulfed.*

*He shivered, his ass muscles clenching tight. His balls drew
closer to his body and his legs tensed. It was absolute torture. A
tingle raced up his spine. No, not yet. "Oh God, oh—"*

The wonderful warmth left his cock.

Remi half growled, half laughed. "You fucking tease."

A snort answered him, then his dick was gripped, held upright and laved from tip to balls.

Fisting his hand in the thick hair again, Remi pulled his lover's face closer to his groin. "Yessss, that feels good."

His legs were shoved up higher, exposing him more, then that wicked tongue laved his crease.

Remi concentrated on the slick caress over his perineum, the breath across his balls. Suddenly it stopped and saliva dripped down his crease.

More spit landed on Remi's hole. A finger circled, spreading it around his anus.

"Tease!"

The finger pressed inside.

Remi moaned. "God...Billy, would you just fuck me already?"

"Mmm..." Another finger joined the first then both slid out and the blunt tip of a cock took its place.

Remi's eyes snapped open. Reaching toward Billy, Remi tried to get him to hurry.

After pushing in just a little, Billy pulled out. Again and again, he stabbed at Remi with his prick, barely breaching him until Remi had had enough.

Remi wrapped his legs around his lover and squeezed, bringing Billy closer.

Falling forward on his hands, Billy laughed. His brown eyes danced as he dipped to kiss Remi. Billy's long hair tickled Remi's cheek, and his tongue flicked over Remi's lips. "Fuckhead."

"Yeah, yeah, bite me. You've gotten off once already this afternoon, asshole. Remember the blowjob?" Remi dropped his legs, looping them over Billy's to get more leverage. Pumping his hips up, he impaled himself further on Billy's cock. "Harder," he

gasped into Billy's ear.

Thrusting forward, Billy grunted, his balls smacking against Remi.

A loud roar echoed through the quiet room. Billy's head jerked backward and he yelped.

Suddenly, Remi's body was cool where Billy had been.

"Son of a fucking bitch!" Dirk stood at the side of the small twin bed, his face twisted in an enraged scowl. He reached for Remi.

Remi backpedaled until his back hit the wood headboard, making it knock against the wall behind him. Throwing his legs over the other side of the bed, he lunged, but he wasn't fast enough. Hands wrapped around his throat, jerking him backward and lifting him completely off the bed.

Remi clutched his father's hands, gasping for air. His leg kicked frantically, trying to get purchase on something, anything. Oh God, he had to get loose, he couldn't breathe. His eyes hurt, his face felt like it was going to explode.

Dirk's breath was foul, heavy with alcohol, as he hissed in Remi's face. "I will not have a fucking faggot for a son." He shook Remi, his fingers digging into Remi's neck.

Remi's vision went white. His short nails raked at Dirk's hands, to no avail.

"Let go of him!" Billy screamed. The sound of skin slapping against skin registered at the edge of Remi's consciousness, then the vise grip around his throat abruptly ceased. He fell, his face hitting the cold wood. Pain slammed into his head. He gasped for air, trying to relieve the tight burn in his chest. His arms felt heavy, but he managed to get them under him.

"Get off me, you little fag!"

A loud crash and a gurgling sound followed.

Remi's clouded vision cleared and he raised up, trying to see what had happened. His throat hurt so much he couldn't yell.

Because of the tears, he saw the black boot aimed at his face too late. It clipped his chin, knocking him to the ground.

Billy lay on his back, his arms and legs at odd angles. There was a jangle and rustling, Dirk mumbling something. But Remi couldn't tell what, it sounded like he was in a well. Then pain exploded across Remi's shoulders. A deafening crack rent the air seconds after the sting sliced into Remi's skin. He tried to escape but the heel of Dirk's boot across his cheek stopped him. Again and again the pain flared, over Remi's back, his butt and thighs. It hurt so badly he just wanted to die, anything to make it stop. He stared at his best friend, his lover, willing him to get up.

Billy never did. He didn't even move.

The sharp jab of a boot toe met Remi's ribs repeatedly until his whole body went numb.

Billy's broken body blurred and eventually everything went black.

Remi sat straight up, gasping for breath. It was like someone was squeezing him so tight he couldn't breathe. His chest burned and he could almost feel the hand around his throat.

Arms encircled his body, pinning his own arms to his side. *Oh God no.* He had to get away, he had to—

"Shh... It's okay, it's only a bad dream. I've got you, pup. You're all right. I'm not going to let anything happen to you."

Jake. It was Jake. Remi relaxed, collapsing back into his mate's arms, trusting Jake to hold him. He stayed there for several minutes, his head on Jake's chest, listening to his heartbeat and his reassurances.

Wrapping his arms around Jake's wide back, Remi

squeezed tight. He was safe now, Jake was here and wouldn't let— No, no, he wasn't in danger, it was a dream.

Jake rubbed his back, making circles. "Talk to me, pup. What was that about?"

Remi closed his eyes, slipping down until his arms rested on Jake's waist and his head was in Jake's lap. He liked it when Jake called him pup.

Over and over, Jake stroked his hair, combing his fingers through it.

"I keep having this dream. I've always been woken up before anything happened, but this time..."

"This time you didn't. Tell me about the dream, Remi. Maybe together we can figure out why you keep having it, and why it turned into a nightmare this time."

ভিত্তি

Jake caressed Remi's cheek, pleased to find his mate snuggled into his touch even in sleep. It lessened the ache in his chest somewhat, knowing Remi was aware of his presence. Being careful not to disturb Remi, Jake lifted his mate's head and scooted down in the bed. Once he got settled, he kissed Remi's forehead.

Blinking back tears, he rested his cheek on Remi's for a second, trying to gain his composure. His heart hurt—that was the only way he knew how to describe it. The physical pain as deep as the mental one. Hell, his stomach was queasy too. Fuck, how had Remi survived? No wonder he'd repressed the memory. And Jake was convinced it was a memory. What Jake knew of the injuries Remi had suffered that night were consistent with Remi's scars.

Reaching past Remi, Jake grabbed his cell phone and flipped through his phonebook. He kissed Remi's cheek as the phone began to ring. "I love you, pup."

Remi made a soft sound, almost like a sigh. A little smile tugged at the corner of his lips.

Rolling onto his back, Jake stared at the ceiling while his hand idly stroked Remi's hair. He had to tell Rhys. If they could prove Dirk had murdered Remi's first lover, the son of a bitch would go away for a long time. He'd never be able to hurt Remi again.

Chapter Thirteen

Remi stepped just inside the kitchen door, blinking at the sunlight streaming in through the window over the sink. The smell of coffee and bacon filled his nose. *Ahh...* The first thing he registered after his eyes adjusted was Jake, ass encased in a pair of tight jeans, bent over getting things out of the refrigerator. *Oh nice.* He was wearing the clothes he had on yesterday. Remi made a mental note to clean out some space in his closet so Jake could bring extra clothes over if he wanted. Remi grinned, remembering last night.

"How old is Rhys?" Sterling stood at the stove in a pair of shorts and a tank top. He was turned toward Jake with his bottom lip caught between his teeth and a spatula in his hand. Eggs dripped off the end of the spatula onto the white linoleum, but Sterling didn't seem to notice.

Remi yawned and started forward, but Jake beat him to it.

"He's twenty-six. Why don't you set the table and I'll scramble the eggs." After taking the spatula from Sterling, Jake set it on the stove, grabbed a towel off the counter and wiped up the mess.

Sterling leaned against the cabinets next to Jake. "He's hairy. I've never seen an Apache with a beard."

"He isn't Apache. His father was Cherokee and his mother is Scottish."

"Is he married?"

"No." Jake stood, handing the dirty towel to Sterling.

Sterling took it and tossed it in the sink. "Girlfriend?"

Jake chuckled and shook his head. "No, he doesn't have a boyfriend either."

"So he *is* gay?"

Jake turned to Sterling, pointing at him with the spatula. "Yes, he is. Why all the questions?"

"I was just curious. Can't a guy ask questions anymore?"

Going back to the stove, Jake groaned. He spotted Remi and smiled. "Morning."

"Shhh...don't talk to him yet." Sterling dug through the cupboard for a mug and headed to the coffeemaker. "He's a real dickhead without his first cup." He poured some coffee and brought it to Remi.

Taking the mug, Remi scowled at his brother. He was *not* a dickhead without coffee.

Sterling, the smartass, backed away making bowing motions.

Jake chuckled and turned back to the eggs. "You better watch it, kid. If that's true he's liable to strangle you."

"Nah, 'cause I remembered to make the coffee in the first place." After opening the cabinet, Sterling got three plates and began setting the small card table Remi used as a kitchen table.

"Don't push your luck. You made the coffee for yourself." Taking a sip, Remi savored the strong brew. *Ah.*

"I haven't even had my cup yet." Sterling went to the drawer and pulled out silverware.

Jake turned around, his mouth hanging open. "Oh God. Sterling on caffeine?"

Remi nodded. "Yeah, it's not pretty, but I can't seem to break him of the habit. Mom and Dirk have been letting him drink it since he was seven. I've, at least, gotten him down to one cup."

A phone rang. It wasn't the house phone or Remi's cell phone.

Jake took his phone off his belt and looked at it. "Not mine. I forgot to turn mine back on apparently." Pushing the button, he clipped the phone back to his belt and went back to filling the other plates.

"Hey, that's *my* phone." Sterling ran toward his room.

Remi groaned. What if that had rung when Sterling was with Dirk? "If he's been giving his number out to his friends I'm going to kill him. I told him not to, it's supposed to be for emergencies only."

With the pan held out in one hand, Jake grabbed Remi behind the neck with the other and kissed him on the lips. "How do you feel?"

"Umm..." Remi kissed back. "Fine."

Jake grinned and let go of Remi. "Sterling questions everything. He's been hounding me for info on Rhys for the last thirty minutes."

"Sorry, you should have woken me." Why was Sterling so interested in Rhys? What else had Sterling been asking about?

"Sorry? Why are you sorry?"

"Sterling can be a little, er, talkative at times if you haven't noticed." Talkative was an understatement. Sterling was a motormouth.

"I like Sterling. He doesn't bother me in the least, pup." Jake put the pan in the sink. After getting himself a glass, he poured water in it and jerked his head toward the table. "Let's eat." He set his glass down and went to the microwave, pulling out a plate of bacon. After setting it on the table, he grabbed the dish rag, opened the oven and extracted a plate with several pieces of toast. "Couldn't find the toaster."

Damn, Jake and Sterling had made bacon and toast too? "Sterling broke the toaster."

"Broke the toaster?"

"Yeah, he had three cups of coffee one morning while he was making breakfast. The toaster jammed and he threw it against the wall. That's why he's only allowed one cup now." Remi took another drink of coffee and sat at the table.

Jake sat next to him, scooting his chair close. He picked up his fork, and his brow furrowed. "I hate to bring this up, but last night..."

The dream. *Fuck.* "What about it?" Remi asked hesitantly.

"I need you to think about it. I know it has to be painful, but if you can come up with something to prove it was real, we can nail his ass."

"What if it wasn't real? What if it's all in my head?" Then again, what if it did happen? Remi couldn't recall very much about that period in his life. Hell, he barely remembered Billy. Had he blocked out his relationship with Billy too?

Jake shook his head. "I don't think so. I think it's exactly what happened to you. I've already got Rhys looking into it."

Remi dropped his gaze. *Fuck.* He knew Rhys was Jake's partner, but...

"He's had run-ins with Dirk before."

"Huh?" Remi raised his eyes.

"Rhys worked for the FBI. His ex-boss worked that case. Said it felt wrong to him even back then. Apparently, your father made an impression on most of the agents, and it wasn't a good one." Jake cupped Remi's cheek. "You have nothing to be ashamed of."

"I know. I'm not ashamed of that. Dirk is fucked up, he always has been, I've always known that. But what if it really happened and I didn't tell anyone? What if I let Dirk get away with it?" Not only would he have failed Billy, but all this time he could have been rid of Dirk.

Jake kissed Remi's forehead. "Even if you had remembered it sooner, do you honestly think you could've made a difference? On reservations the FBI oversees murder investigations, but even they dropped the case. Who the hell knows who Dirk has in his hip pocket? Let me find out more and we'll go from there."

Remi nodded. Jake was right. They should make certain the dream was real and see who all was involved first. He'd have to rack his brain and see what he could come up with. Maybe talking to his friends would help jog some memories. If that dream had been real, he didn't want to remember it, but remembering would help Remi get Sterling away from Dirk. Speaking of Sterling... "Sterling."

"Coming," Sterling yelled from the other room.

Jake ran his finger down Remi's cheek. "You look damn good this morning."

Remi smiled. He felt damn good this morning. He'd never imagined actually having a real relationship, much less one like he and Jake had. He'd never thought that far ahead. "Thank you, sir. Thank you for saving me...for changing me."

A slow grin spread across Jake's lips. He blinked a few times, his eyes misty, then kissed Remi again. His lips were soft and gentle. "I hate to admit it, pup, but I did it for selfish reasons."

"Because I'm your mate?" Remi whispered against Jake's lips.

Jake nodded. "You're mine."

"I'm glad."

"Hold on and I'll let you talk to Jake," Sterling said, coming into the kitchen. Handing the phone to Jake, the little shit grinned from ear to ear. What had he seen? "It's Rhys." Did he just sigh?

Nah, must be Remi's imagina— Rhys? What was Rhys doing calling Sterling's phone? More to the point, how'd he get the number?

Frowning at the phone, Jake gave Sterling a hesitant look and put the phone to his ear. "Hello?"

Jake asked what Rhys wanted and how he got that number, but Remi turned to Sterling. "How does Rhys have your number?"

Taking the seat across from Jake, Sterling shrugged. "Don't know. He wouldn't tell me. He said he was a PI, it was his job to find out things."

Hmm... "You need to keep it turned off unless you're calling me. What if you got a call at home or something and Dirk heard it ring?"

"I usually keep it turned off. I forgot last night after I called Jake." He picked up his fork and took a bite of his eggs. Grabbing a piece of toast and bacon, he put them on his plate and went to get himself some coffee. He had a strange smirk on his face.

Jake hung up the phone and handed it to Sterling, his mouth tight.

"Everything okay?" Remi asked.

Shaking his head, Jake took a drink of water and stood. "I have to go." He kissed Remi's head almost absently, then walked around and ruffled Sterling's hair.

Okay, that was strange. Remi watched him leave the kitchen. Something was up. Did it have to do with pack stuff?

As if Jake heard his thoughts, he peeked back in the kitchen door, his helmet in hand and his saddlebags over his shoulder.

"I'll see you tonight. Meet me at my house at seven." He glanced at Sterling, then back at Remi as if he wanted to say more. "Are you taking him home?"

Remi started to say yes, but Sterling looked up from his food. "Me? Nah, I called Mom. She's going to pick me up after Dirk goes to work today."

Jake nodded and turned his attention to Remi. "I'll tell you about it tonight." Then he left.

Remi stared at the empty doorway until the front door clicked shut and he heard Jake's bike start. What had happened? He noticed Sterling smiling. "What?"

Taking a bite of toast, Sterling smiled.

"Did Rhys say anything to you? What were you talking about for so long?"

Again Sterling shrugged. "I told him Jake said his bike was acting screwy and asked him if Gadget got it fixed. Then we started talking about football and motorcycles and..." Sterling went on about the things he'd talked about with Rhys, but Remi stopped listening.

Remi grinned thinking about poor helpless Rhys stuck on the phone with Sterling. The poor man had looked absolutely pitiful the day they played football and Sterling followed him around talking. Rhys didn't talk much himself. Then again, with Sterling around no one talked much. How could they? They couldn't get a word in edgewise.

"Are you listening to me?" Sterling waved his hands in front of Remi.

"No."

"I'm telling you something important."

"I'm sorry, tell me again." Remi picked up his coffee cup, still grinning as he took a sip.

"I said I think I'm gay."

Remi dropped his cup. *What?* It felt like someone had stabbed him in the gut. Memories of Dirk calling him a faggot and kicking him in the face flashed through his mind. Then he saw Billy lying in a puddle of his own blood. *Oh God.* He was going to be sick. Using the heels of his hands, Remi rubbed his eyes.

Jumping up, Sterling got a dishtowel and wiped the table off. "What's wrong with you?" He tossed the towel at the sink and put his hands on the table, glaring at Remi.

Remi stood, pointing his finger in Sterling's face. He gritted out each word to be sure Sterling heard him. Maybe if he said it slow, Sterling would realize it was the truth. "You. Are. Not. Gay."

"I think I am. And why the hell do you care? Obviously you are too."

"What? I am not! It's a were—" *Fuck, fuck, fuck.* Remi slammed his fist on the table, making food jump off plates and Sterling's coffee slosh onto the table. He'd almost said it was a werewolf thing.

"Fine, bisexual. Whatever." Sterling kicked his chair out of the way, sending it clattering to the floor, and stomped past Remi.

Remi caught his arm on the way by.

"Leave me alone." Sterling tried to jerk his arm away.

"I'm sorry."

Tears streamed down Sterling's face. His lip trembled. It tore Remi's heart out.

Remi tugged him close, hugging him tight, his own eyes filling with tears. "I'm so sorry. I love you, I could never be mad at you for being who you are. I'm just...scared."

Nodding, Sterling hugged Remi back. They stood there for several minutes. Remi wanted everything Dirk had done to go away.

"I thought you'd understand," Sterling whispered in a shaky voice full of tears.

Fuck, he wished Jake were still here. And how weird was that? Remi had never had a hard time expressing himself to Sterling, but he couldn't tell Sterling how afraid he was. Or how Dirk may or may not have nearly killed Remi for the same damn thing Sterling was now confessing to.

Oh God. He was gay and had been all along, but he'd never had the courage to admit it. How could he have ignored his sexuality? He'd shut out who he really was deep inside to protect himself. Sterling was what he wanted to be. Sterling was comfortable with himself in a way Remi never had been. He'd made Sterling that way and now he'd yelled at Sterling for it.

"I love you, and..." Remi pulled back, making sure Sterling was looking at him. "I do understand, but no matter how hard it makes things you can't let anyone know right now. Do you understand what I'm telling you? You can't let Mom and Dirk ever find out about you or me...or Jake. Okay?"

Jake ran his hands over his face. Looking up at the office's fluorescent lighting, he groaned, before turning his attention back to Rhys. "I swear to you, if you'd seen his face, you'd have no doubt that it happened."

"I *don't* doubt it. What I can't figure out is how the fucker got them to that field without getting caught. And why the hell no one figured out they'd been moved there. I know forensics have come a long way in the last fifteen years, but this shit could have been determined back then. So why the fuck wasn't it?"

"Because he's a crooked son of a bitch and he had the time and opportunity to do it."

Rhys gritted his teeth, giving a crisp nod. "I can't seem to get Caspari to call me back. I know damn well he could point me in the right direction to find out who else might be in on this and why."

"You think your ex-boss was involved?"

"No, but Caspari knows something he doesn't want to tell me. Apparently I'm going to have to corner him and make him talk to me." Rhys would do just that too. He was a good investigator. He paid attention to everything and filed it away for later use, and he wasn't above blackmail. Not many people were ballsy enough to call his bluff.

Jake got up, stretched his legs and walked to the window. It wasn't much of a view, only an alleyway, but it let the sunlight in. He needed something to do to distract himself from the images rattling around in his head. After listening to the vivid description of Remi's dream, Jake could not help but imagine it. It was like a horrible movie playing over and over in his mind. He wanted to hunt Dirk Lassiter down and make him pay for what he'd done.

Shaking his head, he stared out at the brick wall of the office building behind theirs. He was going to do this the right way. Killing the bastard would be too easy, but Jake wasn't going to go to jail for the bastard or sign his own death warrant by going rogue, unless he had no other recourse. "What did the other kid's family say? You said on the phone you'd talked to them."

"Yeah, I stopped to talk to the brother on my way in to the office this morning—"

The intercom buzzed.

Rhys growled and pushed the button. "Yes?"

"Can I go to lunch now?" Matt asked so softly he could barely be heard even over the intercom.

Jake opened the office door so he and Rhys could watch the front with Matt gone. "Go ahead, Matt."

Matt swiveled his chair toward Jake, making it turn all the way around once before he stopped and smiled. "Thanks, Jake. I'm just going to go get a burger and bring it back. I won't be long. You want something?"

"No thanks, Matt."

"Okay." Matt hopped up and headed out the door with a wave.

Jake and Rhys watched him leave, both shaking their heads. Jake turned to Rhys. "Do you think he dresses in the dark?" Matt was wearing khaki shorts, a long-sleeved pink shirt with a gray striped tie and black dress shoes with no socks.

"I was leaning more toward him being colorblind, but that doesn't explain the shoes."

Which would support Jake's theory that Matt dressed in the dark. Matt was a wolf so even in the dark he could see. Rhys was right, what the fuck was up with the shoes? Jake shrugged and sat back down in the chair across from Rhys' desk, positioning himself where he could see the front office. "Tell me about the brother."

"Jonathon Ikaz, thirty-five, married with two kids, a boy and girl, the boy is named William after his deceased uncle. Ikaz works at the casino as a cashier. He has no love lost for Lassiter. He didn't seem to have anything against Remi though. He made a point to tell me what a good kid Remi had been and that he was always very polite when he was at their house. He also hinted Remi and Billy were maybe more than friends, but he wouldn't come right out and say it. I got the impression Ikaz's parents suspected it as well."

"Which adds validity to Remi's dream."

"He also said no one questioned him or his parents about Billy's whereabouts, possible enemies or anything. Said it sort of fizzled out and went cold, no investigation by the police whatsoever." Rhys raised an eyebrow at Jake. "And Dirk was the one who told them Billy was dead."

"He told them himself?"

Rhys nodded. "Ikaz said Dirk told them Billy was dead and Remi wasn't going to make it. Ikaz remembers smelling alcohol on Lassiter's breath. And get this...apparently after talking to Lassiter, the whole family got in the car and headed up to the hospital to see what was what, and not only had Billy's body not been taken in, but Remi hadn't arrived at the hospital either."

Fuck me. Jake sat there staring at Rhys, not believing what he was hearing. "You think he came from the scene? After he dumped them in the field?"

Rhys shook his head. "Not sure. The report says he was the first on the scene and called it in."

The door opened and Remi's scent assailed Jake's nose, making him smile.

Remi came to the office door and leaned against the doorway, looking dazed. "Hi."

What was he doing here? He seemed sort of down. His scent was off, not scared or mad but not exactly normal either. Jake stood, going to his mate. He caught Remi's chin and kissed him. "Everything okay?"

Remi nodded, then stopped and shook his head. His stare was unfocused. "No—no it's not. Sterling told me he thinks he's gay." Remi raised his face, meeting Jake's gaze almost pleadingly.

Oh shit. Jake got a hollow feeling in his stomach. He drew Remi into his arms. "He won't say anything, will he? He knows not to tell Dirk or your mother that, right?"

"Where is he?" Rhys asked.

Jake had forgotten all about Rhys.

Pulling back, Remi peered over at Rhys. "At home with my mom." Then he glanced up at Jake, his eyes almost blank. "Yeah, I told him not to let anyone know."

It was all Jake could do to keep from pulling Remi back to him. "We've got to hurry this up."

Remi was quiet for a few seconds. Then he swallowed audibly and nodded. "Yeah. I've got to remember. I wish I knew if that dream was real."

"I think it was," Rhys said from his seat. "Both of you sit, we need to talk."

Rhys told Remi about his meeting with Billy's brother and suggested Remi talk to the man. Hopefully Ikaz would tell Remi more than he had Rhys.

After a few minutes Remi got up. Jake went to stand too, but Rhys caught his gaze and shook his head. Jake opened his mouth to tell his best friend to back off when Remi started pacing back and forth.

"I heard you say Dirk was the first on the scene?" Remi

asked Rhys.

"That's what the report says. And Ikaz talked today like Lassi—your father had come from the scene while the investigation was still going on to tell them Billy was dead."

Remi stopped pacing and looked at Jake. "He was off work that day."

"Are you sure? I thought you didn't remember much about what led to the attack?" Jake asked.

"I don't, but it makes sense that he'd be off. Wouldn't he?"

Jake must have missed something because it didn't make sense to him at all, but judging from the look on Remi's face it made perfect sense to Remi. "Why, pup? Why does it make sense?"

Remi stopped pacing, turning toward him and Rhys. "I think that was the day Sterling was born."

"What?" Rhys pinched the bridge of his nose.

"And why would I go to a movie instead of going to the hospital? It was a weekday when Sterling was born, but..." Remi closed his eyes and planted his hands on the side of Rhys' desk. "I was at school. There was a note when I got home telling me Mom and Dirk were at the hospital and Dirk would be back around five o'clock to pick me up." He opened his eyes, staring right at Jake, and bobbed his head. "I remember it. I remember the note, that's why we..." He shot a glance at Rhys then back to Jake, his cheeks tinged red. "Well, I know what Dirk is like, I'd have never risked getting caught if I thought he'd be home earlier."

"Fucking A." Rhys stood, slamming his fist on the desk. "Are you telling me it was the middle of the afternoon when you were attacked?"

Remi nodded.

"What's up, Rhys?" Jake motioned to Remi, wanting him closer.

Rhys' jaw ticked. "Dirk reported the incident in the evening. It was already dark. That son of a bitch killed the kid hours before and left Remi lying around to die before getting him help."

Snagging Remi's hand as he walked closer, Jake pulled him into his lap. Resting his head against the top of Remi's head, he closed his eyes. He felt sick again. *Remi is here, he's alive and safe. But Sterling.* Oh God, they had to work fast. They had to get Sterling away from that monster. Dirk was getting closer and closer to meeting an angry werewolf in a dark alley.

Remi patted Jake's back like it was no big deal and turned to face Rhys. "Yeah, that sounds about right."

The door opened and Remi jumped out of Jake's lap, looking toward the door. His forehead wrinkled, then the corner of his lips turned up.

Matt. Jake didn't even have to look. He smelled the kid and McDonald's French fries. Jake grinned. Apparently he and Rhys weren't the only ones amused by Matt's sense of style.

"Oh my God." Matt ran into the office, so excited he must have forgotten Rhys was there. Amazing, as terrified as the kid was of Rhys. He dropped his bag of food in Jake's lap and reached for Remi. Remi stepped back but Matt managed to snag his hands and pull him into a hug.

Chuckling, Jake just watched. The look on Remi's face was part surprised, part cornered wolf.

Finally, Remi patted Matt on the back, sort of hugging him in return.

Matt drew back without letting go of Remi's shoulders. "I'm so happy to finally meet you. I've wanted to since I found out Jake found his mate. Dad said you are coming to dinner
178

tomorrow night. I was going to see you then, but, wow, just wow." He leaned forward and lowered his voice. "You think you can talk to Jake about letting me be a beta?"

Remi's eyes widened and he shot Jake a panicked look.

"This is Matt. Our office manager."

The phone rang. Rhys answered it, "Romero and Waya investigations."

"Matt? Gadget's son?" Remi blinked.

Matt opened his mouth to speak, but Jake beat him to the punch. "Yeah, Matt is the oldest." *Wait. Did Matt say—* "We're going to Gadget's for dinner tomorrow?"

Matt nodded, a lock of his black bangs falling into his eyes. "Yeah, he said you were bringing Remi."

"Motherfucker." Rhys slammed the phone down.

"What?" Remi and Jake asked at the same time, turning toward Rhys.

Matt grabbed his lunch from Jake and darted out the door. "Nice to meet you, Remi. See you tomorrow night." He closed it behind him.

"He's checking on you." Rhys turned the phone around and pushed the caller ID button.

It read: *Lassiter, Dirk.*

The smell of fear surrounded Remi for the first time since he came into the office, and Jake growled, unable to hold it back. "What did he say?"

"Nothing. He hung up as soon as I answered it."

Chapter Fourteen

"Cut it out, fag!"

Remi winced at the slur from his fellow firefighter and continued reading his book. It wasn't directed at him, but damn it was hard not to take notice of it. Funny, the word had never bothered him before. He'd thought nothing of calling one of his friends a fag or queer when they did something less than manly.

Jamison launched himself at Cortez. They fell off the battered brown firehouse couch and rolled across the floor. Tortilla chips came raining down in their wake. One pelted Remi in the cheek and landed on his book.

Remi picked it up and ate it, flicking the salt off his page. Catching Baker's gaze in the chair across from him, he shrugged.

Baker shook his head and went back to his Game Boy.

"You fucking faggot, get off me," Cortez snarled, shoving at Jamison's shoulder with one hand while still holding the TV remote above his head with the other. They flipped over again, heading toward the small end table next to Remi's chair.

Remi rescued his can of coke off the table just in time to keep them from spilling it.

"I was in here first, asshole." Jamison grunted. "Give me back the damn remote. We aren't watching fucking TV Land."

"Fuck you, dick breath, no one else wants to watch NASCAR, you damn redneck," Cortez shot back.

They rolled again, crunching chips and plowing into the rickety particleboard coffee table someone had donated to the firehouse when Remi first started working there.

"No one wants to watch *Leave it to Beaver* either, you fucking cocksucker."

Finally, Baker turned his game off and got up. "I'm going to the grocery store for more chips, wanna come with me, Lassiter?"

Remi closed his book and stepped over the two firemen wrestling around on the floor like a couple of punks and followed Baker to the door leading into the garage. He turned back. "Hey, assholes, clean up the fucking mess. We're going to get shit to make dinner."

"Fuck you, Lassiter," Jamison growled out before bursting into laughter.

Cortez soon joined him. "Hey, Remi. Get stuff to make cookies."

Grinning, Remi flipped them both off and jogged past two more of his coworkers—Duncan and Thomas, who were straightening hoses and talking—to catch up with Baker.

Duncan hailed Remi as he went by. "Hey, Remi, y'all going to the store?"

"Yeah."

"Get some chocolate ice cream."

"Got it." Remi slid into the seat and buckled his seat belt, looking out the passenger side window. The number two engine towered over the truck as they drove out. It looked like shift three had washed the big red beast yesterday. Someone needed to wash the truck too.

"Does that bother you?"

"What?" Remi glanced over at Baker. Baker was one of the two paramedics on first shift. He was also the only white man on first shift. The rest of the men were Latino or Apache.

"The gay jokes."

Oh shit, had he given something away? Remi's stomach sank. "No. Should it?"

Baker shrugged. "Just wondered since your friend is gay and all."

How did Baker know Jake?

"The vet?"

"Oh, Chay."

"Yeah, the animal doc. That was wild. Never would have guessed he was gay. Lots a folks were surprised."

"Tell me about it." Remi squirmed in his seat, trying to think of something to change the subject without being too obvious he was doing so. Sadly, his father wasn't the only person in town who was homophobic. If anyone suspected Remi was gay... Actually, he didn't much care what people thought so long as Dirk didn't find out, but in this town that would be a long shot.

They pulled up in front of the grocery store, and Baker cut the engine and got out. "We should get a cart. The cupboards are bare. We can take up a collection when we get back."

Yeah, they were, someone forgot to put the lock on their fridge and someone from second shift had eaten their leftovers from the other night. Remi got a shopping cart and shoved it toward Baker. He hated pushing the damn things. Which was why he always took Sterling shopping with him. Sterling loved to push them. Unfortunately, not only did he play on them, but he snuck things in behind Remi's back. A small price to pay as far as Remi was concerned. "Whose turn is it to cook dinner?"

Groaning, Baker took the cart and pushed it toward the first aisle. The right front wheel wobbled, not touching the bright white floor. "Mine."

Remi laughed and followed his coworker. The smells of different produce tickled Remi's nose, making him have to concentrate to keep it out.

Most of the guys hated to cook, but they all took turns. Remi didn't like to cook, but he was used to it. He had been cooking for himself and Sterling almost from the day Sterling was born. Something niggled at the back of Remi's memory.

Sterling was crying.

Remi could barely walk, fresh out of the hospital. Why wasn't Mom getting the baby?

Getting up, Remi slowly made it to his parents' room where the bassinet was.

Sterling was red-faced and screaming his lungs out. His little fists were balled up so tight his tiny knuckles were white.

Lifting the baby up, Remi realized not only did it hurt his ribs, but the kid was sopping wet. Somehow he managed to get Sterling changed and into the kitchen.

Sterling quieted for a little bit when Remi found his pacifier, but it didn't last long. He spit it out and started wailing again.

Remi just wanted him to shut up. He was tired and he hurt and his pain medication was making him sleepy. He found a note in the kitchen telling him his mom had gone to the store, and who the hell knew where Dirk was, probably at work.

With Sterling screaming in his ear, he had to figure out, by himself, how to make a bottle.

"Remi, you all right?" Baker asked, stopping in front of the produce area.

"What? Oh yeah, sorry. I was just thinking."

"Yeah? What about?" Baker started pushing the cart again.

Remi picked up a head of lettuce and put it in the cart. "My little brother." He frowned. He never thought about that period in his life. Come to think about it, he'd never really had many memories of it. That was the first time he'd remembered how he'd started feeding Sterling.

"Remi."

Jake. Remi turned around.

Jake was coming up behind him, smiling and holding one of the blue handbaskets.

Remi smiled back and almost reached for Jake before he caught himself. "Hey, Jake." Oh damn, Jake smelled good. Would he ever be able to be around Jake and have it not affect him? In a way, he hoped not. He loved how Jake made him feel.

"Glad I ran into you. I wanted to talk to you about something. You got a few minutes?" Jake extended his hand to Baker. "Jacob Romero."

"Ted Baker. Nice to meet you." Baker looked at Remi. "I'm going to go ahead and start getting stuff, catch up when you get done talking." Baker pushed the cart off toward the next aisle.

Remi nodded. "Thanks."

"Listen, I forgot to ask you before you rushed off today. Will you come to dinner with me at Gadget's place tomorrow? I didn't want to say anything in front of Matt, but Gadget wants you to meet his youngest, Eddie. He's pretty bad off. I told Gadget not to get his hopes up, pup. So no worries if nothing happens."

After seeing the cut on Keaton's hand disappear, Remi

wasn't at all sure what he could and couldn't do, but he was positive there was something to the healing. "It won't hurt to try. I wish there was someone who knew more about it. This weird healing stuff I mean."

"I'll talk to Carter and see if he knows anything. The way omegas and their powers are kept secret, he may not, but—" Jake shrugged. "Who knows? You okay? You smell agitated all of a sudden."

"Oh, just wishing I knew more about it. I wanna help the kid."

"Remington?"

Mom? Remi turned.

His mother stood a few yards away behind a blue grocery cart. Damn, the harsh fluorescent store lighting made her wrinkles stand out. Age and life had not been kind to her. She was only fifty, but she seemed much older. Her light brown hair had recently been dyed, covering the gray, but the lines and bruises on her face couldn't be disguised by the makeup. The haunted look in her pale green eyes never disappeared anymore. Even the slight twinkle in them when she had first seen Remi didn't last but a second. "I thought it was you, honey. How are you?" She hugged him. "I never see you anymore, except to drop Sterling off." Drawing back, she kissed his cheek and looked him over. Her eyes widened when she glanced past him and spotted Jake.

"Mom, this is Jake. Jake, this—"

"Karen Lassiter, Remi's mother." As she reached out to shake hands with Jake, Remi noticed the dark bruises around her wrist. "It's nice to finally meet you, Jake. Sterling has told me all about you." Frowning, she darted a glance at Remi. "Your father doesn't..." She trailed off, biting her lip.

"Doesn't want me hanging out with Jake, yes I know,

Sterling told me."

His mom blushed. "It's not that, dear, it's—"

"It's okay, Mom, I don't have any secrets from Jake. He knows all about Dirk."

"Remington," she snapped, giving him the look. The one that said she was disappointed in him.

Remi snarled before he could stop himself. He was tired of her games, tired of feeling sorry for her. Let her be disappointed. He'd kept her secret far too long. If she was embarrassed or ashamed by her husband, it was her own damn fault. How many times had he begged her to leave?

"Mrs. Lassiter—" Jake shot Remi a disbelieving look.

"No, no. It's all right. Remington is right." She waved Jake away and caught Remi's hands. "I worry, is all. I—" Squeezing Remi's hands, she averted her gaze and swallowed hard. When she looked back she was smiling, but tears rimmed her eyes.

Fuck. Remorse gnawed at Remi. He shouldn't feel guilty, but damn it, he hated hurting her. "Mom, I'm sorry."

"No, you don't need to be sorry. Listen. I have something you need. Maybe you can come by the house sometime next week? You can come inside the next time you come get Sterling, okay?"

"Okay, Mom, I'll come in next time." Remi kissed her cheek, feeling more like an ass. She obviously missed him and he avoided her whenever possible because she made him uncomfortable.

She kissed him back. "I love you, Remington. I know you don't believe it, but I do."

Remi opened his mouth to argue, but nothing came out. How could he deny it?

Patting his cheek, she smiled and turned toward Jake,

dabbing away a tear. "It was nice to meet you, Jake."

"Nice to meet you too, Mrs. Lassiter." Jake hugged her and watched her walk off.

"Okay, that was weird." Staring at her back, Remi tried to shake off the odd feeling. It was like she was trying to warn him, or was she giving him her blessing to go against Dirk's wishes? He didn't know, but something felt wrong. Normally, she would have pleaded with him to *behave* and not give Dirk any reason to be angry with him. "Sorry you had to see that, Jake."

Jake touched his arm, rubbing it briefly before stepping away. "If you want to talk, you know where I'm at. I'll see you tomorrow, okay?"

"Yeah. I'll see you tomorrow as soon as I get off work." Remi shook his head. Why did his mom always affect him that way? He was torn between being pissed at her and pitying her. Why didn't he have a happy, healthy, loving damn family?

Halfway across the store, he looked over his shoulder. Jake was staring after him.

Smiling, Jake waved and mouthed the word, "Tomorrow."

Remi nodded and grinned back. He did have a happy, loving family, just not the one he was born with.

ༀ

Jake leaned back in his chair and closed his eyes. Matt was playing solitaire on his computer and from the sound of it Rhys was next door getting ready to leave. *Almost five o'clock.* Jake wasn't in any hurry, he still had two hours until Remi got off work.

There were ups and downs to Remi being a fireman. Remi

had a lot of time off, but the days he did work he worked twenty-four-hour shifts. That sucked. And tonight as soon as Remi got to Jake's house they had to turn around and leave to go to Gadget's for dinner. He wouldn't get Remi alone until probably ten or eleven o'clock.

"I got an appointment with Caspari the day after tomorrow."

Opening his eyes, Jake spotted Rhys leaning against his doorframe. "Couldn't you get one sooner?"

"He's out of town until tomorrow evening."

"You believe that? Or you think he's still avoiding you?"

"He's in Kansas City, I checked it out. He didn't seem too keen on talking to me about the case, but I reminded him of a favor he owes me."

Jake could imagine how the conversation had gone. He grinned. Caspari didn't stand a chance, poor fucker. "Good, I'm anxious to get something going. I met Remi's mom yesterday."

"Yeah?" Scratching his chin, Rhys glanced behind him at Matt, then shut the door and took a seat in front of Jake's desk.

"Yeah. It was fucked up, man. Really fucked up. Remi seemed resentful of her."

"Can you blame him?"

Jake thought about it for a moment. He supposed he could understand it, it just wasn't what he'd expected. Remi was the protective type. He bent over backward to keep Sterling safe. Hell, he had fussed over their pack the night of the challenge. Jake shrugged. "Guess I was surprised. He's normally pretty understanding, good at empathizing with people. He's got a big heart."

"Yeah, he does. But he also doesn't seem the type to stick his neck out for someone over and over when they won't help themselves."

That was true. Funny, but now Jake could see Remi protected and cared for people because he wanted to, not because he felt like he had to. He'd sat in Rhys' office yesterday upset because he couldn't remember more. Because he wanted to help, he wanted Dirk gone. Remi hated what his father had done, he hated his father, but Remi hadn't let it ruin his life. He'd done what he had to cope and he didn't feel sorry for himself and he hadn't let it destroy who he was. More to the point, he'd raised a well-adjusted kid despite his parents, a kid who wasn't even his responsibility. "Yeah he is. You think he'll be able to help Eddie?"

Rhys stood. "Don't know. Would be nice if he can."

"Yeah it would."

Stretching, Rhys headed toward the door. "Get the fuck out of here and go home and wait for your mate."

"My mate doesn't get off work for another—"

Something thudded against the door to Jake's office. "Sir, you can't barge in here like this." Matt sounded more nervous than agitated.

Rhys' face hardened and his posture stiffened as he reached for the doorknob.

Inhaling, Jake came to his feet. He didn't recognize the other person's scent but Matt was afraid.

Opening the door, Rhys caught Matt as he fell into the office. "Can I help you?" Rhys' voice was a low, menacing rumble as he maneuvered Matt into Jake's office behind him.

"I want to see Jake Romero."

Dirk Lassiter. Jake knew the voice. He'd heard it over and over in his head after hearing the man talk to Remi the other day out behind Remi's apartment complex.

Matt held up his hands. "I'm sorry, I tried to tell him we were closed for the day, Jake."

Pushing Rhys out of the way, Jake stepped into the doorway. "What can I do for you, Mr. Lassiter?"

Lassiter stood inside the main office, right outside Jake's door, in his tan police uniform. He was about Remi's size, but broader, more built. The smell of anger surrounded the man. If you could ignore the nasty gleam in his eye, he wasn't a bad-looking man. However, his looks didn't compare to either of his sons, even though there was a slight resemblance in the face. Especially around the eyes and brow line, but Remi's face was softer and less angular, as was Sterling's.

Odd. Anger and alcohol were the only things Jake could smell on him. Most men, gun or not, would be a little intimidated facing two men bigger than themselves, but then maybe it was the alcohol giving him courage.

Lassiter looked Jake up and down, then took in Rhys as well. His eyes narrowed on Jake. "I heard my son hired you."

"You heard wrong, Mr. Lassiter. Your son and I are friends, we hang out sometimes."

Lassiter snorted. "That's not what I heard." Glancing over Jake's shoulder, he jabbed a finger in Rhys' direction. "And you can tell your boy here if I hear about him poking around in my business asking any more questions he's going to be looking down the wrong end of my police revolver."

"Are you threatening me?" Rhys asked in a cold, flat voice.

Having heard that voice before, Jake knew it never boded well. He held a hand up without looking at Rhys, and raised a brow at Lassiter. "Mr. Lassiter, I don't know what you're talking—"

Stepping closer, Dirk got in Jake's face.

Rhys' hand landed on Jake's shoulder, and he stepped to the side, positioning himself where he had a clean shot at Lassiter.

Shit, this could get ugly in a hurry. "Rhys..." Jake put his newfound power behind the warning, but it didn't seem to work.

Rhys stepped closer to Lassiter. "If you have nothing to hide, Mr. Lassiter, I'm sure there won't be any problems." There was no mistaking the malice behind the calm and steady voice.

"Damned right there won't be any problems. I'll have your licenses revoked. I suggest you drop your investigation." Lassiter glared at them both one last time and turned to leave. When he got the door open he pointed at Jake. "And you stay the hell away from my son. I don't need you stirring shit up." He let go of the door, got in his squad car and left.

"I'm sorry, Jake." Matt came out of the office behind them, more jittery than normal. The kid's hands were shaking and his eyes were wide.

Jake squeezed his shoulder. "It's all right, Matt. Why don't you go ahead and go home."

"You hurt?" Rhys grumbled.

Face blanching, Matt shook his head.

Jake waved Matt away. "I'll see you tonight. Drive carefully."

Nodding, Matt hurried to the door, peeked out, and looked both ways before opening it fully.

"Matt." Jake put power behind his voice, wishing Remi were here to calm the boy. If it didn't work, he was going to drive the kid home.

"Yes, sir?" Matt blinked at him.

"It's okay. Calm down." He gave the kid a smile.

Taking a deep breath, Matt seemed to relax then he

191

grinned. "See you in a few, Jake."

Hmmm, the voice worked on Matt fine, but not on Rhys. Jake turned around, catching his beta's gaze. "We need to get something on that son of a bitch, fast. Do whatever you have to do to get your ex-boss to spill what he knows."

Still glowering, Rhys dipped his chin in recognition, then he shook his head, the corner of his lips twitching. "I can't believe you tried to use your *voice* on me."

"My *voice?*" Jake grinned. "Yeah, it doesn't work on you, does it? I don't think it works on Remi either. Damn it." Which was kind of scary. Remi and Rhys were the only two who would really challenge him on anything. They were the ones most likely to fight for Jake, even if Jake didn't want them to.

Rhys snorted. "Of course not. Remi is your omega and I'm your beta, it's our job to take care of you."

"You have it backward. I'm supposed to take care of the pack, including you and Remi." Jake went into his office and closed his computer down and got ready to leave, knowing Remi would see things exactly like Rhys. What was he going to do with the two of them?

Turning off the office lights, Rhys opened the door and waited for Jake to exit so he could lock it behind them.

Jake extracted his keys from his pocket and stepped out the door.

"If you try to use your *voice* on me again, I'm going to kick your ass."

Great. Jake smiled and headed toward his Tahoe. "Yeah, well let's hope you're not about to get yours kicked when I use it."

Chapter Fifteen

Closing his front door, Remi made sure it was locked and jogged down the stairs. Oh, man, he'd been dying to see Jake all day. Running into him at the grocery store had only whetted his appetite, so to speak. He'd gotten to where he either saw or called Jake every day. When had that happened?

Remi opened the door to Jake's SUV and tossed his bag in the backseat. "Hey." Leaning across the seat, he kissed Jake. "I missed you today."

Jake sat there staring at him with a stunned expression on his face.

Chuckling, Remi climbed into the seat and shut the door. "What?"

"I never thought you'd be like this." Jake reached behind Remi's head and maneuvered him closer. His lips brushed across Remi's softly, then he stared into Remi's eyes. "Maybe I should have seen it, you're naturally affectionate."

Remi started to move back, but Jake stopped him, almost as if he couldn't help himself. He threaded his fingers through Remi's hair and pressed their lips back together.

Opening up his mouth and resting his hands on Jake's chest, Remi melted. He loved the way Jake's lips tasted and felt. The way Jake took over. Moaning, he let Jake know how much he enjoyed this.

Jake traced Remi's lips with his tongue. Catching Remi's bottom lip between his teeth, he nipped. He kissed Remi's cheek before dropping his head to Remi's shoulder and nuzzling his neck.

Remi's fangs elongated without warning. Arousal rushed through him and his cock went rock hard at the thought of Jake biting him. Oh God, he could feel Jake's teeth, knew they'd shifted. Squirming closer, he pressed his neck into Jake's face. "Please, sir." That felt so natural to say, which was sort of strange. He'd never have thought... No that wasn't true, he'd always enjoyed taking a less aggressive role with lovers. But Jake was the only one who actually saw it and acted on it.

"Shh..." Jake slid his hands out of Remi's hair.

Whimpering at the loss, Remi closed his eyes and sat back.

Jake brushed his knuckles over Remi's cheek and relaxed into his own seat.

It had only been about two days since they'd fucked, but it felt like forever. Remi's nipples got hard remembering the last time, the clamps. He'd always liked sex, but with Jake it was mind blowing. Remi craved him. Last night he'd lain in his bed fantasizing about Jake. No matter how hard he tried, he couldn't stop thinking about Jake. Finally, he'd gotten up and gone to the bathroom to jerk off so he could get some sleep. Even then, his mind hadn't let go of his mate. He'd imagined Jake there with him, holding him, kissing him, telling him what to do.

"How was work?"

Okay, that was weird. Now Jake was reading his mind. Remi chuckled and glanced over, noticing Jake sitting straight and tall in his seat. His eyes were still closed, like he was trying to regain composure too. "Long. I kept thinking about you."

Jake groaned.

They sat there for several minutes. Neither of them said a word, but Remi was even more aware of Jake's presence. He could smell Jake's arousal. *Oh wow*, he could tell the difference. Jake smelled...muskier, warmer, kind of spicy. He probably tasted wonderful right now. *Shit.* "Hey, Jake."

"Yeah?"

"It's not working."

"What's not working?"

"Trying to ignore each other to get our minds off of fucking. I'm sitting here wondering how you taste right now."

Jake half laughed, half groaned. "Remi?"

"Yeah?"

"Shut up and put your seat belt on." Jake started the engine.

"Okay." As Jake put the SUV in gear and began backing out, Remi reached for his belt. He got it buckled and Jake slammed on his brakes, making Remi bounce against the seat.

"Son of a bitch. Where the hell did he come from?"

Huh? Adjusting the belt, Remi looked out the back.

A scraggly old man walked past the parking lot. He glanced up at them, then kept going, slow as you please.

"Beats me. Sure have been a lot of them around here lately. I hate to sound like an old fart, but I'm beginning to agree with my neighbor, Mr. Morris. The neighborhood is going to hell in a handbasket."

Jake chuckled and got them moving again. "Well, if you promise not to run children off the lawn and complain about the newspaper not making it all the way to the porch, you can move in with me."

"Really?" *Damn, damn, damn.* He hadn't meant to say that out loud. He'd been surprised. He hadn't thought about moving

195

in with Jake, but logically he supposed he should have. Jake *was* his mate. Oh, man, that really sounded good. If he moved in with Jake he could see him every day.

"Yes, really." Jake looked both ways at the apartment exit and drove out. "We can even turn my office into a bedroom for Sterling. I don't use it much, I do most of my work at the office or on my laptop. Eventually we'll have to move, but for now, there isn't any reason for you to have to keep the apartment, unless you want to."

Whoa. Remi blinked. His stupid eyes were all watery. None of the women he'd dated had ever understood his relationship with Sterling. They tended to be jealous, but Jake got it. Remi wasn't sure why he was surprised. Jake was always thinking of Remi's needs. He truly was the perfect match for Remi. If he hadn't recently discovered werewolves, he might have laughed at the idea of soul mates, but now he wasn't so sure it wasn't a very real possibility. "I'll think about it." Lots of people had roommates. There was nothing unusual about that. He'd be moving to a better neighborhood and into a house. Dirk couldn't really say much about it. *Wait.* Did Jake say—? "Why will we have to move? I thought the house was yours. I mean I thought you were buying it, not renting."

"Eventually we are going to have to move the pack, pup." Jake reached over and squeezed his thigh. "We need to go somewhere where no one has the least inkling you're different. I don't want to risk one of John Carter's pack deciding you should submit to them."

Remi glanced over at him, watching the business lights and streetlamps cast moving shadows across his face. Jake was concentrating on the road, but Remi wasn't fooled. Jake was focused on him. Why was Jake concerned? "Jake, I can't leave Sterling. Even if Dirk is out of the picture, I'm not leaving Sterling here and moving off someplace. I can handle myself against other wolves. And besides, I seriously doubt my mom can handle things on her own when Dirk is gone. She's..." *broken.* And she would be even more without Dirk.

"I know you can take care of yourself, but I'd rather not chance it. But don't worry about it right now. We've got time. We'll get your mom to move. I promise you, we won't leave Sterling. Something tells me your mom is going to need our help too." Jake turned onto a residential street.

Jake sounded so sure Remi decided to let it go for now. But it worried him. What if John Carter wanted them gone sooner than later?

"Here we are." Jake pulled into the drive of a two-story stone home.

It was in a newer subdivision, with fairly large houses. Remi was sort of surprised. With Gadget having nine kids, he was expecting a little less...well, nice. Mechanics didn't make that much, did they? Then again, what did he know, he'd been raised on the reservation. He was used to poorer houses.

"You ready?" Jake cut the engine and peered over at him.

"Yeah. I'm ready."

Jake unbuckled his seat belt and tilted forward.

Remi did likewise, meeting his mate halfway. As their lips were about to touch Jake groaned and looked past Remi.

Huh? Remi was expecting a kiss. Turning his head, he bumped his nose into Jake's cheek.

"What are they doing here?"

Their core pack members, all but Gadget, were standing on the lawn waiting on them.

Dago and Nick smiled and waved. Tank tipped his head and Rhys stood there, scowling as usual. Zack came forward and opened the passenger side door. "Y'all coming in?"

At the door, they heard a woman yelling about something.

Remi raised a brow at Jake.

Jake shrugged. "Gadget's wife."

"Are we welcome?" Remi asked hesitantly and glanced behind them at the rest of the guys. They'd dressed for the occasion. There wasn't a leather jacket in sight and all but Dago had on slacks instead of jeans. But Dago made up for the jeans with a tie, so it sort of evened out.

Tank leaned forward to whisper something, then the door opened.

An attractive blonde with short hair, wearing tight jeans and an even tighter shirt stood in the doorway, her mouth pinched together. She gave them a hostile glare and huffed out a breath, making her bangs move. Stepping out of the door, she left it open and barged past them without a word.

Matt strolled past the entryway with a baby on his hip and spotted them. "Hey, guys, come on in."

Jake was the first one to move. The rest of them followed.

The foyer of the house was large, with a carpeted staircase to the right. Past it led to a big open den area. It was very neat and tidy but for a few toys in the middle of the floor.

Three boys about ten or so crowded in front of the TV, playing a video game. Two more closer to five or six played with cars behind the boys at the TV. They ran them around in circles making *vroom vroom* sounds and crashing them into one another.

Matt stepped over them. "Dad's in the kitchen finishing dinner. Looks like it's just going to be us. Mom had a meeting or something."

A boy about four came running in from what appeared to be the hallway, squealing and holding out an action figure. He ran to Matt, flopped onto the floor at Matt's feet and threw the broken toy.

"Darren, get up from there right now," Matt growled.

Falling backward, Darren started wailing.

"Darren? Are you throwing another fit?" Gadget's voice came from the left, the kitchen Remi assumed.

Jumping to his feet, Darren shook his head. He said, "No," at the exact same time Matt said, "Yes."

"Matthew?"

"Yes?" Matt asked.

"Put him to bed, I'm tired of his temper tantrums," Gadget answered back.

"No, I be good." Darren held his hands out to Matt, shaking his head. "I be good, Maff. I be good."

Chuckling, Jake headed toward the kitchen. Zack trailed after him. Tank, Nick and Dago walked further into the living room. Tank and Nick went straight for the video game. Dago got on the floor and started playing cars. Rhys followed Zack and Jake.

Matt turned to Remi. "Umm, Remi, would you, ah?" He dipped his chin toward the kid on his hip.

"Sure." Remi held out his hands. "Hey there. What's your name?"

The boy shied away, clinging to Matt.

Darren got to his feet and tugged on Matt's pants. "I sorry, Maff."

Leaning toward Remi, Matt tried to hand the clinging child off. "This is Eddie. Eddie, this is Remi. Be careful with his knees, Remi. They've been bugging him. I gave him some Motrin a few minutes ago."

Remi took the boy from Matt and realized the child's hands were held in. This was the kid Gadget wanted him to see. "Hi, Eddie. How old are you?"

To Remi's surprise Eddie blinked his big brown eyes and smiled. "I'm two."

Remi grinned at the clear, precise voice. "Oh, you're a smart one, aren't you?"

Eddie nodded, making hair fall in his eyes.

He reminded Remi of Sterling at that age. Remi had loved playing with Sterling as a baby. Sterling never failed to make him happy and forget about the other things in his life.

Chuckling, Remi headed toward the kitchen as Matt hefted a squalling Darren and went up the stairs.

Laying his head on Remi's shoulder, Eddie rested his hand on Remi's chest.

Wasn't that just the sweetest thing? Remi rubbed the baby's hand out of habit.

Stiffening, Eddie lifted his head off Remi's shoulder and peered at his hand.

Crap. Remi let go. "I'm sorry. Did I hurt you?"

"No." Eddie raised his hand and studied it.

Remi looked too. Eddie's fingers were still bent. Remi held out his hand. "Can I see?"

Eddie put his hand in Remi's.

The action was so trusting and innocent, it made Remi smile. He petted the back of the boy's hands and knuckles with his thumb. Babies' hands were fascinating. So small and delicate. It was the one thing that reminded you they were little people. His hand was just like Remi's only tiny. Remi rubbed the knuckles softly. "Does that hurt?"

Eddie shook his head.

"Does it feel better?"

Eddie nodded.

Remi let go. Could it have possibly helped? Such a simple thing?

Eddie lifted his hand and it was straighter than it had been. Wiggling his fingers, he blinked at Remi and held up two fingers. "I'm this many."

Tears welled in Remi's eyes and he laughed. He massaged Eddie's knee that was resting against his stomach then moved on to his chubby little leg. Being able to heal was amazing. It made all the trouble that came with being a werewolf worth it. He made a vow to stop bitching about the weirdness. How could he when it also gave him the ability to do this?

Halfway to the kitchen, Eddie stopped Remi, pointing to something on the floor by the dining room table. "Woof Woof." It was a stuffed animal of some sort, but it was shaped more like a human. It had brown fur on its back and head, but its butt was covered in denim.

Retrieving the plush toy, Remi turned it over and laughed. It was a werewolf. Sitting Eddie on the edge of the table, Remi pulled out a chair and sat in front of him. He held Woof Woof up and growled, "Oh no. He's growling at us. What should we do?"

Eddie grinned really big and giggled, shrugging his little shoulders.

"Here, give me your hand." Taking Eddie's other hand this time, Remi rubbed it in his own, then wrapped it in his fist and gently punched the stuffed animal. Still holding Eddie's hand in one of his and the doll in the other, he made the werewolf fall to the table and gasped out exaggerated dying sounds. Sterling used to love to play with his action figures like this.

Laughing, Eddie reached for the doll. He pointed his finger;

it was nearly straight. "Bad, Woof Woof."

Remi laughed too, marveling over the boy's hands. They weren't miraculously healed, but they didn't seem to be bothering him as much. Any improvement was good. Maybe some of it was the medicine Matt had given him, but Remi didn't see how it could make this big of a difference. Some of it had to be Remi's new powers. He rested his hands on the boy's knees, rubbing them a bit while Eddie made Woof Woof bite Remi.

"Ah, he got me. Save me, Eddie." Remi went limp in the chair, hanging his tongue out of his mouth.

Eddie giggled again. Swinging his feet a little and pretending to scold the stuffed animal, he touched Remi's chin. "Okay, Remi?"

"Whew, yeah that was a close one. Good thing you made him leave me alone, I thought I was a goner."

He'd gotten so carried away playing with the toddler, he hadn't realized they had an audience until Gadget spoke.

"I knew you could help him." Gadget's eyes were wide with amazement and there were tears in them.

Jake stood right behind him, a huge smile on his face.

"I didn't, but I'm glad." Taking the doll from Eddie again, Remi made it growl.

The boy cackled and shrugged his shoulder to his head, laughing and trying to keep the werewolf from getting him.

Gadget laughed. "Eddie, are you supposed to be on the table?"

Eddie pointed at Remi. "Remi did it."

✍

"You think it will continue to get better?" Remi glanced over at Jake from the passenger side of the Tahoe. "You think it will last?"

Jake shrugged. "Don't know, pup. I hope so."

"Me too. I like Eddie."

Jake grinned. "I couldn't tell." Jake wasn't sure if Remi had latched on to Eddie or vice versa, but Remi had spent all evening with the kid in his lap. It really wasn't all that surprising, Remi was a kid type of person. It was easy imagining him as a teen with Sterling hanging off of him.

Remi snorted. "Kids and animals like me. What can I say, it's a gift." Then more quietly he added, "I miss Sterling being that little sometimes."

The wistful tone went straight to Jake's heart. He'd had a hard time not pulling Remi into his arms all night. Seeing Remi playing with the kids and asking after their pack mates was something. Jake had never considered himself the domestic type, but boy Remi sure was. He was the perfect mate for a pack alpha. Taking care of people and organizing things seemed to come naturally to him.

He hadn't batted an eye when Gadget's boys started shoving at one another, fighting over something. He'd stepped between them and pointed Blake, the nine-year-old, to one side of the table and Scott, the seven-year-old, to the other. They had both stalked off and not said a word. Gadget had been thoroughly impressed and Matt demanded Remi teach him that trick.

"Jake, I liked helping him. I wanted him to be better and he seemed to be improving. I wish I knew what all I am capable of."

"Once we get things taken care of with Dirk, we'll talk to John Carter and see if he knows anyone who can teach you.

Have you asked Keaton?" Jake needed to tell Remi about Dirk's visit to the office, but it could wait. Remi was in such a good mood, he couldn't stand to ruin it.

"Not really."

"You want to go by there and see if he knows anything?"

"No, let's go home."

Oh, hell yes. Jake sped up a little. The smell of Remi's arousal filled Jake's nose and his whole body responded. His cock was hard and his gums itched.

"Mmm... Oh, man, I smell you. I'm getting better at picking out scents. You've always known I wanted you, haven't you?"

Oh fuck. He had known, but what a confession. "Yeah." Jake pulled into the drive and got out with Remi on his heels.

As soon as Jake got his front door opened and they were inside, he shoved Remi against the back of the door and reached around him to lock it.

Remi's peridot eyes shifted all of a sudden, making him blink.

"Damn." Jake's eyes reciprocated, losing color and focus momentarily. Slanting his mouth over Remi's, Jake pushed his tongue in. He couldn't wait.

Remi melted, purring into his mouth and following Jake's lead.

Tracing his tongue over Remi's teeth, feeling them lengthen, Jake moaned into Remi's mouth. His own gums tickled, threatening to make his teeth extend.

Leaning in, Remi rested his hands against Jake's chest. They were warm and trembling. It was enough to make Jake pull back. He didn't let go, instead he slid his hands around and cradled Remi's firm jaw. "I want to see you in those chaps I promised you." He kissed Remi's forehead and led him down the hall.

Jake entered the bedroom and crossed to the closet. He opened it, looking for the chaps.

The smell of Remi's arousal strengthened. Then his hand squeezed Jake's ass. "I bet you'd look great in leather chaps, sir."

Jake nearly moaned aloud. Remi had taken to calling him sir and submitting so beautifully. Jake was willing to bet that the guys had been right, that it was part instinctual, something Remi needed as much as Jake did. Reaching to the far left, he got the chaps and held them out to Remi.

Remi's eyes were still canine, his teeth elongated and damned if his cock wasn't perfectly outlined in those tight jeans. He took the leather from Jake, holding it to his waist.

Jake went to the end of the bed and sat. Closing his eyes, Jake took a deep breath to clear his mind and immediately wished he hadn't. The smell of Remi's arousal was even more intense. It made Jake's balls draw tighter. Running his hands over his face, Jake opened his eyes.

Remi had the waistband of the chaps snapped and was trying to zip the inside of the legs.

"Come here, pup, and I'll fix them for you." Jake crooked his finger.

Coming to the edge of the bed, Remi positioned himself close to Jake. When he turned, his butt was right in Jake's face, incased in tight denim. It made Jake's cock throb.

Jake zipped the zipper on the inside of the right leg, doing his best to ignore Remi's constant fidgeting. It wasn't easy. Remi managed to get his ass against the top of Jake's head. Jake had to adjust his prick before he finished zipping Remi up. He tapped Remi on the ass. "Turn a little and let me get the other one."

Remi shifted.

As soon as Jake bent over, Remi stepped backward, mashing his ass right into Jake's face.

Groaning, Jake fought the urge to nip his mate's fine ass. Fuck, Remi smelled good. Running his tongue over his gums, trying to soothe the itch and keep his teeth from changing, Jake moved Remi forward a little.

"Maybe I should earn this leather, sir."

Jake sucked in a breath. "Remi..." He finished fastening the chaps and turned Remi around. "Do you have any idea what you are asking for?"

Remi dropped to his knees, placed his hands on Jake's thighs and stared right into his eyes. "I want this, Jake."

He picked Remi up and threw him onto the bed face down. Maybe he could just go with the flow for a bit and see how Remi responded?

Remi gasped and tried to turn over onto his back.

Jake clasped Remi's right hand. Feeling around under the bed near the headboard at the corner, he found the chained leather restraints he'd had welded to the wrought iron frame years ago, and put it on Remi's wrist.

Remi tugged, but otherwise stopped trying to turn over.

Quickly, Jake straddled his back and got hold of the other cuff from under the bed. He captured Remi's other wrist and buckled it as well. Grabbing Remi's shirt, Jake ripped it off and slid down Remi's body.

He spotted the tanned back with its crisscross of scars that had bled and likely been infected wounds at one time, and his legs almost gave out. It felt like someone punched him. His erection even flagged a little. Closing his eyes, he tried to calm down. He'd forgotten all about the scars.

Snapping his eyes open, Jake watched Remi try to see over his shoulder. Was he blushing?

"Ugly, huh?" Remi dropped his gaze, not meeting Jake's eyes.

He couldn't let Remi think the scars bothered him. And they didn't for the reason Remi thought. But they did support his fear about doing this. "No. Nothing about you is ugly." He gathered the back of Remi's jeans in his hands and jerked. Thanks to werewolf strength, the jeans tore down the middle and exposed Remi's bare ass.

Sucking in a deep breath, Jake moved back. *Holy fucking shit.* The elastic of a red jockstrap was visible at his waist and small straps framed each muscled cheek.

Remi tried to see over his shoulder, but the restraints didn't allow enough movement for him to look Jake in the eye.

"You still want this?" *Please say yes.*

"Yes, sir." His voice was loud and assured, not the least bit hesitant.

Remi truly loved being told what to do, he was naturally submissive. Everything they'd done so far reinforced the fact that Remi wanted this relationship as much as Jake did. He had to give Remi the benefit of the doubt.

Goddamn, Remi looked good lying there chained to the bed with his ass exposed. Remi was completely at his mercy. Or was he? After catching a glimpse of those eyes... Jake decided that it might be the other way around.

The dark skin of his sinewy backside was gorgeous against the white comforter and even the scars didn't mar his perfection. The man was simply beautiful. Jake had thought that from the beginning. He ran his hand over his mate's ass before getting off the bed and undressing.

Remi lay there listening. He knew Jake was still there, could hear him moving around, but he couldn't turn enough to see him.

The air rushing over his skin with Jake's movements felt good on his heated skin, like a cool breeze. He couldn't remember ever being this turned on. He squirmed a little, pressing his cock against the mattress. *Fuck.* He was going to go crazy. How the hell long could his eyes and teeth stay shifted anyway? "Please..."

Moving against the bed again, he tried to get some relief. His cock was already leaking.

Jake's hand stroked his ass. *Oh damn, what is he going to do?* Remi moaned and lifted toward it.

"Get your knees underneath you. Ass in the air, pup."

"Oh God, yes, fuck me, please." He wanted it, needed it. Remi turned his head instinctively, but Jake's hand came to the back of his neck, pinning him to the bed. His other hand slid over Remi's ass, caressing. He closed his eyes, letting go and trusting Jake.

Being bound was a new experience for him, but he liked it. His entire body was one big bundle of nerves. "Please fuck me, sir."

Growling, Jake removed his hands from Remi's neck and ass. The bed moved.

Remi couldn't see, but Jake's smell teased his nose then something warm and wet slid down the crack of his ass. *Spit.* Jake's finger followed the trail of saliva, circled his hole and pressed in.

Sucking in a breath at the sheer pleasure, Remi pushed back against Jake's finger.

Jake slapped him on the ass. "Be still."

"Yes, sir." *Oh God, please hurry.*

Repeating the process with two and then three fingers, Jake drove him insane, teasing him. Remi shook with the effort to hold still as commanded.

"Very nice, pup." Jake's fingers retreated, then the head of his cock pressed against Remi's hole and shoved in, inch by slow torturous inch, until his balls rested on Remi's ass. Jake rubbed more saliva around his cock and Remi's stretched hole, making it slicker.

Remi moaned and tried to push back. He was so damn close.

Gripping Remi's hips with both hands, Jake started fucking him hard and fast. He dropped forward, bracing himself on one hand, and pulled Remi's jock aside, grasping Remi's cock. He stroked in time with his thrusts, driving Remi forward into his palm as he hit Remi's prostate. "Come for me." His teeth clamped over Remi's shoulder, piercing the skin.

"Oh fuck!" Remi's whole body jerked. The pain in his shoulder radiated out as the hand over his prick tugged hard. Pleasure crashed over him, bowing his back. He came, his ass clenching around his mate's cock.

With a hoarse groan, Jake lifted his mouth from Remi's shoulder. He continued to stroke Remi's dick, now slick by his come, until he thrust forward one last time and came deep in Remi's ass.

Easing him down to the mattress, Jake withdrew from his body and quickly unbuckled Remi's wrists. He scooped Remi into his arms and kissed the top of his head. "You did good, pup."

Remi snuggled into Jake's warm, sweaty chest and kissed him on the chin. He loved how Jake held him, how he praised him. He...loved Jake. "Thank you, sir."

Chapter Sixteen

Remi signed his name on the application but left the date blank and set it on the coffee table by his laptop. Getting up from the couch, he stretched out his back and turned to look at the paper. He'd done it, he'd actually filled out the paperwork and it felt damn good. But he couldn't turn it in, not yet. He would talk to his boss and put in for the EMT position as soon as Dirk was behind bars. Dirk had never laid a hand on Sterling for anything Remi had done, but he wasn't willing to chance it.

The threat to Sterling weighed heavily on his mind, but now he had hope it wouldn't be forever. He was tired of living by that asshole's rules. Remi had always loved helping people, but last night helping Eddie cinched it. Maybe he could only heal wolves like that, but he would learn to help humans too. If he could remember more about his beating and Billy's murder to help speed things up... He shook his head. Forcing it would likely make it take longer, wasn't that what they always said on TV?

Where is my cell phone? Gazing around the living room of his apartment, he tried to remember where he'd put it. He wanted to tell Jake about his decision.

Whoa. Remi stopped halfway to his bedroom. This was the only time he could remember not wanting to share something with Sterling first. Not that he didn't want to tell Sterling or that he wouldn't, but his initial thought had been Jake. Somehow it just felt right to tell his mate first. Remi smiled, knowing Jake would approve of Remi doing something he wanted to do.

Continuing into the room, he spotted his phone on the nightstand. After picking it up, he flipped through the numbers. It was midafternoon, so Jake would be at the office.

Someone knocked on the front door. Probably Sterling. He wasn't supposed to come over today, but Sterling had a way of talking people into rides. Looked like the kid was going to find out first after all.

Remi tossed the phone onto the bed and jogged toward the living room. "Coming."

As soon as he got the door unlocked it slammed open, nearly hitting Remi in the face, but he jumped to get out of its way.

Dirk barged in and shut the door behind him, looking like he could spit nails. "What in the holy hell are you doing, boy?"

Oh shit. Familiar fear flared to life. Out of instinct Remi backed up further, putting himself out of reach. "What do you mean, Dirk? I haven't done anything." What in the world did he think Remi had done? He had done many things lately that Dirk loathed, but Dirk didn't actually know about them. Did he? Darting his attention around, Remi looked for an escape route while still trying to keep Dirk in his vision.

"Look at me when I talk to you." Dirk stepped closer. His breath smelled like cheap whiskey. Which was pretty much the norm. He wore plain clothes, so he'd either had the day off or hadn't gone to work yet. Whichever, it meant he didn't have a gun or nightstick with him now and that was what interested Remi.

Remi stepped backward, his stomach tying in knots. *Please, don't do this.* Meeting Dirk's gaze, he tried not to seem defiant or scared. Either appearance would piss Dirk off. Then again, you couldn't predict what would set the old man off and make him detonate. Remi tensed. God, it was hot in here all of a sudden.

"What is this I hear about you hanging out with a bunch of bikers? What the hell do you think you're doing going to a dive like Hell's Kitchen? No son of mine is going to hang out with a bunch of criminals."

"I—I went there with Jake. It was only the one time." Remi shook his head and glanced at Dirk's hands. They weren't fisted yet. Remi's own hands felt sticky, and he wiped them on his jeans.

"Why did you hire a detective to follow me, Remington? What are you trying to find?" Spit flew from Dirk's mouth, landing on Remi's cheek. He didn't dare acknowledge it, knowing it would get him backhanded.

Dirk kept coming closer.

"Nothing, Dirk." Remi raised his hands in front of his face.

"Get your hands down, boy." Flinging his arm up, Dirk knocked Remi's hands away and caught Remi across the cheek with his knuckles. "Goddamnit, boy. Don't you lie to me. What are you looking for?"

Remi stumbled backward, bumping into the wall. *Please, just go away.* What if he saw the EMT application? "Nothing, I promise. Jake is my friend, we hang out sometimes. You told me not to hang out with Chay anym—"

Dirk's eyes blazed, his face got redder and his voice lowered. "What did you say? *I* told you not to hang out with that fag? Are you saying you want to hang out wi—"

Oh shit. "No, no, I didn't mean it. I was only saying I have new friends." Backpedaling, Remi tried to get himself out of range. How could he have screwed up this badly? *Fuck*, Dirk got him so flustered he couldn't think. "I—" As Dirk stepped closer to him, Remi cringed away, which was a huge mistake. It only made Dirk madder and gave him space to get in a good hit.

Pain slashed through Remi's face and his eyes blurred with tears. "Uh." Blood poured out of his nose onto his shirt and the gray carpet. Trying to see through watery eyes, he grabbed his nose.

"I swear to God you're as dumb as your fucking mother. When are you going to learn not to cross me, boy?" A slap followed the hateful voice. "Huh?"

Remi's head jerked to the side and blood flew, hitting the white wall next to the front door. It hurt like a son of a bitch. Before he could recover, Dirk struck him in the stomach and swept his feet out from under him. Remi didn't have time to brace for the fall, and he hit the floor with a loud thud. Pain shot through his leg and spine from the jolt with the floor. His face throbbed.

"And what the hell did your worthless bitch of a mother say to you? What did she tell your detective friend at the store?" Not giving Remi a chance to get to his feet, Dirk advanced. "Answer me, Remington."

Curling into a ball out of habit, Remi protected himself as best he could with his back against the bar overlooking the kitchen and the living room. How had they gotten this far into the apartment?

Dirk gave him a kick to the ribs and pain sliced through them where Dirk's boot landed again and again.

৻৵৵

Matt leaned back in his chair, looking into Jake's office. "Jake, do you know a Sterling? He says—"

Jake snagged the phone and punched the button before Matt finished talking. "Sterling? What's wrong?"

A split second later, Rhys poked his head into Jake's office.

"Remi." Sterling sounded upset. "Dirk and Mom got into a fight about Remi. Someone told Dirk they saw you, Remi and my mom talking. He thinks you're investigating him."

Jumping up, Jake turned his computer off. "Sterling, are you okay, do you need me to come get you?"

Rhys came into the office, his head cocked.

"No, I'm fine. Dirk left. You gotta go check on Remi. I think Dirk went to Remi's. You have to make sure Remi is okay. I can't get him on the phone. It's not like him to not answer. I called from my cell phone and he always answers that number." Sterling sounded on the verge of tears.

Jake grabbed his keys. "All right I'm leaving now."

"Wait! Jake—"

"I'll call you when I get there." Jake hung up and jogged out of the office.

Rhys started out of the office behind him. "What do you need me to do?"

"Nothing. Just take care of things here. Find something on that asshole, damn it." Jake ran to his Tahoe. Grabbing his cell phone as he backed out of his parking space, he punched in Remi's number. It rang and rang. No answer. "Damn it, Remi, pick up the phone." It forwarded to his voice mail. Peeling his tires, Jake got out of the parking lot and onto the main road.

It was the longest drive of his life. He could swear he hit every damn stoplight on the way over and every slow person on the road got in front of him. No one knew how to merge onto the damn highway either. How in the hell did these idiots get driver's licenses?

When he dialed Remi's number again, he got voice mail. His heart raced and his palms started to sweat. So much so that his hand slipped on the steering wheel twice. The image of Remi lying in a puddle of blood, like he'd been when Jake first met him, flashed through his mind. He slammed his foot on the gas, speeding through a yellow light.

ல்லை

"You better call the detective and his goon off or both of them are going to get a whole heap of charges on their heads. They won't work in New Mexico again." Dirk punctuated the statement with another kick to the ribs. "Did you think I wouldn't know? You got shit for brains, boy. You want me to ask Sterling what you've been up to?"

Remi saw red. All the fear evaporated instantly and his protective instincts kicked in. He just snapped. *No fucking way. Not this time. Dirk had best keep his hands off Sterling.*

He stopped trying to dodge Dirk's boot, and with a burst of energy, he launched himself at Dirk's legs.

Dirk hit the ground, his head bouncing off the floor. The air whooshed out of him. He struggled, trying to get his breath.

Using the opportunity, Remi crawled forward and straddled Dirk. He still couldn't see very well but he didn't need to. He knew about where Dirk's face was and he started punching.

The feel of Dirk's face under his knuckles and the sound of his fist connecting with skin created a rush of euphoria. Suddenly, Remi could see again, only everything was in black and white.

Holding his arms up, Dirk attempted to block Remi's blows. Even now, in this position, the bastard was shouting out insults about how he was going to kill Remi and how Remi was a worthless piece of shit.

"No more. No more, you son of a bitch. Do you hear me? No more." Pounding over and over, Remi yelled until his voice gave out. The smell of blood and something else pierced his attention. *Fear.* It was fear. He could smell Dirk's fear.

It felt wonderful. He wanted to kill the son of a bitch. He could, so easily. Then it would all be over. As he smiled his fangs exploded in his mouth. He was damned close to shifting. He could tear Dirk to shreds in wolf form and no one would miss him.

No. He couldn't do it. Remi stopped.

Still trying to cover his face, Dirk laid there. His fear and helplessness felt good, but Remi relented.

He stood. His arms were tired. They felt like they weighed a ton and he couldn't breathe. He was so out of breath his lungs burned, and sweat dribbled down Remi's temple. "Get the fuck out. You so much as lay a finger on Sterling or Jake and I will fucking kill you."

Scooting toward the door on his butt, Dirk tried to glare, but he still reeked of fear. "We aren't done with this, Remington."

"I think we are done. Get out." Remi pointed at the door.

Gasping, Dirk crawled backward. His eyes were wide and his face had drained of color. "What are you on?" Dirk asked in a soft whisper.

Shit. His eyes. Dirk could see his canine eyes. Remi hauled back his foot, ready to kick Dirk again. He growled, trying to make him leave.

Dirk scrambled up and out of the apartment, leaving the door open.

Remi should've felt relief, even humor and a sense of victory. Instead he felt sick. His eyes changed back so fast he had to blink several times to clear his vision. His teeth shrank and all the pains and aches flared to life.

Sinking to the floor, he wheezed out a breath and rested his back against the wall next to the door. Vomit rose in his throat, but he swallowed it back. His eyes teared up again and his hands shook as he slid onto his back, keenly aware of the twinge in his ribs. Covering his face with his quivering hands, he felt the fine sheen of sweat covering his body. It began to cool, making him shiver. *Jesus, what have I done?*

Chapter Seventeen

There was no sign of Dirk, and Remi's bike was under the awning in the place it usually sat. Jake whipped into the spot next to it, cut the engine and jerked his keys out. Opening his door, he smelled blood. *Fuck.* It was Remi's blood. His eyes and teeth shifted.

He slammed the door shut and ran up the steps to the front door. It was standing open. A fear like he'd never felt coursed through him. Oh God, why was the door open? He felt ill. It meant Remi wasn't able to shut it. Pushing the door open further, he frantically searched for Remi.

He sat in the entryway against the wall with his knees pulled up to his chest and his hands over his face. Moving his hands, he blinked up at Jake. His muscles tensed like he was preparing to bolt.

Jake took a deep breath, willing his racing heart to slow. Remi was alive. He smelled of blood and fear, his chest rose and fell rapidly with erratic choppy breaths, but he was alive. "Remi." Jake fell to his knees in front of his mate.

Remi's pale eyes weren't quite focused. There was dried blood under and around his nose and on his chin and cheeks. He looked like hell.

"Oh God, Remi—" Jake reached out toward his cheek, intent on checking his injuries.

"Unh." Flinching away, Remi moved out of range. He winced and clutched his left side.

Dropping his hand, Jake gritted his teeth to keep from punching the wall. Overwhelming anger surged through him. He wanted desperately to find Dirk Lassiter and tear him to pieces, not only for the pain he'd caused physically, but for putting the haunted look in Remi's eyes.

Taking several deep breaths, Jake flexed his fingers, releasing his tension. The last thing he wanted was to traumatize his mate more. He had to get it together. Like a magnet, his gaze was drawn to the wall above Remi. Dark splatters blared at him from the sea of white. There wasn't a lot of blood, but the fact that it was Remi's had Jake's heart in his throat. He'd promised he'd never let his mate be hurt again. He'd failed.

Scrunching his face a little, Remi closed his eyes. "I'm sorry."

Sorry? What the fuck? Jake growled and stood. Dirk was going to pay for this. "Are you all right? Where all are you hurt?"

Remi winced again. "I'm okay."

"I'm going to have Rhys come stay with you. I'm going after your father. He's not getting away with this." Jake grabbed his phone off his belt. Fuck, he was so pissed, he couldn't even operate the fucking phone. His hands were shaking.

Remi jumped to his feet and pushed the phone down. "Don't. Dirk isn't worth it."

Jake clasped Remi's hand with his other one. "How can you say that? Look at you. Look at what he did. He had no right. I'll be damned if that son of a bitch lays another hand on you." Realizing he was yelling at Remi, he lowered his voice. "I promised you'd never have to go through this again."

Remi tugged on the phone, pulled it out of Jake's hand and tossed it to the couch. "You can't go after Dirk. And you can't promise something like that. This isn't your fault any more than it's mine. It's Dirk's, but murdering him isn't the answer."

Seething, Jake looked away. Remi was his. His to protect and care for.

"Jake, I nearly killed him myself a few minutes ago. We're close to finding something on him, I know it. Let's just keep doing what we're doing. Rhys is supposed to meet with his ex-boss today, right? Give him a chance to find something." He touched Jake's cheek with tears in his eyes. "I don't want to risk you going to jail. Sterling and I need you."

They stood there staring—almost glaring—at one another for several moments before Jake gave in. How could he not when Remi looked at him like that? The gnawing anger didn't disappear, but the need to comfort Remi grew stronger. For all his bravado, Remi was still scared. His scent hadn't changed much.

With a pleading look on his face, Remi caressed Jake's cheek. "Please."

He loves me. It was there in his eyes. He wanted Jake with him more than he wanted Dirk gone. Jake closed his eyes, nodding. For once it was he who leaned into Remi's hand and enjoyed the feel of his mate's touch. Remi needed him here. Dirk would have to wait.

"Your eyes and teeth shifted." Remi's voice was soft, almost a whisper.

"It's the smell of your blood." Closing the door with his foot, he reached for Remi. This time Remi didn't shy away, he let Jake help him. "Come on, let's get you taken care of. Where do you hurt?"

"I'm not that hurt, just pissed off mostly."

"You and me both." Jake traced his hands over Remi, trying to assure himself Remi was really okay. He seemed to be. Now Jake felt like an ass for not seeing to his mate's care sooner. He steered Remi toward the bathroom. "What happened? Sterling called me in a near panic saying Dirk was headed here."

"Yeah. He told me to call you off or you and Sterling were going to get hurt."

Jake ground his teeth together. Guilt ate at him. He should've told Remi about Dirk's visit. "He came to my office the other day. I was going to tell you about it tonight. I didn't want to ruin your evening yesterday. You seemed happy and in such a great mood, I didn't want you to worry. I figured he was confronting me, so he'd let you be."

"There isn't any way you could have known he'd come looking for me too. You can never tell what the asshole is going to do. Where are we going?"

"Bathroom to clean you up."

Remi was limping a little and Jake had to quash down the anger threatening to take over again.

"I scared him." Remi leaned against Jake more, groaning softly. "I lost it, Jake. I just wigged out. I started beating the hell out of him and my eyes and teeth shifted." Stopping, he turned to Jake and worried his lip. "He saw them."

"What did he do?" Swooping Remi gently into his arms, Jake carried him the rest of the way to the bathroom.

Remi wrapped his arms around Jake's neck. "He thought I was on something. I don't think it really registered. I shouldn't have fought back. What if he tells everyone about what he saw? What if…?" Shoulders slumping, Remi sighed. He seemed exhausted. More mentally than physically, but then physically he wasn't so hot either. The dried blood on his face and clothes

222

was turning crusty.

"Who the hell is going to believe him, if he does tell?" Setting Remi on the vanity counter next to the sink, Jake turned on the water to let it heat and got a washcloth from the linen cabinet.

Remi reclined against the mirror and shut his eyes, a small smile curving his lips. He looked pleased with himself, or maybe he was resigned to let things be for now and allow Jake to care for him. Whatever the case, he was still and compliant.

Placing his hands on Remi's knees, Jake bent forward and brushed their lips together. Thank God Remi wasn't more seriously injured.

"Mmm..." Remi's eyes opened. With the dark smears of blood on his face, his pale eyes appeared even lighter, almost white because of Jake's monochrome vision.

"What are you smiling about?" Brushing Remi's hair out of his face, Jake picked some dried blood out of it.

"I fought back. It felt good."

Jake smiled and kissed Remi again. "I'm glad. Wish I could have seen it. Lift your arms."

Remi raised his arms, allowing Jake to pull the T-shirt over his head. After tossing it toward the hamper, Jake inspected Remi's ribs. There was a bruise halfway up on his right side, but it wasn't too bad. There wasn't any swelling. Likely whatever injury he'd sustained was already healing but Jake ran his fingers over it lightly.

"That tickles."

Pulling his hand back, Jake straightened. "Sorry." He wet the washcloth with warm, soapy water and cleaned Remi's face and neck.

He had the urge to bite into Remi's neck and taste. The

smell of Remi's blood was going to Jake's head and had been since he opened the SUV door. Now his cock was getting hard too.

He bathed Remi's shoulders and chest, ignoring his arousal. There was nothing on Remi's stomach, but Jake washed it, too, enjoying the feel of Remi's ab muscles rippling under his ministrations.

Yawning, Remi closed his eyes, and Jake gave up all pretense of cleaning wounds. He tossed the washcloth aside and turned off the water. Threading his fingers through Remi's soft black hair, Jake situated himself between Remi's thighs.

Sitting forward, Remi put his hands on Jake's shoulders and offered his mouth. "Sir?"

Jake groaned. How could he ignore the plea in Remi's tone? It still amazed him Remi had switched to calling him sir so effortlessly. He captured Remi's mouth in a slow, gentle kiss and traced Remi's lips with his tongue, feeling where it had been split. It wouldn't take long to heal, but until it did... He drew back, studying Remi.

They stared at each other for the longest time with everything Remi felt on his face for Jake to read. The last of Jake's anger melted away. He couldn't remember ever sharing silent communication with another. Sure Rhys and he used grunts and nods on occasion, but with Remi it was different, special. The more they were together the closer they grew. It was an amazing feeling. One he didn't know he could feel until Remi came along.

Yawning again, Remi leaned forward and rested his head on Jake's shoulder.

Grabbing Remi's legs, Jake wrapped them around his waist and picked his mate up.

"Where are we going?" Remi nuzzled Jake's neck.

"To put you to bed."

"Thank you."

Jake smiled and continued to the bedroom. He lay on the bed, situating Remi on top of him, and rubbed circles on Remi's back. He felt the scars and closed his eyes. The welts reminded him once again of his hatred for Lassiter and his desire to go after the man. But he wouldn't, at least not now. He had a mate to take care of.

For the longest time, Remi laid there. His breath was slow and even, and Jake thought he'd fallen asleep, until he kissed Jake's collarbone. "I hate how good it felt to hit him. I don't want to be like that and I don't want you to be like that. Killing him would be too easy and it would feel really good for a while, but in the long run it would make us no better than he is."

Remi was right. They needed to try to do it legally first, like they'd planned. But if it didn't work... "Okay, pup, we'll keep going at it the way we have been." Sighing, Jake continued to rub Remi's back.

Remi's cell phone rang.

Damn. "It's probably Sterling calling to see if you're all right." Jake loosened his grip on Remi so he could get up. He'd forgotten to call the imp back.

Oh no. What if Dirk had gone home and beat on the kid? Jake had been so preoccupied with caring for his mate, he hadn't thought of it before. "Do you think Sterling is okay?"

Remi crawled off of Jake and down to the foot of the bed to retrieve the phone. "Yeah, Sterling's okay. Dirk was mad at me, not him."

Pushing himself to a sitting position, Jake watched his mate. *Fuck me.* That was a pretty sight. He grinned and went to get his own cell phone as Remi answered. He got to the couch where his phone had been tossed and realized Remi hadn't said

225

any more than, "Hello."

Something was wrong. Fear and the need to protect besieged Jake. He hurried back down the hall.

Remi still sat at the foot of the bed, the cell phone held in his hand. His face was blank, confused. Remi's eyebrows pulled together. "I'm not allowed to see Sterling anymore."

∽∾

Rhys hurried across the field, with his ears back and his tail down, until he could clearly see the small white house. Hopefully, anyone who saw him would think he was a dog, but he'd stayed out of public view, keeping away from high traffic areas anyway. Now it was getting dark and he blended in.

Raising his nose, he sniffed, trying to find his target. The soft, wild and fresh, almost evergreen scent was easy to find. It was getting stronger.

The back door opened and Sterling clambered out, holding a bowl of something. *Milk.* It smelled like milk. Looking left then right, he hurried down the porch steps and into the grass.

What was he doing? Rhys crept closer on his belly trying to see.

Glancing back at the house, Sterling set the bowl on the ground. "Come on, boy, it's okay." He stared toward Rhys.

What? Can he see me? Rhys looked around him, fairly certain he was concealed by the dark and the tall grass.

"Oh, there you are." Sterling turned his attention to his left.

A small orange tabby cat wandered up and meowed a greeting. He went right to the bowl and began drinking.

Sitting down in the grass, Sterling talked to the cat like he was a long-lost friend.

If Rhys had been in human form, he'd have smiled. The kid would talk to anyone or anything. It was endearing.

Lying there, Rhys could see that Sterling was unharmed. Dirk Lassiter's scent lingered around the home, but it was faint. The man wasn't in residence. The tension in Rhys eased and he closed his eyes, listening to the smooth cadence of his mate's voice, content that the kid was all right.

Chapter Eighteen

"Goddamn it, Jake, get out of my way."

"No. You are not going over there by yourself. You told me your mom said everything was fine and Sterling was safe. If you think you have to go, I'll take you, but you're only going to make him madder." Jake leaned against the door and crossed his arms over his chest. Remi was being completely unreasonable. After the phone call from his mother informing him Dirk no longer wanted him around Sterling, Remi got up and grabbed his helmet and keys. He was intent on going to check on his brother, which was probably exactly what that asshole, Lassiter, was counting on. No way in hell was Jake letting Remi go near Dirk Lassiter after what had happened.

Jake was trying his damnedest not to get mad at his mate, but he was nearly at the breaking point. It amazed him how quickly Remi could go from sweet and lovable to growling and snapping. Sometimes it was like he was two different people.

"I can't take you with me. I have to make Dirk think I'm doing what he wants." Remi looked down at the helmet in his hand, then back at Jake. "Jake, please."

"No."

Remi's eyes shifted as he snarled at Jake. "I just want to make sure he's—"

Someone knocked on the door.

Holding up his hand, Jake stalled Remi and inhaled deeply. Pack. It was their guys. Jake recognized their scents. He turned and opened the door, letting them in and ignoring Remi for the moment. "What are y'all doing here?"

"Son of a bitch." Remi stalked further into the living room.

Dago's eyebrows rose as Zack pushed past him into the apartment. Dago came in behind him, his eyes zeroing in on the blood-splattered wall to the left of the door. "Whoa."

Jake shut the door.

"We heard what happened and came to check on Remi." Zack walked around Remi, studying him. "Are you okay?"

Jake grinned, not at all surprised. They'd taken to Remi as quickly as he'd taken to them. Following the guys into the living room, he extracted the helmet and keys from Remi's hands. He set them on the coffee table and sat on the couch, crooking his finger at Remi. "Come sit." He looked at Dago. "How did y'all find out?"

"Listen, guys. I'm fine, but I need you to go. You can't come here. If I'm seen around all of you—" Remi stopped when Jake turned back to him.

Immediately, Jake felt the unease in the air. The men were reacting to their omega. "Remi, come here."

"He's having me watched, somehow. He knew about me going to the bar. I bet you anything he's paying those homeless men we keep seeing around here to report back to him." Pinching the bridge of his nose, Remi closed his eyes for a minute. He dropped his hand and glanced at Jake. "He knew about you and I running into my mom at the grocery store. If he finds out about all of them"—he waved his arms around, indicating the room as a whole—"here, he's going to keep Sterling from me."

Which was a moot point as far as Jake was concerned

because Dirk was already doing that. Jake stood and went to his mate, wanting to ease his worries even though he knew there was little he could do. Remi was right. Dirk had to be keeping tabs on Remi somehow, which was exactly why, from now on, Jake was staying with him at all times.

So far, he'd kept his cool and tried to calm Remi that way. Earlier, Remi had done the same to him. It wasn't easy though, he couldn't remember ever hating another person as badly as he did Lassiter. His resolve to keep from killing Dirk was slipping a bit more each second. "Remi, he's already forbidden you to see Sterling. There isn't anything you can do about it. What will alienating our friends, your pack, do?"

"He did what?" Dago asked, outrage clear in his voice.

"He doesn't want me hanging out with all of you." Holding up his hands, Remi turned back to Jake. "I tried it your way." Shaking his head, he took a seat on the arm of the couch, next to Zack. "I can't not be around Sterling, Jake. With me out of the picture, Sterling will end up hurt. You can keep investigating, but until you get something on Dirk..." He stood and his eyes were misty. "I can't." He gazed back at the guys. "I'm sorry. All of you have to go."

Feeling his mate's fear and sorrow so keenly, Jake had to blink back tears. How could he get Remi to understand? How could he assure Remi they'd get something on Dirk? Maybe he *should* just go kill the bastard.

Zack came forward and began kneading Remi's shoulders.

Shrugging him off, Remi stepped away.

Looking like a kicked dog, Zack went and sat beside Dago on the couch.

Jake studied them with their heads hanging and had no clue what to say. Jesus, this was not only destroying Remi, it was tearing their pack apart.

There was a knock at the door.

Growling, Remi grumbled, "Who now?"

Nick and Tank. Jake could smell them. He opened the door, allowing them in before shutting it.

"Goddamnit." Remi threw his hands up again and groaned. "Gee, let's put a sign on the door to make sure everyone knows who all's here."

Nick's eyes widened. "Is he okay?"

"Yeah, he's fine." Stepping aside, Jake extended an arm toward the couch.

"No, he's not." Remi flopped down on the carpet.

Something scratched the door.

Jake frowned.

"And that would be Rhys, Keaton and Chay." Covering his face with his hands, Remi groaned.

All the men looked at Remi, then one another.

"Who is that?" Tank asked.

It smelled like...*Matt?* Opening the door, Jake spotted a black wolf. He stepped out of the way, letting the wolf in, and closed the door.

Sighing, Remi sat up.

The wolf began to shift. Muscles shrank and bones popped as tanned skin took the place of black fur. In a matter of seconds, Matt picked himself up off of all fours and stood, naked, in the living room. Shaking his head, he stretched his arms. His lithe body flexed. He turned, looking at Jake. "Rhys sent me to tell you that Sterling is fine."

Remi jumped to his feet and rushed forward, nearly tripping over the coffee table. "What? How does he know? Where is Sterling? What—?"

Jake wrapped his arms around Remi's waist. "Shh. Let him talk, pup."

Matt smiled at Jake and addressed Remi. "After Jake left, Rhys shifted and headed out. I, ah—" Matt blushed and darted a glance around the room. "I decided to follow. So, after I let Rhys out the front, I locked up, stripped and went out the back." His gaze met Jake's. "I locked the back door first and hid the key before I shifted. Then I followed Rhys' scent. When I got there, Rhys told me to come let you know."

Remi actually relaxed a little, his shoulders lost some of their tension and he leaned against Jake. "Tell me about Sterling?"

"He's at the house with your mother. We caught glimpses of them through the windows. Your father came home, got changed into his uniform and then left again. Rhys is going to stay until he comes back, to make sure everything is okay."

"Thank you." Remi stepped away from Jake. "I'm going to have to ask you all to leave now."

Ignoring the gang's reaction, Jake reached for Remi and turned him back around. This news should have made him feel better. It sure as hell had made Jake's anxiety lessen. "What gives? Rhys is watching after him."

"It doesn't change anything. The fact that Dirk is at work makes it worse. You all have to leave. What if he comes by and sees all the bikes?"

What if he did? No way in hell was Jake leaving Remi, knowing Dirk was out there. And if Remi thought otherwise, he'd lost his damn mind.

The guys all got up and gathered around Matt, talking at once, but Jake tuned them out. "Remi, don't do this." He smelled tears, but Remi never let them fall.

Blinking them back, Remi looked at the ceiling. "Sterling

needs me."

So do I. "So do we." Jake pointed to their pack, his anger growing despite his promise to remain clam. Remi was being stubborn and he wasn't thinking straight.

Shaking his head, Remi went to the couch. "Get out." He didn't say it with much conviction but he dropped his head in his hands, dismissing Jake.

Caught between the urge to shake the shit out of Remi and start punching things, Jake turned back to their pack.

They stood gathered around the door, looking like they'd gone to a funeral. Matt was gone.

"Where's Matt?"

"He went to go back and help Rhys," Tank answered.

If Jake hadn't been so pissed at his mate, he'd have smiled. It appeared Matt had found something more important than his fear of Rhys. Jake bobbed his head. "Listen, why don't you guys split for right now and let—"

Dago was already opening the door, his head hanging.

Fuck. Jake ground his teeth together.

"Hi. We came to check on Remi, is he—" Gadget stepped in the door, Eddie on his hip. Frowning at the guys, he met Jake's gaze. "What's wrong?"

"Remi wants us to leave," Zack mumbled.

The pack's mood pressed in on Jake's anger. He was starting to sense their depression, their feeling of rejection from their omega.

Eddie squirmed in Gadget's arms, making little grunting sounds, and reached toward Remi.

Jake just stared. The boy's hands weren't twisted up in pain, his color was normal. Before, even when his arthritis wasn't bothering him, he had a grayish cast to his skin. Remi had truly healed him.

Jake smiled in spite of the situation. He couldn't ever remember seeing the child do that, he always clung to whoever was holding him.

"Shh..." Gadget patted his leg and hefted Eddie up higher on his hip.

Jake held his arms out to Eddie.

Gadget frowned, but handed him over.

Setting him on the ground, Jake let him go where he wanted.

All the men watched. There were several soft gasps as Eddie ran to Remi. The baby wasn't limping and favoring his legs like he normally did.

Eddie stood in front of Remi for several seconds, waiting. When Remi didn't lift his head, Eddie crawled down into Remi's sight and peeked up at him. "Remi? Okay, Remi?"

"What are you doing here?" Remi sounded surprised.

"Come to see you." Eddie climbed into Remi's lap. It was awkward as little as he was, but he managed it nicely.

Remi steadied Eddie on his leg. His eyes widened. Catching Eddie's hands in one of his, he studied them. Tears ran down his cheeks and a smile crept over his lips. He glanced at Jake, then at their pack.

Jake smiled back, aware of some of the guys tearing up. "We need you too, pup."

Eddie pulled his hands free and hugged Remi.

Remi nodded. "I'm sorry. Please shut the door and come back in here."

"We're going to go hide our bikes first. But we'll be back if you really don't mind," Tank said.

Remi hugged Eddie harder. "I don't mind."

They all filed out the door, their unease gone.

Gadget grinned. "Looks like we made it just in time."

Chapter Nineteen

"They *did* cover for Dirk, but not for murdering Billy—"

"What?" Remi stopped his pacing, his green eyes wide, his gaze boring into Rhys'. "Sorry, go on." He continued to pace a rut in Jake's carpet.

"The story was that Dirk killed a pedophile who attacked the boys."

"He told them he killed an attacker?" Remi threw his hands in the air then let them fall. He gripped his hair, pulled, and made a sound caught halfway between a groan and a yell. "What the fuck? So these great wondrous civil servants took it upon themselves to play judge? Didn't they think it was a little odd there wasn't another body?"

Jake watched his mate. Fearing for Remi's safety was only half of his dilemma, albeit the most troubling. "Remi, come sit down."

Remi turned and glared.

Groaning in frustration, Jake got up from the couch and went to fetch him. "Cops, oh hell law enforcement of all kinds, hate child predators. Think about it, especially one who'd prey on young boys." He caught Remi's hand, guiding him to the couch cattycorner to the chair Rhys was sitting in.

As badly as Jake wanted to get rid of the threat to Remi and their happiness, he didn't dare rush something like this. He wanted to make certain everything would stand up in court. But at the same time the urge to get things rolling was paramount. To do that he needed to keep a clear head and hear the rest of what Rhys had learned.

"They had a body," Rhys added.

"What?" Remi and Jake both stopped at the end of the couch.

Jake sat.

"There was a body, a Geoff Clifton." Rhys leaned forward, his gaze focused on Remi. "According to the story Caspari uncovered, Dirk went to pick you and Billy up. The two of you had gone to the movies, with Dirk's permission, to kill time while waiting for Sterling to be born. Dirk had gone to the movie theater first. When he didn't find the two of you there, he assumed you'd started walking back home. He got back to the house and neither of you were there, so he traced his way back to the theater. He was about to go see if the two of you had gone to Billy's house when he heard you yelling."

Growling, Remi flopped on the couch next to Jake. "Heard me yelling?"

"Yes." Rhys held up his hand.

Jake rested his hand on Remi's thigh because hearing this made his blood boil. "Let him finish, pup."

Rhys took a drink of his water. "He heard yelling and parked the car. He didn't see anything at first, but followed the direction of the cries for help. Upon searching the field, he stumbled over Billy's body, at which point he panicked and called out to Remi. Allegedly, Remi called back and then went silent in the middle of yelling 'Dad'."

Remi scoffed, his back going rigid. "I've never called Dirk

dad."

Jake patted Remi's leg, trying to get him to quiet. He did his damnedest to remain calm, but Remi's anger was infectious.

"Finally, Dirk said he saw something in the knee-high grass. He raced forward, pistol drawn, but only found Remi unconscious and unresponsive. The day after, a drunk they were holding in the pen had an accident and fell down the stairs on his way to questioning. According to what Caspari heard, the man confessed to raping the boys, killing Billy and leaving Remi for dead."

"Un-fucking-believable." Jake leaned back on the couch. Goddamn, he'd love to get his hands on Lassiter. "You're telling me that the FBI found this out and let it drop? Instead of investigating the prisoner's murder as well?"

Rhys nodded. "You said it yourself about law enforcement and pedophiles. And with a cop's kid being involved..." Rhys shook his head. "Cops take care of their own."

Remi leaned closer to Jake and Jake wondered if he realized he'd done it. Probably not, it seemed automatic, but it gave Jake a bit of reassurance. Some of his own tension ebbed away with Remi's nearness.

"What's the word on the alleged pedophile?" Remi sounded tired and defeated.

Rhys shrugged. "I'm looking into that now, trying to find out who the man was. I'm looking for a report. I'm anxious to see how his death was explained and where they supposedly found him."

Running his hands through his hair, Jake huffed out a breath. Dirk was a fucking genius. If they dug stuff up on the son of a bitch, they'd find *this* cover-up story. They were going to have their work cut out for them proving Dirk set that scene up to cover for himself.

Apparently, Remi drew the same conclusion. His shoulders slumped, his head hung and the scent of fear poured off of him again. "What a clusterfuck." Standing again, Remi paced in front of the coffee table. "So basically, it's my word against his and he has not only the rez police on his side but the fucking FBI too. There is no way in hell all those cops are going to admit to being duped and covering a crime." He walked over to Jake's fireplace and ran his hands over the mantle. His gaze was unfocused and far away. "There is nothing else I can do." He sounded as if he'd given up all hope.

Jake's chest felt like it was being crushed. Any minute Remi would turn to him and break off all ties in hopes he'd be able to see Sterling again. With tremendous effort, Jake swallowed the urge to scream and yell. Why couldn't Remi love him as much as he did Sterling? No, that wasn't fair. Remi would do whatever it took to take care of anyone he cared about who was in trouble, Jake knew that as sure as he breathed. He even understood Remi's logic, but it still hurt. He wasn't being at all rational. Dirk wouldn't let Remi see Sterling just because Remi was no longer hanging out with Jake. Hell, Dirk had no idea they were lovers. It came down to the fact that Dirk was concerned Remi remembered something...or at least that was Jake's take on things. And Dirk knew his son well enough to know Sterling was the key to keeping Remi quiet. He was dangling Sterling as bait until Remi came clean, telling Dirk what he knew and promising to keep it secret.

And Remi would do just that, if Jake allowed him. But it wouldn't solve anything. It wouldn't keep either of them from danger, even if it would allow him to see Sterling.

Okay think, Jake, think. Which was way easier said than done. He had to fight back. Now that he had Remi, he wasn't letting go. Remi had done well with what he had to work with, but Jake was here now and it was up to him to break this cycle.

If he didn't, Remi would always be under Dirk Lassiter's thumb.

There was a file folder sitting next to Rhys. Rhys had glanced at the folder a few times but hadn't opened it. Why? "What's in the folder?"

"Crime scene photos." Rhys shook his head. "You don't want to see, trust me. Hell, *I* don't want to see them again." Rhys' voice sounded rougher than normal.

Swallowing the lump in his throat, Jake held out his hand. "Let me see them. Maybe we can find something that doesn't add up."

"Jake..."

He continued to hold out his hand, glancing at Remi, who was still lost in thought by the fireplace. "Rhys."

"Fine. But I warned you." Rhys slapped the folder into Jake's palm, got up and stalked to the kitchen.

Staring at the manila file folder, Jake heard the refrigerator door open and noticed the water bottle Rhys had been drinking from sitting on the coffee table empty. The fridge door shut and a can popped open. Okay, he was being ridiculous. Stalling wasn't going to make what was in the folders less harsh. The descriptions from Remi's dream painted a horrendously vivid picture, how much worse could the actual pictures be?

Flipping open the folder, he found what he recognized as an official report. He scanned it. It was what Remi had told him to begin with. The boys were walking back from the movies and attacked by unknown assailants, for unknown reasons. He set the document aside. A boy's sightless eyes stared back at him.

He was Apache from the looks of it. In spite of the ugly bruise on one cheek, he was handsome, with tanned skin, big brown eyes, long black hair and a hawk-like nose. This was Billy. Remi's first love. The kid looked so innocent, almost peaceful with his red shirt open just enough to show off his

With Caution

bruised throat.

Jake flipped to the next picture. Another of Billy. He lay in the yellowing grass, arms and legs spread like he'd been positioned there.

Rhys came back and set a beer in front of him. "You're going to need this."

Great. Ignoring the beer, Jake picked up the picture of Billy and moved it.

The first thing he saw was the slender back, legs and buttocks covered with bloody welts. Remi's long hair fanned out around him and his head was turned, leaving one side of his face clearly visible. Dried blood covered his cheek and chin, his nose was purplish black and swollen. *Jesus.* He was barely recognizable.

"My God," Jake whispered to himself. Tears threatened his eyes. It was like being punched in the stomach so hard he lost his breath. How could anyone do this? To Remi? Remi, who always thought of others before himself.

Jake moved to the next picture.

It was a closeup of Remi's battered face. Jake closed his eyes, trying to hide his overwhelming anger from his mate. Before Remi, Jake had thought he, Rhys and their group were some tough sons of bitches. Now he realized they were nothing compared to Remi. Remi took what life dished out and never once complained. Even his abusive upbringing he tried to ignore, except when it came to Sterling.

Remi's cell phone rang.

Snapping open his eyes, Jake watched as Remi fumbled for the phone.

Turning toward Jake and Rhys, he flipped it open. "Hello?" His eyebrows pulled together like he was trying to hear.

241

"Sterling? I can't hear you. You're breaking up." He walked closer to the front window. "Sterling?"

Jake was on his feet in a second. Tossing the folder aside, he hurdled the coffee table and caught Remi's shoulders. "What is it?"

Remi's face went blank. "I don't know. I could barely hear him. He sounded like..." Pulling away from Jake, Remi stuffed his phone back onto his belt and dug out his keys, running toward the kitchen door.

Jake caught him before he made it to the garage. "Sounded like what?"

"Like he was crying."

Oh fuck. The pictures of Remi's beaten face flashed through Jake's brain. It gave Remi enough time to hit the garage door opener and go to his bike.

Jake ran back inside and grabbed his keys and helmet off the kitchen counter. Putting his helmet on, he passed Rhys on his way to the garage. "Stay here in case Sterling calls."

"Fuck that." Rhys had his keys out and phone in hand, already heading out the front door.

The sound of Remi's bike motor echoed through the house and Jake didn't have time to think, much less argue. He shook his head and ran out the garage door, trying to keep up with his mate. "Remi. Wait!" *Damn.*

Remi took off.

Jake started his bike, hit the garage door opener, then jumped on and headed out of the garage with the door closing behind him. His heart leapt into his throat. Remi shouldn't be driving. He didn't think straight when it came to his brother.

He drove onto reservation land, and Remi was still nowhere in sight. Had he taken a different way? He hadn't said anything, but Jake was certain he'd go to his parents' house. That's where Sterling would be.

Rounding the first of three curves on the way to the Lassiter house, Jake hit the dirt road. Feeling the bike try and get away from him on the dirt and loose gravel, he slowed a little. That's when he saw the cloud of dust and Remi's bike laying in the middle of the road, the tank and front wheel crumpled, the back wheel still turning.

Oh God no. Jake stopped so abruptly his bike almost slid out from under him. Alarm stabbed through him. Everything went still and quiet. It was like watching a movie in slow motion with the volume turned down. He scanned the area for Remi and inhaled, trying to find him through the dust. "Remi!"

ক৹ঞ

Rhys watched Jake's taillight speed away as he put his car into reverse. It was getting dark out. He'd been taking nightly trips to the Lassiter house in wolf form and so far Sterling had come to no harm, but he'd be lying if he said he wasn't concerned now. He was tempted to try and call the kid's cell phone, but he didn't want to chance Dirk Lassiter hearing it.

Those pictures of Remi as a teen haunted Rhys. Even knowing they were Remi, when Rhys had first seen them he'd envisioned Sterling lying there. He'd been so unsettled, he'd shifted and gone to the Lassiter house in broad daylight just to check on the kid. Luckily, Sterling had been unharmed. Which was a damn good thing. Rhys wasn't sure he had Jake's restraint. He'd have to kill Lassiter for harming the boy.

His cell phone rang as he drove onto the reservation. Recognizing Sterling's number, he hit the talk button. "Sterling?"

J. L. Langley

"Rhys? I...can't...get...Remi." His voice was soft and slow, like he was having a hard time talking.

Rhys didn't like the wheezing sound of his voice. Something was very wrong. "I'm on my way, tell me where you are."

"There's a fiel—" He coughed, the sound almost gurgling. When the coughing ceased, a long, pain-filled moan started.

Fuck. Rhys stepped on the gas. "What are you closest to? Did you walk toward town or toward the Winston's house?" He tried to reach that inner calm he always obtained in a dangerous situation, but it wouldn't come.

"I don't...know. I went str—" There was more coughing. When Sterling spoke again, his voice was softer. "—out the back door and kept going."

A field. Out the back door. Rhys racked his brain. There were a lot of fields on the reservation. Turning onto the road behind the Lassiter house, Rhys rolled down all his windows and slowed. He concentrated on making his eyes shift so he could see better. Taking a deep breath, he pulled the outside air in through his nose and made his voice calm and stern. "Keep talking to me, kid. Are you walking in the field?"

There was more coughing.

A wave of nausea hit Rhys. *Hang in there, kid.* "Sterling! Where are you? Are you in a field? Can you see your house from where you are?" He hated sounding so rough, but he had to get Sterling to answer him.

"In the field. I can't see the house, I'm lying down." His voice was so slight Rhys wouldn't have been able to hear it without his sensitive hearing.

"Can you hear any cars?"

"No."

Damn, damn, damn. He gripped the steering wheel harder

244

to keep his hands from shaking. He couldn't remember ever being this unnerved. Rhys honked his horn. He was directly behind Sterling's house, overlooking a field he himself crossed in wolf form to check on the kid. "Can you hear a horn?"

There was no answer.

"Sterling?" Rhys stopped the car and pulled over to the side. God, please let him be right. Please let this be the field Sterling was crossing. He got out, taking his phone with him. "Sterling?" Why wasn't he answering? Lifting his face, Rhys scented the air. Blood. His fangs dropped. He sniffed again and took off toward the appealing aroma. His heart pounded so fast and hard he could hear it. Scanning the ground, he didn't see the kid anywhere but the scent was getting stronger. Sterling was here in this field...somewhere.

Closing his eyes, Rhys stopped and listened. To his left there was the sound of labored breathing. He turned and ran.

Sterling lay on his back in the tall grass.

The picture of Remi flashed through Rhys' mind, making him shiver. The similarities were staggering. Dropping the phone, Rhys fell to his knees, already reaching for Sterling.

Sterling was still. Even the rise and fall of his chest was faint and shallow. Rhys couldn't see color, but he knew Sterling's was off. His lips were the wrong tint and dark splotches of liquid dotted and ran down his face. He'd been coughing up blood. He was bleeding internally.

Tears gathered in Rhys' eyes, making him blink them away. Ingesting blood helped heal human mates, but there was no way Sterling could swallow anything. Scrambling for his back pocket, he retrieved his pocketknife and opened it. *God, please let this work.* It worked for Remi. Maybe because Sterling was his mate, it would work for them to.

He'd never been so afraid in his life. He slashed his wrist

with the knife, then cut open Sterling's shirt and cut a gash on his slim chest above his heart. As quickly as Rhys' pulse raced, his arm was already dripping at a rapid rate. He held it over Sterling's cut, getting in as much as he could. When his incision closed he cut it again and repeated the process.

It seemed to take forever.

Glancing down, Rhys noticed the phone on the ground next to Sterling, still clutched in his hand. His hands were almost elegant, with long slender fingers. No wonder he was so good at catching a football. Closing his eyes, Rhys let go and allowed himself to cry.

He'd learned quite a lot about the kid by watching him. The name Sterling fit him, he was so vibrant and full of life. He truly never stopped talking. It was like he had way too much energy and excitement to contain. It bubbled over by means of singing or carrying on a conversation with himself. Hell, not just himself, he talked to inanimate objects, strays, insects, everything.

Rhys had found himself enchanted.

Feeling the cut on his hand heal, he turned his attention back to his mate.

The cut on Sterling's chest closed. *Please, let that mean it worked.* Rhys dropped to sit on the ground and pulled Sterling into his arms.

Sterling coughed and blood flew out of his mouth onto Rhys' face and shirt. He turned his mate's head, trying to help him get the blood up.

While Sterling heaved the last of the blood from his lungs, Rhys took a deep breath and let relief wash through him. Sterling smelled like pack now. Like a wolf.

Finally, Sterling stopped coughing and fell into a peaceful sleep. Cuddling him closer, Rhys held him, listening to the sound of his breathing. It was calm and even...normal.

Sterling snuggled against him, burrowing his nose in Rhys' chest. There was even a soft snore.

Smiling, Rhys turned his face into his shoulder and brushed the tears off his face. In the background, wind rustled the grass, the crickets chirped, there were even some cars on nearby roads, but Rhys didn't want to move. Not yet. He just wanted to sit here and hold Sterling. It might be the last chance he got for several more years. But at least he'd have several more years. Sterling was here, safe.

"Sterling? Rhys?" Remi's frantic voice rang out, breaking the silence. Jake's followed. "Rhys? Sterling?"

"Over here." Rhys didn't yell, he knew they'd hear him. Grabbing his and Sterling's phones, he laid them on Sterling's chest and for the first time noticed a hardback notebook. Hmmm...that was odd. It must have come with Sterling, so Rhys picked it up and put it on Sterling as well. Getting his feet under him, he stood.

Remi ran to him, looking like death warmed over. "Oh God. No!" He reached for Sterling.

"Whoa." Jake scrambled to get Remi and pulled him back. He looked up at Rhys. "Hey, buddy. Everything okay?"

Huh? Rhys realized suddenly that he was growling. Taking another step back, he nodded.

"What's wrong with him?" Remi struggled against Jake's hold and reached for Sterling again.

This time Rhys was very aware of his growl and he made sure they saw his teeth. He wasn't ready to hand Sterling over yet.

Chapter Twenty

If Remi smoked he'd have gone through a pack already. As it was he was ready to collapse. Remi glanced at Sterling, lying on Jake's couch, and his anxiety kicked up a notch. "You're sure he'll be okay?"

Lifting his head from his hands, Jake sat up straight. "He'll be fine. You slept for a bit too." Jake narrowed his eyes, studying Remi intently. "Are you sure you're all right?"

"Yes." Remi looked down at his torn jeans and dirty shirt. He was achy from wiping out, but okay. Likely, he'd feel more pain after he was certain Sterling was fine, but at the moment he had too much on his mind. He forced himself to sit on the love seat next to Jake.

Sterling rolled over, his arm flopping off the couch and hanging over the edge. Remi, Jake and Rhys stared at him expectantly, but other than that he didn't budge.

After Rhys had stopped growling at them, they'd put Sterling in a pair of Remi's shorts and a T-shirt he'd left at Jake's. Between Remi and Rhys, they had managed to clean him up.

Sterling seemed peaceful, like he was asleep, and the bruises on his face were nearly gone. Whether it was Remi touching them or Rhys changing him into a wolf, Remi couldn't say, but he was glad. As nervous as he was over the fact that

Rhys had claimed Sterling as his, Remi was damned glad Rhys had gotten there when he did. If not, Sterling would have died.

"Do you know what happened?" Remi made a move to put Sterling's arm back on the couch, but Rhys beat him to it.

Lifting Sterling's feet out of his lap, Rhys got up from the end of the couch and put Sterling's arm across his chest. "No, he wasn't in a condition to tell me what happened. Did the two of you go by the house?"

Jake nodded. "There was no one there, just the smell of blood. Sterling's and their mom's from what I could tell."

Which was another thing that had Remi concerned. His mom's blood had been all over the place, but she'd been nowhere in sight. Her car was missing. Had she gone looking for Sterling after he'd left the house? Why hadn't she called Remi?

Scooting closer, Jake put his arm around Remi and hauled him close.

Remi gave in and rested his head on Jake's shoulder, needing the closeness of his mate. He felt his anxiety slowly ebb away and fatigue start to take over. But he couldn't go to sleep...not yet. He had to wait and watch after Sterling. Whatever happened, Sterling wasn't going back. Remi had already decided. He was going to take off with the kid as soon as he woke. Jake had assured him if it came to that, he'd go too, as did Rhys. So no matter what, Remi would have his brother and his mate.

Man, his eyes hurt. Maybe he could just close them for a second.

He must have drifted off to sleep, because the next thing he knew, his head was in Jake's lap. Jake's hand rubbed over his shoulder and the soothing tones of his deep voice tried to lull Remi back to sleep, but something kept pulling at him, telling him to wake up.

"I left while he was arguing with her. I'm not sure what happened after that. I just knew I had to get help," Sterling said.

Sterling? Sterling was awake. Blinking his eyes open, Remi sat up.

Jake gripped his shoulder. "Slow down, pup, he's fine."

Sterling came and squatted in front of him, touching his face. "Are you okay? Jake said you wrecked."

Ignoring the brief growl coming from Rhys' direction, Remi grabbed his brother and hugged him. "I'm okay. Just worried about you. You almost died."

"Yeah, I know, I could tell." Sterling drew back with a strange expression on his face and looked down at himself. He lifted his shirt, showing off a tanned, flawless stomach. "How am I not dead? I don't even hurt." Dropping his shirt, he cocked his head. "He beat me with the baton he carries when he's at work."

Oh God. Remi felt like someone had dumped ice water down his back.

"How am I okay? I was badly hurt. I was coughing up blood." Sterling frowned and turned so he could see Rhys. "I called you and you were coming to find me..."

Glancing at Jake, Rhys raised a brow.

Sterling spun around, his forehead furrowed at Jake.

"Rhys turned you into a werewolf." Jake rolled his eyes. "Chay is right. There just isn't an easy way to tell someone that."

Remi couldn't help himself, he burst into laughter. It really wasn't funny. His life was totally shit right now. His brother had been beaten to the brink of death then changed into a werewolf, his father was still out there somewhere, his mom was missing, his only transportation was now gone, yet here he was laughing so hard he had tears in his eyes.

Sterling, however, wasn't at all impressed. He glared. "Y'all are freaking me out."

Patting Remi's back, Jake grinned. "You gonna make it?"

Remi nodded, wiping the tears from his eyes. His mind had snapped, that was his only excuse.

"Well, who's going to show him?" Jake asked.

Rhys growled and got up from the couch. Walking over to Sterling, he put his hands on Sterling's shoulders and peered over his head at Remi and Jake.

Remi resisted the urge to tell Rhys to get his hands off Sterling, since Rhys hadn't done anything wrong. He'd been absolutely wonderful at looking out for Sterling. In fact, Remi couldn't have asked for a better guard, but somehow the sudden protectiveness made Remi's hackles rise. *He* was supposed to take care of Sterling. Sterling was *his* responsibility, not Rhys'. "I'll show him."

Standing, Remi stripped his shirt off and started to work on his jeans.

Sterling looked at Rhys. "What's he doing?"

"Shh... It's okay, kiddo, watch." Rhys' voice was so gentle, it made Remi pause. He hadn't heard that particular tone come from Rhys.

Apparently, neither had Jake. He was staring at Rhys like he'd never seen him before.

Remi shook himself out of his daze and finished undressing. He'd worry about the change in Rhys later, with all the other things on his list to worry about. First, he had to put his baby brother at ease. Rolling his shoulders back and stretching his neck out a few times, Remi began shifting.

His eyes changed first. Instead of blinking through it like he normally did, Remi just closed them and let the change overtake him. His teeth lengthened, poking out from under his lip. Then the goose bump sensation that came with growing fur hit him in a wave, rushing up and down his arms and legs.

He heard Sterling scream, like he was in a well. It sounded hollow and distant. Remi resisted the urge to stop and comfort him, knowing Jake and Rhys would take care of him. This was something Sterling had to see.

Remi's joints popped as his legs and arms reformed. It happened so quickly he was standing one moment and on all fours the next. The pulling sensation of his snout almost tickled as it lengthened. Last, the prickle along his spine that signaled his tail forming occurred and he was completely transformed.

The sound of rapid breathing breached Remi's senses, along with the occasionally whispered, "Oh my God." Slowly, Remi opened his eyes.

Sterling leaned back against Rhys, his face pale and his eyes unblinking. He stood there staring for several seconds, then a slow smile crept over his lips. "That is so freaking cool."

Getting up from the love seat, Jake knelt beside Remi and stroked his fur. When Sterling came forward, Jake moved back, allowing Sterling to touch Remi.

Rhys stood perfectly still, but Remi wasn't fooled. He was beginning to realize that Rhys was ready for anything. As if Remi would harm his brother. But then, since they'd found him a few hours ago, Rhys wasn't being exactly logical where Sterling was concerned.

Oh man. That's when it hit Remi. Sterling was Rhys' mate. Rhys acted like Jake did in regards to Remi. He was overprotective.

Petting Remi's fur, Sterling dropped to his butt and looked

Remi in the eye. He touched Remi's nose. "Remi?" Scrunching up his nose, Sterling grabbed Remi's face in both hands and looked at him. "It is you, isn't it?" Sterling started laughing and launched himself at Remi, wrapping his arms around Remi's neck and nearly knocking him to the ground.

Letting out the breath he'd been holding, Remi lapped at his brother's cheek. He should've known Sterling wouldn't freak. Hell, he should have known Sterling would think it was cool.

"I've always wanted a dog." Laughing harder, Sterling ruffled the fur on the top of Remi's head.

Jake and Rhys both groaned. One of them mumbled, "Wolf not dog," but Remi would have laughed if he'd been able. Sterling was taking this very well. Much better than Remi had. Remi had fainted when he'd found out. That still chafed at his ego.

Suddenly, the laughter ceased and Sterling's arms disappeared from around his neck. "You asshole." Sterling shoved him hard, nearly knocking him down, then his brother jumped to his feet.

Stumbling sideways, Remi tried to figure out what the hell had happened.

Jake was there instantly, putting himself between Remi and Sterling. "Sterling?"

"No." Walking to Jake's side, Sterling glared at Remi and pointed his finger. "You didn't tell me. How could you keep something like this from me?" His face grew red with anger. "You lied to me, Remi! This is where you've been. Hunting, my ass." Scoffing, he turned away.

Remi changed back so fast he got dizzy and would have fallen if Jake hadn't caught him. *Whoa.* Clutching his mate's arms for a minute, he tried to get his bearings.

"Slow down, pup. He's had a shock." Jake tipped his chin and kissed him.

Easy for you to say. Remi let himself lean into the kiss for just a second before letting Jake go. "Sterling, we couldn't tell you. Would you have believed us?" He felt a little on the ridiculous side, having this conversation naked. Where were his fucking clothes?

Rhys was talking to Sterling, trying to get him to understand.

"What is the world coming to? What is with all the damn lies? First Mom lies then—" Sterling stopped. "Oh God." He looked around, suddenly frantic. "Where is it?"

Remi froze. "Where's what?"

Sterling started lifting couch cushions. Running to Rhys, he grabbed his arms and tugged. "Where is it? Where's the book?"

"What book?" Jake asked, handing Remi his jock and jeans.

"The diary." Sterling jerked on Rhys' arms again. "Where is the diary?"

Rhys untangled his forearms from Sterling's grasp. "Shh... Calm down. I got it, it's in my car. Let me go get it." He headed for the front door and Jake followed, standing at the door watching as Rhys went out.

As soon as he jerked on his jock and jeans, Remi went to his brother. "Sterling?"

He blinked at Remi. "I found it in my nightstand today with a piece of paper between the pages. She must have put it there."

Rhys came back in with a leather-bound book, and Jake locked the door behind him.

Racing over to Rhys, Sterling snatched the book and began

thumbing through it. "She claims that Dirk killed someone." He stopped and frowned at Remi. "Did you have a friend named Billy?"

♋∽⧏

"I don't like him going with Rhys."

Jake sat on the edge of his bed, feeling tired to the bone. What a day. "I know you don't, but it's better than him being here. If Dirk comes here with the police to get him back, he's shit out of luck."

Remi dragged his hands through his hair. "I know, but—" Wincing when he hit a tangle, he put his hands down. "He's Rhys' mate. You realize that, don't you?"

Jake had decided the same thing, although Rhys hadn't said so.

"Sterling is too young for a relationship, he's just a—"

Whoa. Remi didn't honestly think... "Remi... Rhys is a lot of things, but he's not some sicko pedophile. With Rhys, Sterling is completely safe...from everyone."

Remi sighed but he nodded. "I just worry about him. How long do you think it will take Rhys to get that diary to the FBI?"

"He and Sterling are going tonight. He said he'd call when he had it in the hands of the authorities." Jake heaved himself up and snagged his mate's hand. "Come on, we need a shower. You're covered in dirt." And Jake didn't want to think about why Remi was filthy. That wreck was going to haunt him for weeks to come. He pulled Remi toward the master bathroom and started undressing him.

Remi just stood there, still thinking things through, Jake supposed.

"You want to drive my bike or the Tahoe until we get you another vehicle?"

"Huh?" Looking down at Jake, Remi stepped out of his jock and pants. "Jake, I can't afford another vehicle right now. You said you thought Gadget might be able to fix it."

If anyone *could* fix it, it would be Gadget. He'd gone to pick it up, but Jake hadn't heard anything back from him, not that he expected to tonight.

Standing, Jake turned on the shower to let the water heat up. After getting them both towels, he shucked his own pants. He'd taken the rest of his clothes off in the bedroom while listening to Remi fret about every little thing. "You're getting awfully lippy lately." He swatted Remi on the bare ass. "Get in the shower."

Chuckling, Remi climbed into the shower and held the glass door open for Jake. "I've got a lot on my mind."

"Don't we all?" Jake shut the door, hauled Remi under the spray and kissed him. "Trust me. Everything is going to be okay. Rhys will get the book to the FBI and get them to re-examine the case. Dirk will go to jail. In the meantime, Rhys will keep Sterling hidden and safe."

"He's mad at me, Jake." Remi's shoulders hunched. "He was really pissed about me not telling him about wolves."

"He'll get over it." Catching Remi's chin, Jake made him look up. "The important thing is that he's alive and now he's gonna be damn hard to kill." He caressed Remi's cheek with his thumb, staring into his pale green eyes.

Remi melted and nuzzled like he always did.

Brushing his lips across Remi's, Jake pulled him close and rested their foreheads together. "You scared me tonight. I thought I might have lost you."

"I'm sorry." Remi caught Jake's lips with his teeth and wrapped his arms around Jake's waist. His cock began to harden against Jake's hip, and the smell of arousal filled the shower.

Jake rubbed his body back and forth, touching Remi's, enjoying the feel of the hard warmth on his own. He loved the way Remi felt and how Remi responded so quickly to his touch. His prick was rapidly approaching hard. "No more pulling away. I'm not letting you go. Whatever comes, we'll get through it together."

Snaking a hand down to capture Jake's erection, Remi tilted his head and offered his throat. "No more, I promise."

Jake growled, spun Remi around and put his back toward the spray. "Put your hands around the showerhead, pup, and don't move them."

"Yes, sir." Remi's gaze skimmed over his body. When it got to Jake's cock, he licked his lips.

Good God, he'd missed that eagerness. Groaning, Jake grabbed the mesh sponge and shower gel off the shelf to Remi's right. He soaped the sponge and let his gaze linger over his mate.

Remi swallowed hard and his belly contracted. Was that a small shiver?

Working up the suds, Jake put the bottle back and started on Remi's arms. He took his time running the sponge over the planes of Remi's firm chest and shoulders. When he got to the cobbled stomach, he couldn't help but play a little and follow the intriguing ripples of Remi's abs. Slipping further, he grazed Remi's cock with the sponge.

Remi moaned and went on his tiptoes, arching his hips toward Jake, but he didn't drop his hands.

Good. Jake decided to reward him for it. Squeezing the

suds onto Remi's cock, he wrapped his hand around it. Damned if Remi didn't whimper. Jake stroked up and down a few times, enjoying the way Remi's prick tensed in his palm. He kept it up until Remi started fucking his hand, then he let go. "No one gave you permission to move, pup."

"Unh." Dropping his chin, Remi relaxed. His damp hair hung in front of his face and onto his chest. His prick bobbed out, begging to be touched.

Desire speared through Jake, but he wasn't going to rush this. He hadn't gotten to play with his mate in days. He wanted Remi mad with lust and to forget about all their problems for a while. Hell, he wanted that himself. Quickly, he washed Remi's legs and feet.

Remi peered down at him through a web of wet black hair. His canine green eyes glowed almost eerily, and the tips of his fangs peeked out from under his lips.

Standing, Jake kissed him and let his tongue slip into Remi's mouth for a brief caress. "Turn around and put your hands back around the showerhead."

"Yes, sir." Remi turned, presenting Jake with a delectable view of his pretty little ass.

Fuck me. Jake shook off the need in favor of tormenting his mate, but it wasn't easy. His cock was aching to be buried inside Remi's body. Already precome was seeping from his prick, and he knew Remi's was as well, he could smell it.

Jake dragged the sponge down Remi's spine so faintly he knew it tickled, but Remi stood still. Making small circles, Jake lathered the wide shoulders, narrow waist and firm globes of Remi's butt. He worked his way down one leg, then up the other, pleased with the sounds of pleasure echoing in the stall. Washing out the sponge, Jake stood back and admired the view.

White suds cascaded down Remi's body, mixing with the water swirling around his feet.

Jake moaned. He would never get tired of looking at this man. "Lean back. Leave your hands where they are and step back. Stick your butt out." He'd only meant to guide Remi into the spray to rinse the soap, but damned if that wasn't a nice position.

Remi stood there with his ass presented so nicely. A shudder wracked his body, making the skin on his back ripple and the scars dance.

Jake set the sponge back on the ledge and knelt. His hands went to his mate's ass. "Let go of the nozzle and put your hands flat against the wall." Once Remi complied, Jake snaked his tongue through Remi's crease and probed his hole. *Mmm... Rich, tangy, completely Remi.* His eyes blurred and his fangs pushed through his gums.

Remi moaned and mashed himself back onto Jake's face.

Continuing the exploration, Jake didn't let up. He laved, circled and even stabbed his tongue at Remi's hole. His cock jerked at the long, drawn-out mewling sounds Remi made. If that wasn't the sweetest...

Remi pressed back and his breath sped up slightly. "Oh God yes, please..."

Tracing the tight pucker with his tongue, Jake slipped his hands down and rubbed his thumbs against Remi's balls. They were close to his body, testifying to his arousal as loudly as his scent and sounds.

Cupping his hand around them, Jake pulled them closer and licked his way down to the taut sacks before lightly sucking on them.

"Please...I need you to fuck me." Remi's legs shook.

Jake could no longer bear it. He wasn't just torturing Remi, he was torturing himself as well. He was dying to be buried in his mate's body. Snagging the shower gel off the ledge, he coated his cock with it and dripped some down Remi's crease. He pushed one finger into Remi's ass then another.

Remi whined and pushed back, impaling himself further as Jake replaced the bottle on the shelf.

Extracting his fingers, Jake lined up his cock and thrust. He clutched Remi's hips and sank all the way into Remi's greedy body with a hiss.

Nodding, Remi whined and arched his back. "Please..."

Jake growled, feeling his mate's need as keenly as his own. He slipped one hand around Remi's chest and clutched Remi's hip with the other as he shoved in. He fucked Remi hard and fast. The wet slap of skin grew louder than the water hitting the shower floor. The steam made it harder to breathe, or was that exertion? Jake hammered into his mate and Remi was with him the whole way, pushing himself back on Jake's cock. It was the best proof he was okay that Jake could ask for. He was never going to let Remi go.

"Mine." Jake was so close, his balls tight, he had to make sure Remi was with him. Sliding a hand down Remi's chest, he gripped Remi's cock and pumped a few times.

"Yours." Panting, Remi nodded. "Bite me. Please bite me." His voice was hoarse, strained, as he continued to writhe.

Just the thought of Remi's blood flowing over his tongue catapulted Jake over the edge into orgasm. He thrust forward one last time before his body tensed and tingled. A shiver raced up his spine, taking his breath. Not even bothering to move Remi's hair, he bit into the top of Remi's shoulder.

Remi's cock jerked then he arched forward. His ass gripped Jake's prick and he moaned as the musky aroma of spunk pierced the air.

Jake wasn't entirely sure how it happened but they both ended up slumped against a shower wall staring dazedly at one another.

Blood trickled down Remi's chest. Even as exhausted and sated as he was, Jake had the urge to lick it off. God, Remi was handsome with his hair plastered to his face, sprawled in the shower and... He was sound asleep.

I love you, pup. Grinning, Jake got up and turned off the water. He was pretty damn exhausted too. Remi and Sterling had taken years off his life tonight. But at least now the hard part was over. Dirk would soon be out of the picture, and Remi and Sterling were safe.

Remi woke when Jake opened the shower door. Blinking heavy-lidded eyes up at Jake, he smiled. "Hey."

"Hey." Jake helped Remi up and dried him off before allowing him to stumble into the bedroom.

When he got to the bedroom, Jake found his mate sprawled out on the bed. Gathering Remi to his chest, he covered them both up. He loved how Remi fit in his arms.

Jake was nearly asleep when Remi raised his head off Jake's chest. Jake cracked open one eye to see what his mate was up to.

Inhaling deeply, Remi turned his head. "Jake?" Remi whispered. "Do you smell that?"

Jake sniffed. He did smell an unusual scent. Unusual for his house anyway.

"It smells like alcohol." Remi's nose wrinkled and his brow creased.

It *did* smell like whiskey. But now there was something else...something stronger. Smoke.

Chapter Twenty-One

Jake was right, there *was* smoke. Remi hadn't first smelled it. Where was it coming from? He hurried into his pants, not bothering with a shirt, as Jake hopped and skipped toward the door while putting on his jeans. "Don't open the door without feeling." Racing to the bedroom door, Remi felt it for heat. There wasn't any. Touching the doorknob to check it first, he opened the door.

Jake stepped beside him into the hall, inhaling through his nose. "The backyard." Hurrying toward the back door, he reached for the knob, but Remi got there first and knocked his hand away.

"Check it."

"It's outside."

"Fires happen outside too. How do you know you aren't opening the door and walking into flames? Besides, it's a fire-rated door. It will help keep it from spreading if it's closed." Remi touched the surface and didn't feel anything so he opened it.

Heat fanned his face immediately. The glow of flames came from beside the door. The back deck had not yet become an uncontrollable blaze. How had it started? "Get me the fire extinguisher."

"Let go of me, you son of a bitch." A hoarse yell came from the back fence line followed by a canine yelp.

Jake brushed past Remi and ran out the door.

What the—? People were fighting. No, not people. Dirk was trying to fight off a couple of wolves. *Fuck.* Remi frowned but didn't have time to think about it right now. He had to get this fire under control before it grew too big. Where in the hell was the fire extinguisher? *Garage.* He'd seen one on the wall next to the big toolbox.

Running to the garage, he located the extinguisher and yanked it off the wall. He pulled the pin out and had it ready to use by the time he got outside. Luckily, since most of Jake's house was stucco but for some wood railing and the back deck, the fire hadn't gone any further and Remi was able to get it out without much difficulty.

Confident that the fire was out, he ditched the extinguisher and turned his attention to the yelling and cursing going on in the backyard.

"Call these fucking dogs off and get that little bastard out here," Dirk yelled at Jake and charged him.

The wolves let out a deep, rumbling growl and bared their teeth.

Jake sidestepped and faced Dirk as he rushed by. "I don't know what you're talking about."

The wolves hurried to flank Jake, still snarling, then two more came over the fence and joined them. What were they doing here?

Remi ran into the foray with his adrenaline already high from the small fire. He guessed he had his answer as to how the fire started. Jake had been right in sending Sterling with Rhys. At the moment all he wanted was a little revenge for his brother. "What the fuck do you want?"

263

Dirk turned on him, his face red and twisted. He looked like hell. His clothes were all over the place, his white, blood-splattered shirt half tucked in, half not. His long hair was tangled, sticking up in all directions, and had leaves clinging to it. "You little fucker, this is your fault. All of it."

Expecting Dirk to lunge, Remi braced himself. But Dirk didn't move forward. He stood there, a blank look on his face. "You killed her just like you killed that fucking faggot."

What? Killed her? Who? Dirk had finally gone completely mad. He was blaming Remi for Billy's death? The odd realization zapped the energy right out of him.

Jake rushed to Remi's side, as did their other four pack members, but Remi remained focused on Dirk.

He appeared every inch the madman. Remi almost pitied him...almost. Then it occurred to him what else Dirk had said. *Her. Oh God, no.* It felt like someone had taken a baseball bat to his stomach. "What did you do to my mother?"

"If it weren't for you, none of it would've happened." Tears streamed down Dirk's face and spit flew from his mouth. "She would have been happy if you'd never been born. She blamed me for running you off. I tried to help you. I tried so hard to make you do right. It worked for awhile, then you got caught up with this"—he raised his hand, indicating Jake—"loser." Dirk shook his head and the volume of his voice lowered. "You made me do it. You made me kill that little fag. Just like it's your fault Sterling got what was coming to him. He upset your mother, telling her he wanted to live with you. Then she started talking about leaving and how she'd lost you boys. Like the two of you meant more to her than me."

"What are you talking about?" Remi's stomach sank. It felt like he'd swallowed rocks and they'd gotten caught on the way down. What had Dirk done? "Where is she?"

Dirk reached under his un-tucked shirt. "Gone. You killed her."

Tears stung Remi's eyes. No, she couldn't be. Not now, when they were so close to freedom. She'd survived too many beatings to be dead.

Jake stepped in front of Remi, knocking him down, then a blur of black fur jumped at Jake.

A loud pop sounded.

Jake roared and leapt forward over a black lump.

Remi blinked, trying to focus. A wolf lay on the ground. The smell of blood slammed into him. Crawling forward, he grabbed his pack member.

Another wolf had Dirk's hand in his mouth, and was growling and shaking. Something fell and Dirk ran. Jake took off after him. As did three of the four wolves.

A gun, Dirk's service revolver, lay in the grass several feet above them. No. Remi glanced down at the wolf in his lap. Zack. It was Zack. He didn't know how he knew, but he did...he could feel it.

Tracing his hands over Zack's fur, Remi found the blood right dead center of the chest where the heart was. "Hang on, Zack." He put his hand over the fur and willed it to heal. He'd helped Rhys and Eddie. He'd made Keaton's cut close. He could do this.

Zack's heart was still pumping, Remi could feel its beat. The rhythm grew slow and the blood felt as though it was gushing out, but there was still a heartbeat. Zack's chest rose and stuttered back down several times. More and more time passed between each breath. Blood continued to soak Remi's hands.

Remi pushed harder. Wolves could heal anything, couldn't

they? Why wasn't the bleeding slowing? Remi's eyes blurred. Tears streamed down his cheeks, but he brushed them away with the back of his hand. He was aware of the other wolf, and that the yelling had stopped, but he kept his hands on Zack. Closing his eyes, he pictured Zack well. *Heal, damn it.* It had to work. *Please be better.* The inconsistent thud against Remi's hand stopped and Zack exhaled.

No. Remi moved his hands, bringing them up to look at them. They were covered in blood. It dripped down his forearms into the grass with the rest of Zack's blood. This couldn't be happening. Shaking his head, Remi wiped at his eyes again with the back of his wrist. Zack couldn't be dead. He'd saved Jake. He couldn't— Remi shivered, freezing all of a sudden in spite of the fact he was sweating. A sense of emptiness overwhelmed him and took his breath away. *Zack is gone.* Remi could feel it. A connection had been severed. Not only was Zack a friend, but Remi's body seemed to know he was also pack. He could feel where all the men were, at least his mate and their immediate pack. It was strange and he hadn't been aware of it until now, but he had a bond with the six men who made up their core pack. It wasn't like he was psychic or anything, but he was always aware of their presence...their feelings.

The wolf that stayed in the yard with Remi and Zack shifted. Remi didn't know him.

"Remi?" The muscular, dark-haired man tugged him away. "We have to take Zack away. The police will be here soon."

"He's gone. I couldn't help him, I tried but—" He shook his head. Zack was dead, his mom was dead. Dirk was— Remi tried pulling away from the stranger, even though his senses told him the man was pack.

The other wolf who'd been there from the beginning, Nick— how could he have ever thought all wolves looked alike?—was standing over Zack. He lifted his head skyward and let out a mournful howl. Somewhere in the distance another wolf howled back, then another and another.

Jake came through the back gate followed by the wolves he'd left with. "We lost him."

Remi looked at the unknown pack member lifting Zack into his arms. He had tears in his eyes. Remi started forward and two strong hands pulled him back.

"It's okay. Bambi is Zack's brother." Jake wrapped one arm around Remi's chest and addressed the others. "Shift and get dressed. Did someone call the police?"

Bambi? Remi stood there feeling numb all over and stared at Zack's lifeless body.

Gadget nodded, watching Bambi carry Zack out of the yard. "The police are on their way. So are Rhys and Sterling." He followed Zack's brother.

ↂↂ

Sitting on the back porch, a cup of coffee in hand, Remi stared at the spot where Zack had been. The police were still swarming all over the place, talking to Jake and Nick. Bambi, Zack's brother, had come back a few moments ago and was standing with them. Someone—Gadget, Remi thought—had pushed a cup of coffee in his hands and wrapped a blanket around his shoulders. All of his and Jake's inner circle were here, except for Zack and Rhys. From what Remi had gathered, Rhys had called them to patrol the house and make sure Remi and Jake were safe for the night.

His mother was still missing, but Dirk had been caught and arrested. Not just for arson and assault, because Rhys had gotten the diary to the authorities and Dirk was being held for questioning by the FBI as well.

Remi was trying his best not to worry about his mother. She'd survived beatings before, maybe...

He glanced up to check on Jake again, even though he didn't need to. Nick and Dago stood guard as Jake talked to a policeman. Jake turned his head in the middle of his conversation and gave Remi a weak smile.

Remi tried to smile back, but he didn't think he was all that successful.

"Lassiter?" A cop Remi knew from working fire, came up. Douglas, something? Sheffield? Yeah, that was it, Douglas Sheffield. Sheffield looked like he was going to a funeral. He glanced around, his gaze not meeting Remi's for a few moments.

Remi closed his eyes, barely holding back his tears. He already knew what Sheffield was going to say. "You found her body?" He opened his eyes and glanced up at the officer.

"Yes, I'm sorry." Sheffield seemed like he didn't know what to do and Remi felt for him. Delivering that kind of news wasn't easy. He'd done it once, accompanied by a policeman after a fire had swept through an apartment complex.

"Can you give me any information? Where you found her? How she was killed?"

"Out back of her house. Officially, it's under investigation"—Sheffield glanced around—"but from what I heard it looks like blunt force trauma to the head."

"Thank you."

Sheffield nodded. "Is there anything I can do for you?"

"No. Thanks though."

He nodded one last time and walked off. The rest of the policemen finished taking pictures and talking to witnesses as

Remi stared at his bare feet. *Oh God, how am I going to break it to Sterling?*

"I'm sorry, pup." Jake sat next to him, putting his arm over Remi's shoulders and kissing his temple.

"Jake?" Tank stepped up to the porch. The rest of the men came up with him.

Catching Remi's face in his palms, Jake made him look up. "We need to take a new member in Zack's place."

What? How could he think of that right now? Remi shook his head.

"Yes. We cannot leave the pack vulnerable. The core members must be replaced."

"Jesus, Jake. He just died." Zack wasn't just a pack member, he was a friend. Didn't Jake feel his loss? Couldn't he feel the emptiness?

Jake nodded. "Very bravely, protecting his alpha and his omega." Jake held out his hand to Zack's brother.

The man, Bambi—what an odd name—stepped forward. He was big and burly and, well, he appeared every inch the biker. He was Native American and big like Jake, Rhys and Tank.

Bambi knelt and peered up at Jake. He gave Jake his oath, vowing to protect the pack. A strange tingly sensation raced up Remi's spine, making him shiver. It was the weirdest thing. It was like...he could feel Bambi. The bareness that Zack's death created was full.

How had he never noticed this strange connection? Had he been too busy finding his way as Jake's mate to recognize it? He felt guilty. Zack was his friend and he couldn't be replaced so easily, yet the strange blank feeling was gone. The sadness remained.

Bambi turned to Remi. His eyes were red, his face tear-stained, but he managed a smile. "It's an honor. Zack spoke very highly of you."

Remi didn't know what to say. He touched Bambi's shoulder and nodded, still feeling like a traitor.

"Remi!" Sterling came bursting through the wooden gate with Rhys on his heels. "Remi!"

Bambi hurried to his feet and Remi stood, raising his arms just in time to catch Sterling. He hugged him tight, looking over his shoulder at Rhys. *Thank you,* he mouthed.

"You're welcome." Rhys dipped his head and greeted Bambi, welcoming him.

Holding on to his brother, Remi tried to focus. He had to figure out how to tell Sterling about their mother, but he wasn't sure he could. Then Jake's arms encircled Remi from behind, giving him strength. Jake was okay. Sterling was okay. Eventually, everything else would be too. It felt wrong for him to think that, yet he couldn't help but feel a sense of relief even with all the misery. In a way, he'd already grieved for his mother. He'd known she would die by Dirk's hand.

Later that night after Sterling had cried himself to sleep, Remi sat on the edge of Jake's bed.

Jake came in the room and sat beside him. He didn't say anything, just stayed there next to Remi, his hand on Remi's thigh. It was the most peace and comfort Remi had felt in hours. Jake always made him feel that way, but now even more so. "How are you holding up?"

"Better, because you're here." Remi gazed at his mate. "Guess it's really over."

"It is." Jake drew Remi close, pulling him into his lap.

"I love you, Jake."

"I love you too."

That was all it took. Remi let it all out. He cried for his mother, for Zack, because his brother nearly died and he could have lost Jake. He cried because it was finally over. And when he had no more tears, he just sat there, leaning into his mate. It was going to be all right.

Epilogue

Sterling popped his head around the doorframe of Remi and Jake's bedroom. "Jake says if you don't hurry up, he's leaving you here."

Groaning, Remi closed the laptop and followed his brother. He was halfway down the hall when Sterling came running back around the corner and plowed into him. His nose mashed up against Sterling's forehead.

"Oof." Sterling didn't even stop, just continued down the hall to his bedroom.

"Ow." Remi grabbed his nose.

"Sorry."

Groaning and rubbing his nose, Remi went to the living room.

"What was taking so long?" Jake stood by the door with his helmet under his arm and Remi's in his hand.

"I was sending off my acceptance for the EMT position."

Jake handed Remi his helmet. "You already did that."

"No, I sent in the application and got accepted. I just wrote back to confirm that *I* accepted the offer." Remi took his helmet and put it on.

"Why are you rubbing your nose?"

"Because Sterling ran into it."

"I said I was sorry." Sterling came back with his own helmet under his arm.

Remi frowned. They all had helmets and Remi had no bike. Gadget had been unsuccessful in fixing Remi's. "How the hell are we all going to fit on your bike?"

"We aren't. Ster—" The sound of several motorcycles roared up outside and Jake opened the door. "Sterling is riding with one of the guys."

Putting his helmet on, Sterling bounded out the door.

Remi walked out the door and waited for Jake to follow. "Why are we going so early? It's still an hour until nightfall."

Shutting the door, Jake locked it. "I thought it might be nice to get there early for Sterling's first full moon." Without looking at Remi, Jake headed toward his bike that he'd already taken out of the garage. What was he up to?

Remi turned, studying their pack, trying to figure out what was going on.

Gadget was already starting shit with Bambi, which had become the norm. They were arguing back and forth over the rumble of Harley engines. Remi still missed Zack, but Bambi fit right in—if one could discount the constant squabbling over Gadget trying to tell Bambi what to do.

Matt waved from a bike that looked very much like Dago's. Gadget's other older boy, Logan, looked bored sitting behind Gadget. Nick and Tank gave Remi a flip of their chins in greeting. Where was Dago?

Remi returned the gesture and waved to Matt. He didn't even have to guess where Sterling was. Which was probably the best place for him.

Rhys was proving to be great at keeping the kid in line. The only real issue they had was Sterling's constant flirting, but

Rhys seemed to take it in stride. He'd become pretty good at dissuading that sort of attention. He was also the only one who didn't seem to mind the constant chatter. Last week, he'd spent the day of Sterling's fifteenth birthday with them, and Remi was surprised to find that most of the time Rhys didn't have a problem following Sterling's sporadic conversations.

Remi had been thoroughly impressed. Even after almost a month of living together, Jake still got lost and looked at Remi for translation.

"Come on, pup." Jake started his bike.

Climbing on the back of the Harley, Remi grabbed Jake's waist. He sat back and enjoyed the ride, feeling the wind on his face. They were still planning on moving their pack, but John Carter was giving them time to decide where to go. Jake had bargained with the other alpha and gained them use of pack land until Sterling graduated high school. All in all, everything was really coming together, and Remi was happier than he'd ever been.

A faint growl sounded to the left over the wind. Remi looked over in time to catch Rhys removing Sterling's hand from Rhys' groin. Remi rolled his eyes and joined Rhys' growl.

Sterling jerked his head to the right, caught Remi's gaze and blushed.

Good God. Remi glared and mouthed, "Behave," barely holding back a grin. Knowing Rhys' stance on his and Sterling's relationship almost made the whole thing funny...almost. The kid and his raging hormones were persistent though. Remi actually felt sorry for Rhys. Rhys was all about what was best for Sterling, much to Sterling's chagrin. That included no messing around until Sterling was out of school. Now that had been an amusing conversation to overhear. Remi grinned. Wolf hearing came in handy at times.

His shoulders slumping, Sterling turned his attention forward.

Hey, wait a minute. Remi frowned, taking in their scenery. They'd passed their normal hunting grounds. Jake *was* up to something.

Just about the time Remi decided to ask where they were going, Jake pulled onto a dirt trail and slowed. Coming to a halt in front of a copse of trees, he cut the engine.

"Where are we?" Remi climbed off the bike and removed his helmet.

As the others pulled up behind them, Jake took off his and put it on the handlebars. "We're at our new hunting grounds. It's still pack land, but it's unmarked and on the outskirts of the pack land. John and I thought it would be best to separate our packs as much as possible."

Dago came out from the trees, smiling. "Hey."

How had Dago gotten here? They were all up to something. "Hey."

Running up to them, Sterling bounced on his toes and looked at Jake expectantly.

Jake groaned. "It's killing you, isn't it?"

Nodding, Sterling squinted at the trees, like he was trying to see through them.

"What's going on?" Remi squinted too, but he didn't see anything. He took a whiff and didn't smell anything unusual either. He raised a brow at his high-handed mate.

Chuckling, Jake dug into his pocket and pulled out a key ring with one key on it. He threw it to Sterling. "By all means, show your brother what's going on."

Catching the key, Sterling smiled. "Really?"

"Oh absolutely, you've kept the secret a whole week, it

must be a record. You deserve to be rewarded."

"Jake—"

Sterling grabbed Remi's hand and jerked him toward the trees.

"To the left," Dago yelled from behind them.

Switching directions, Sterling nearly ripped Remi's arm out of the socket. A branch he pushed past came back and whacked Remi in the chest.

"Oof. Sterling, for the love of—" A brand new shiny Harley Sportster with orange tank and fenders sat in the clearing. "What the—"

"Jake and I picked it out last week when you were at work. We even got to test-drive it." Sterling tugged him toward the bike. "It's been at Rhys' for the last three days." Sterling tossed him the key.

Remi stood there, his mouth ajar, and let the key hit him in the chest.

Stepping up beside him, Jake picked up the key. He took Remi's hand and put the key in it.

The bike was for him? No one had ever given him something like that. Hell, he didn't own anything as nice as— What was he thinking? He couldn't accept it. Jake had already done so much for him.

"Stop shaking your head. I'm not taking it back." Jake kissed his cheek and squeezed his shoulders.

"But—"

Jake growled. "Just say, 'I love you too, Jake. Thank you. What a great bike.' Then go look at it before we go hunt."

Remi turned around, still thinking about arguing. He couldn't let Jake buy him—

Everyone else sank into the background talking to one

With Caution

another. Some even started undressing, preparing to shift. They all pretended not to listen, but Remi didn't miss the sideways glances.

Jake stood there, gazing down at him, a soft smile on his face. "Yes?"

"I do love you too, but—"

"Then prove it by taking the bike without giving me any shit." Jake grinned and grabbed his face. He slanted his mouth over Remi's, giving him no room to protest. Jake pulled back. "Congratulations on the EMT position."

Everything in him argued that the bike was way too much, but it obviously made Jake happy to give it to him. Making Jake happy made Remi happy. And it was a fucking great bike. Taking a deep breath, he grinned. "Fine, you win."

"I always do, pup." Jake nipped Remi's bottom lip. "Now say, 'Thank you, sir,' and let's go look at your new bike."

Chuckling, Remi nodded. He couldn't remember ever being this happy. He had Jake, Sterling was safe and Remi was finally allowed to live his own life. "Thank you, si—"

"Oh, man! I thought y'all said this was easy."

Huh? Remi turned toward Sterling's voice.

Sterling stood in the middle of their pack, who'd all shifted already, naked with his back to Remi and Jake. The other wolves stared at Sterling with their heads cocked to the side.

Turning, Sterling held up fur-covered, claw-like hands. "I think I screwed up."

How had he done that? The only wolf Remi knew of who could change more than their eyes and teeth without a full shift was Keaton. And Keaton had three—

"Holy shit, he has three forms." Jake gasped. "I guess it's a good thing we don't have to leave right away. Looks like Keaton

277

just got himself a new student."

Remi nodded his agreement. *Holy shit.*

About the Author

JL has been talking since she was about seven months old. To those who know her it comes as no surprise, in fact, most will tell you she hasn't shut up since. At eighteen months, she was speaking in full sentences. Imagine if you will the surprise of her admirers when they complimented her mother on "what a cute little boy" she had and received a fierce glare from said little boy and a very loud correction of "I'm a girl!" Oddly enough, JL still finds herself saying that exact phrase thirty-some-odd years later.

Today JL is a full-time writer, with over ten novels to her credit. Among her hobbies she includes reading, practicing her marksmanship (she happens to be a great shot), gardening, working out (although she despises cardio), searching for the perfect chocolate dessert (so far as she can tell ALL chocolate is perfect, but it requires more research) and arguing with her husband over who the air compressor and nail gun really belong to (they belong to JL, although she might be willing to trade him for his new chainsaw).

To learn more about J.L. Langley, please visit www.jllangley.com. Send an email to J.L. at 10star@jllangley.com or join her Yahoo! group to join in the fun with other readers as well as J.L.! http://groups.yahoo.com/group/the_yellow_rose/

Talk about a compromising situation!

My Fair Captain
© 2007 J.L. Langley

A storm of political intrigue, murderous mayhem and sexual hungers is brewing on planet Regelence.

Swarthy Intergalactic Navy Captain Nathaniel Hawkins ran from a past he had no intention of ever reliving. But when his Admiral asks him to use his peerage, as an earl and the heir to a dukedom, to investigate a missing weapons stash, he's forced to do just that. As if being undercover on a Regency planet where the young men are supposed to remain pure until marriage isn't bad enough, Nate finds himself attracted to the king's unmarried son.

All Prince Aiden Townsend has ever wanted was to be an artist. He has no interest in a marriage of political fortune or becoming a societal paragon. Until he lands in the arms of the mysterious Earl of Deverell. One look at Nate's handsome face has Aiden reconsidering his future. Not only does Nate make a virile subject for Aiden's art, but the great war hero awakens feelings in Aiden he has never felt, feelings he can't ignore.

After a momentous dance at a season ball, Aiden and Nate find themselves exchanging important information and working closely together. They have to fight their growing attraction long enough to find out who stole the weapons and keep themselves from a compromising situation and certain scandal.

Warning, this title contains the following: explicit sex, graphic language, violence, hot nekkid man-love.

Available now in ebook and print from Samhain Publishing.

Enjoy the following excerpt from My Fair Captain...

The window to Nate's left shattered.

Shit. Nate hit the ground, landing flat on his stomach. A white polo ball rolled across the wood floor and onto the rug, coming to a stop inches in front of Nate's face. *What the...* He picked up the ball, got to his feet and crossed to the broken window.

"Hello there." A young man with wide shoulders and a friendly smile waved from atop a sorrel horse. "Sorry about that. I didn't hit you, did I?"

Nate shook his head. "No, you didn't hit me." He held up the ball. "Would you like this back?"

"Yes, please. Are you the earl?" the horseman asked.

"Yes, and who might you be?" Nate tossed the ball out.

"I'm Prince Colton. Pleasure to meet you, milord." He tipped his head and heeled his mount off toward the ball.

Colton? The second to youngest prince. Judging from the looks of him and the similarity to the other two gentlemen Nate had seen since his arrival, he realized they were probably siblings. Good Galaxy, the royal family was a handful. He was starting to get a suspicion as to why Jeffers was shut down.

Stepping away from the window, a rustling sound made Nate stop mid-stride. Leaves rained down and a grunt came from above. "Bloody black hole and imploding stars," a soft masculine voice hissed.

Way up in the tree closest to the window, a boy balanced precariously on a thin tree limb. He reached toward a flat computer screen of some sort that had snagged on an adjacent branch. At his unbalanced angle a fall seemed imminent. Likely a shout to be careful would bring the teen plummeting to the ground, so Nate raced to a set of French doors on his left. Hurrying outside, he got to the base of the tree just as the branch the kid balanced on snapped.

"Whoa." The boy wobbled and fell against the limb holding the computer, knocking the device loose. "Dust!"

The flat screen clipped only one bough before falling free. Nate caught it before it hit the ground.

The young man gasped, his gaze meeting Nate's.

Nate started. The boy—no, that wasn't right, he was young, yes, but not a lad—was absolutely gorgeous. Nate stared into the big gray eyes, mesmerized. The man was simply beautiful. He had a small frame that had, at first, deluded Nate into thinking him a child. A mass of ebony curls surrounded a handsome face, and a full bottom lip was caught between even white teeth.

"Uh, thanks. I, uh— Whoa." The man's booted feet slid off the tree, leaving him dangling from his hands ten feet in the air.

Nate set the computer screen down and held his arms out. "I've got you. Drop."

"Uh..."

"Drop."

"Okay. Please don't miss." The man let go with a reluctant whimper.

The negligible weight landed in Nate's outstretched arms. He bent his knee slightly to keep from jarring the young man. Nate glanced at the handsome face and his gut clenched. Up close the man's eyes were the color of molten steel. He had flawless ivory skin and full lips. The heat of his body pressed against Nate's chest made his cock stir. The man was slim and not very tall, but he had broad shoulders that spoke of nice muscles under the well-tailored clothes. What he wouldn't give to see this slim body completely bare of clothing and those pretty lips wrapped around his hard cock. Closing his eyes, Nate concentrated on getting his pulse back to normal. He was here on a mission, not to get involved. Besides, this was most likely his hosts' offspring.

He opened his eyes in time to see a pink tongue dart out and wet the beguiling lips. Nate's cock—fully erect now—strained against the placket of his pantaloons.

The man's gaze roamed over Nate's face as long, elegant fingers came up to trace his beard. "Who are you?" he asked in a seductive whisper.

Nate hadn't even realized he'd leaned forward until the smaller man jerked, nearly spilling himself out of Nate's arms. Setting the man on his feet, Nate watched him straighten his waistcoat. When he brushed off his trousers, he seemed to realize he had a problem.

Good, the young lord wasn't unaffected, just surprised. Not, of course, that it mattered. Nate wasn't interested. *Yeah, right.* He bowed. "Nathaniel Hawkins, Earl of Deverell."

The younger man's gray eyes shot wide and he hastily tried to hide his obvious erection. He squirmed before spotting his computer. Picking up the screen, he held it in front of his groin and met Nate's gaze. His enticing mouth formed an "O", followed by an inhalation of air, then the man blinked and shook his head as if to clear it. "Thank you for rescuing me, milord. I, uh, got my screen caught on the way up."

Nate was about to ask the man's name and why he was in the tree in the first place when an older version of the young man appeared in the window. "What in stars happened to the window? Aiden?"

The younger man, Aiden, frowned. He darted his gaze to

Nate and gave a barely perceptible shake of his head. "I didn't do it, Cony. I was trying to get a different perspective on the garden." Aiden glanced back at Nate, his eyes pleading, and bowed. "Thank you again, milord."

Before Nate could respond the vision bounded off toward the back of the castle. How odd. Apparently the imp didn't want Nate to mention his fall from the tree. Or did he not want Nate to mention who broke the window?

"Lord Deverell?"

Nate dragged his attention from Aiden's retreating backside and turned toward the window. "Lord Raleigh?"

Raleigh smiled. "Yes, please come inside. You wouldn't happen to know what became of the window, would you?"

Their love knew no shape, no limit, no boundary.
Until someone destroyed their trust.

Trinity Broken
© 2007 Jamie Craig

Scientist Joshua Ames committed the unforgivable sin. He fell in love with his research subjects, shapeshifters Cameron and Sara. Despite the taboo against humans mingling with shifters, Josh left his life behind and moved into theirs without regret.

Then Sara disappeared.

When Josh and Cam finally find her, she is unconscious, emaciated and shackled. They thought the hard part was living without her. But as soon as Sara wakes, they realize the hard part will be putting their lives back together.

Sara barely remembers life with Cam and Josh. All she remembers is a monster, a shifter who wore Cam's face, who tortured and tested her for two long years. Without a home, conditioned to fear her own abilities, Sara struggles to start over.

Solving the mystery behind Sara's kidnapping is the key to her recovery, because whoever destroyed their relationship is hunting her, intent on getting her back.

The truth could bring the three lovers peace—or send them spiraling apart.

Warning, this title contains the following: explicit sex including m/m and m/m/f, graphic language, violence.

Available now in ebook from Samhain Publishing.

GET IT NOW

MyBookStoreAndMore.com
GREAT EBOOKS, GREAT DEALS . . . AND MORE!

Don't wait to run to the bookstore down the street, or waste time shopping online at one of the "big boys." Now, all your favorite Samhain authors are all in one place—at MyBookStoreAndMore.com. Stop by today and discover great deals on Samhain—and a whole lot more!

Samhain
Publishing
Ltd

WWW.SAMHAINPUBLISHING.COM

Hot Stuff

Discover Samhain!
THE HOTTEST NEW PUBLISHER ON THE PLANET

Romance, fantasy, mystery, thriller, mainstream and more—Samhain has more selection, hotter authors, and everything's available in both ebook and print.

Pick your favorite, sit back, and enjoy the ride! Hot stuff indeed.

GREAT CHEAP FUN

Discover eBooks!

THE FASTEST WAY TO GET THE HOTTEST NAMES

Get your favorite authors on your favorite reader, long before they're out in print! Ebooks from Samhain go wherever you go, and work with whatever you carry—Palm, PDF, Mobi, and more.

CPSIA information can be obtained at www.ICGtesting.com
Printed in the USA
LVOW091706240512

283169LV00003B/77/P

9 781599 989709